Lord of the Eyrie

KATERINA DUNNE

HISTORIUM PRESS
U. S. A.

For more information:

www.facebook.com/Katerina-Dunne-Writer-107262811794150

Contact: katerinadunnewriter@gmail.com

Book design by White Rabbit Arts

Original cover artwork (illustration and borders) by Paddy Shaw

HISTORIUM PRESS

Macon GA 31211 U. S. A.

www.historiumpress.com

First paperback edition February 2022

Copyright © 2022 by Ekaterini Vavoulidou

(under the pen-name Katerina Dunne)

ISBN 978-0-578-35544-3 (paperback)

Contents

GLOSSARY

In Hungarian all letters in a word are pronounced. They have the same pronunciation no matter where in the word they are. For example, the *i* is always pronounced as in *sit,* the *e* always like in *get* and the *g* always like in *give*.

Angyalom (awn-dyaw-lom): my angel

Barátom (baw-ra-tom): my friend

Édesem (eh-de-shem): sweetie (literally: my sweet one)

Erdély (er-dee): the Hungarian name of Transylvania

Huj! Huj! Hajrá! (hooey, hooey, hawee-rah): an old Hungarian battle cry, roughly translating as Hey! Hey! Go! Or Hey! Hey! Forward!

Kedves barátom (ked-vesh baw-ra-tom)*:* my dear friend

Kedvesem (ked-ve-shem): my dear

Kincsem (kin-tchem): my treasure

Preot (Romanian): priest

Sasfészek (shawsh-feh-sek): eyrie (literally: eagle's nest)

Szentimrei (in Latin - *de Szentimre* = of or from Szentimre): The ending -*i* after a place name is used in Hungarian to show where a person comes from. In medieval Hungary, where actual surnames were rare, it was commonly used by the nobility to denote the estate or area they possessed. Eg. the name Hunyadi means that he comes from Hunyad County

Szent László! (sent las-low): medieval Hungarian battle cry, in honour of the 11th century Knight-King Saint László, who was canonised in 1192. He was particularly venerated in the border areas of medieval Hungary and the Székely land.

Úristen (oo-rish-ten): Dear God!, My God!, My Goodness! (literally: Lord God!)

Vihar (vi-hawr): storm – in the novel, this is the name of Sándor's warhorse

PART ONE

1

The Return

Sándor wiped the sweat from his sunburnt face. The midday heat made the horses pant and the knights curse under their breaths. But they were almost home now. He pressed his legs against the palfrey's flanks, urging him to go faster.

Halfway down the mountain pass, the horse shied. "What is it, boy?" Sándor said, stroking the animal's neck. The iron smell of blood hit his nose. He peered ahead. About twenty paces away, in the middle of the path, a body lay splayed on the rocky ground. Flies swarmed about it, their buzzing amplified by the stony silence.

His knights approached from behind. "Sir!" one called.

Sándor halted them with a raised arm. "Shh!"

Was it a trap? He lifted his gaze. Covered with large rocks and thick bushes, the sloping sides of the pass made the perfect spot for an ambush.

He signalled to the men to spread out and search while he

warily drove his palfrey forward. He leaned over to survey the body.

The dead man's colourful clothes and leopard-skin jacket were drenched in blood. An Akinji, an Ottoman border raider. His horse was nowhere to be seen, but his band could still be in the area.

Sándor sat back in the saddle and waited. He twitched at the slightest of sounds – a bird flapping its wings and flying away, a squirrel scuttling in the bushes, a dislodged pebble rolling down the slope. If only he had not left his armour with the baggage train, a long way behind. The Akinjis were keen archers. His light surcoat would not protect him from their arrows. At least, he had his trusted horseman's axe in his hand. The curved, sharp edge of its blade and the long spike on its other side had made many an enemy suffer. His fingers clenched around the haft. After years of fighting and an arduous journey in the height of summer, the last thing he wished for was another skirmish with the Ottomans. But if he had to protect his land, he was ready for the challenge.

The knights returned. No sign of the enemy.

"They must have raided already," Sándor whispered. His face went cold as if drained of its blood. Had he arrived too late? There was only one way to find out. He re-sheathed the axe and took hold of the reins. "Go!" He spurred on his horse so hard that the animal jerked into a frantic gallop, sending small stones and clumps of earth into the air.

As he came out of the pass, his ancestral home, Sasfészek, appeared in the distance – in all its glory. Like a true Eyrie, the proud hilltop fortress dominated the family estate of Szentimre with its lofty curtain wall and red-tiled pointed rooftops reaching into the milky-blue sky.

When he rode farther down onto the expansive plateau below the castle hill, the breath caught in his throat. The countryside was littered with overturned carts, burned haystacks, torn sacks of grain, people's possessions strewn on the dirt, broken weapons, arrows and pieces of armour. Carrion birds were feasting on the flesh of dead sheep, horses and dogs. Although no fire was visible, the smell of smoke lingered in the air. In one of the fields, five men were digging near a pile of Ottoman bodies. As the riders approached, the workers paused, holding their shovels in one hand and shading their eyes against the bright sunshine with the other. The sight of the Szentimre banner, carried by one of the knights, must have put them at ease because they waved and then recommenced their work.

Sándor had seen worse destruction caused by war and raiding countless times before. But this was his land and his people. As he passed through the first village on his way to the castle, he slowed his horse's pace to a walk. His heart ached upon watching the frightened figures of men, women and children, who wandered like lost souls or wept in each other's arms outside farmhouses and barns with blackened walls and smouldering roofs.

A line of gloomy-faced people – many of them with their livestock in tow – trickled out of the entrance to the walled town, which lay at the foot of the hill. Sándor and his knights squeezed their way in, only to be confronted with more suffering and despair as well as utter confusion. Dozens of peasant families from the estate's villages had found shelter there. The ubiquitous smell of smoke blended with the stench of too many people and animals crammed in a small area. The main square had been turned into an infirmary for the victims of the attack. Dead bodies lay on carts, covered with bloodied sheets of rough cloth. Men and women were crying beside their wounded loved ones: some treating the injured, others shouting in Hungarian, Wallachian or Saxon; dogs barked; children ran around shrieking; and dispirited priests, with clasped hands, interceded for the dead and pleaded for the living. A handful of soldiers tried to maintain order, but without success. Those villagers and townsfolk who recognised Sándor, either from his looks or his banner, paused and bowed their heads.

Hastening ahead of the knights, he weaved his way through the crowd – his palfrey almost tripping over clucking chickens that scurried across its path – and followed the steep, narrow grey riband-like road towards the fortress. He crossed the gate under the raised portcullis, entered the cobblestoned courtyard and dismounted in the shadow of the imposing building of the castle keep, leaving his horse with a skinny, pimple-faced adolescent groom.

A brawny armoured man with a large moustache and long, greying black hair greeted him at the steps of the keep. "Welcome home, Lord Szilágyi. I am László Balog, the new castellan."

Sándor acknowledged him with a nod. "What happened?"

"The Turks attacked at dawn, sir. They were not many, and we repelled them, thanks be to God. But your sire was badly wounded in the fray." He lowered his head as he continued, "The priest has administered the last rites."

Sándor looked at Balog in disbelief. Why on earth had his old and ailing father been involved in the fight? Despite his stiff legs – from the continuous riding over several days – he hurried into the family residence and climbed the stone stairs two at a time, his gilded rowel spurs jangling with each step.

2

Grief and Guilt

The chamber stank of blood, sweat, incense and Communion wine. Two men stood in silence by István Szilágyi's bed: the physician and a dark figure lurking in the shadows, partly concealed behind the half-drawn green curtain of the bed canopy.

Sándor took off his feathered hat and approached slowly. His father lay with eyes closed, his face ashen. His shirt and hauberk had been rolled up and his braies and joined hose lowered, exposing a large area of dark-blue skin around a grave wound. The broken shaft of a spear protruded from his abdomen, its metal end lodged deep inside him.

Sándor's hat fell from his hand. The ground moved under his feet. He held on to the bedpost. He knew all about this kind of battle injury: nobody ever survived. The spear had delivered its mortal blow. Pulling it out would rip his father's insides apart, causing massive bleeding and instant death. Leaving it in would lead to slower death from internal bleeding and failure of vital organs. And judging by his father's state, that fatal moment did not seem to be too far away.

The physician gave Sándor a disconsolate look. "My lord, there is nothing more I can do. I shall leave you now to say your last farewell."

The dark figure stepped out into the light of the arched window: a scowling youth, lips pressed into a thin line and nostrils flaring. He was wearing a mishmash of mail and plate armour, soiled with blood and dirt and held together so badly that it would make a professional soldier raise an eyebrow. "The prodigal son has returned," he spat.

"Miklós," Sándor acknowledged him coldly. His younger brother had grown up, but he was still a seventeen-year-old boy, desperately trying to look and behave like a man.

"You only came back to claim your inheritance."

Sándor winced at his brother's words but chose not to respond. He had hastened home as soon as he received news of his father's sudden illness, hoping to spend some time with him; perhaps look after him and help him recover if that were possible. But now...

Kneeling at the bedside, he took the old man's hand in his and kissed it. The skin was cold as ice and dry as leather.

"I beg your forgiveness, Father. I'm sorry I was not here. I'm so sorry."

István's arm twitched. His eyes opened slowly, tears trembling in their corners. He gasped, trying to say something, but no sound came from his mouth. His body convulsed. Then his head tilted lifelessly to the left and remained there, frozen forever.

Sándor covered his face with his hand. Sharp, burning pain ran through him while his heartbeat pounded in his ears. If only he had arrived a day earlier!

He remained on his knees for a little while until the sound of the door opening made him turn around.

She brought the sunshine with her when she entered. "Margit?" He blinked several times. No, he was not dreaming. It was, indeed, Margit. She could not be more different from the fragile and puny fourteen-year-old bride that he had left behind. She stood straight and proud in her floor-length, dark-blue velvet gown. Even the bunch of keys and canvas purse hanging from her brass-studded leather girdle added to her air of elegance and authority. Her face radiant and flawless; her straw-coloured hair partially coiled under a jewelled hairnet, the rest of it hanging loose behind her shoulders. She could be easily mistaken for Heaven's most splendid angel. In her hands she clasped a small Book of Hours.

Sándor rose immediately. He took a few steps towards her, drawn by an irresistible, hypnotising force. He bowed his head. "My lady."

She curtsied in return. And lifting her head, her bright blue gaze met his. "Welcome home, my lord. It has been a long time."

Her voice flowed like the pure water of a mountain spring. Sándor's heart stopped for a brief moment... but then he shook his head. How could he let himself be carried away and think of his own gratification while his father lay dead in the same room?

Gracefully gliding away from him, Margit approached the bed. She regarded the lifeless body of her father-in-law. "He is gone now," she whispered and crossed herself. With a gentle and respectful movement, she closed the dead man's eyes.

She turned towards Sándor. "Did he see you at all?"

He nodded.

"I am sorry. May God rest his soul." She opened her book and read a prayer for the dead.

With bowed head and closed eyes, Sándor listened silently until his brother's angry breathing became too loud to bear.

Miklós pointed at their father. "This is your fault. He had to go out there and fight despite his illness and his advanced age. He had to defend the estate because you were not here."

"Why did you not stop him? He was ill and frail. You should have kept him safe." Sándor glanced at his brother from head to toe. "But what am I saying? You cannot even wear your armour correctly."

"Shame on you both!" Margit interjected. "Bickering like foolish little boys while your father's body still lies warm."

Sándor stepped back in surprise, but Miklós ignored her and continued his verbal attack. "You left us all at the mercy of the Turks – your father, your wife, me. You were far away soldiering while your family needed you."

"How dare you? You know very well it was Father's wish that I serve the Holy Crown as he and our ancestors did before me." Sándor squared his shoulders. He had done his duty, and he was proud of it. He was not going to let anyone question him. "Our family banner has known only glory on the battlefield. And I greatly honoured our name once again when the Royal Council chose me as one of the knightly escorts of our new king, Władysław of Poland, at his coronation last month."

Miklós snorted. "Yes! The 'hero' of the family. Always occupied with 'important' matters. And Father adored you, worshipped you like Mars. His warrior son. Since the moment he was wounded today, the only name he kept calling was yours. He held on as long as he could, hoping to see you."

Sándor raised his hand. "Enough!"

"Let us go, Miklós," Margit said calmly and led him by the arm out of the room.

***

Sándor spent the rest of the day in a daze, detached from reality, like the spectator of a heart-breaking drama in which he was also the main actor. A single thought tormented his mind: perhaps his brother was right; perhaps it was his fault. He had let the sirens of glory and adventure lure him away from his home, his land and the people who mattered to him the most. How could he live with the dark spectre of guilt looming over him now? Even when he slept that night, his dreams were grim and frightening.

The next day, after his father's funeral mass, he leaned on his wife's arm and allowed her to lead him away. A large group of people had gathered outside the chapel, waiting to speak to him. Their muddled voices felt like hammering in his head. He would have turned around and run back into the chapel, but Margit grabbed his hand firmly and spoke in a loud and decisive voice, "The lord needs time to mourn. He will arrange a public audience when he is ready."

The crowd went silent and parted to let them pass. Still grasping his hand, she guided him across the courtyard and then into the house.

Sándor stood in the entrance hall and took a deep breath. Finally, some peace and quiet.

"My lord, you must rest awhile," Margit entreated. "Your counsellors will be here after vespers. I shall call for you when –"

He silenced her with an abrupt movement of his arm. All he craved was to hide from everybody and drown his grief and guilt by drinking himself into oblivion. "Bring me wine," he ordered a passing servant.

Wearily, he climbed the stairs and locked himself in the study. The previous years of continuous training and fighting weighed on him now like armour made of lead.

He settled at the walnut writing desk, breathing in the old, familiar smell of books, paper and ink. That small room had been his father's sanctuary, and Sándor had felt so privileged when he was allowed in. He would spend countless hours there, even at the expense of learning his duties as a future landlord. By the age of sixteen, he had read every book on the shelves, mastering Latin and the art of official letter-writing as much as he had mastered sword fighting. He could have served the king either as a soldier or a scholar. His father made the choice for him two years later...

A knock on the door woke him up. He slowly opened his eyes. The world looked distorted through the empty glass beaker in front of his face. The last light of the day shone through the window, spreading a warm glow around the room.

"My lord!" Margit called from the other side of the door. "Your counsellors have arrived. You have duties to attend to."

"Leave me in peace," he mumbled.

He reached for the wine flagon, but his arm fell limp on the writing desk. He cursed, lay his head down and closed his eyes.

Darkness had fallen when he woke again. He called the servants in for more wine and then staggered towards the window. Sweating heavily and barely able to breathe, he flung it open. The cool, fresh mountain breeze hit him in the face. He stood there, inhaling as deep as he could until everything about him stopped being a blur. What on earth was he doing? If his father watched him now from above, he would be very displeased. He grunted, turned around, grabbed the flagon and hurled it against the wall.

A little later, he was in his bedchamber, immersed in a wooden tub filled with cold water while a male servant stood close at hand, holding a clean towel.

The iciness tingled his skin and stirred his blood. Weariness and daze faded away. He threw more water on his face and rubbed his temples, cheeks and jaw. The prickling sensation of stubble reminded him that he had not shaved for days. He closed his eyes, leaned back and let the servant take care of that.

3
A New Life

Margit was still awake, sitting on a cushioned folding stool and absently running a comb through her hair in the flickering light of the candles. Her husband's behaviour thus far had not provided the comfort and reassurance that the people of the estate needed. If only he came out of his gloomy mood and fulfilled his duty! Szentimre needed a competent new master. Miklós was too young and unsuitable for the task; he did not show much interest either. It was she who always helped her father-in-law in the administration of the estate's business.

And there was the threat of the Ottomans too...

The door creaked open. She jumped to her feet, dropping the comb to the floor. No one ever entered her private bedchamber except for her young maid, Erzsi, who always knocked first and announced herself.

Sándor walked in. He was only wearing his nightshirt. His damp, shoulder-length copper-red hair glistened in the candlelight. "You are right. I have duties to attend to. I shall meet with my counsellors tomorrow. And now, I shall start by doing my duty as a husband."

He came so close to her that his breath warmed her forehead.

He touched her face with the back of his hand. His dark-green eyes twinkled. "Take off your chemise," he said softly but still in a commanding voice. "At last, you are a real woman now. I wish to see you."

A tingle went down her spine. Her heart was racing, her cheeks on fire.

"Very well. I understand you may be a little shy, so I shall take mine off first." With a quick move, he threw off his shirt and stood naked in front of her.

Margit gasped. Long, angular and heavily freckled, his face was far from charming. But his height and his well-built and hard-trained body, marked with a few battle scars here and there, compensated for it. She was not a child any longer, yet the top of her head barely reached the base of his neck. She stared at his shoulders and then his chest but did not dare look any lower.

He put his arm around her waist and pulled her against him. His kiss was as firm and as demanding as his grasp, the muscles of his chest and stomach as solid as the castle walls.

When he let her go, she was out of breath. Her whole body trembled, gripped by a strange and unknown sensation.

Her mind flew back to their wedding night. She had arrived at Szentimre a week late because of the bad weather. The ceremony had been rushed. A small, slight, exhausted and frightened orphan, alone in the world, she had cowered at the edge of the bed, shaking like a leaf in the wind. Sándor had taken pity on her and had not touched her. The next morning, he had left for the king's court.

She could not avoid him this time. She was older, stronger and braver now, and she understood her duty. He was her husband. She had to submit to him. At least, he was young and healthy, and the smell of his freshly washed skin pleased her. But he was much bigger and heavier than her. He could still hurt her.

"How much longer must I wait to have what is mine?" he jested, dragging her out of her deep thoughts.

She slowly raised her hand and undid the laces on the front of her chemise. She then pushed the garment towards the edge of her shoulders and let it slide off.

Just like her face, Margit's body was so perfect that it put to shame all those Greek and Roman statues that Sándor had seen in Italy. He was ready to take her right at that moment, but he did not wish their first time together to be a quick and forgettable experience.

With his mouth slightly open, he took some time to admire every aspect of her rare beauty: her skin as pure and unblemished as fresh snow; the pale-yellow stream of hair flowing down her shoulders and back; her breasts, waist and hips created as if by the most skilled master...

She put her hands in front of her womanly parts.

"What's the matter? Are you afraid?" he asked.

She nodded.

"Don't be. You must trust me and forget about everything else."

He swiftly lifted her off her feet and carried her to the bed. He lay beside her, leaning on his elbow, and kissed her again. This time it was more prolonged. He wanted to absorb as much of her taste as he could. But there was no response from her. She just lay there as rigid as a plank of wood and with her eyes shut tight.

"Let go of your fear. I promise I shall not hurt you," he whispered in her ear while his thumb traced the outline of her lips.

Margit held her breath momentarily. Her eyelids quivered, and her face reddened. She must have liked that, he thought, smiling.

Encouraged by her reaction, he slid his hand down her body, exploring every inch of it – starting from her face and continuing to her neck, shoulders, breasts, belly and then lower. Little by little, her skin warmed, and she softened.

He gently pushed her legs apart and lifted himself over her. Slowly and lingeringly, he placed a trail of kisses on every part of her, moving lower and lower. She moaned, softly in the beginning and then a little louder, while she held his head between her legs.

Sándor stayed there until he could taste her readiness. He had pleased many women before, but none of them mattered to him as much as Margit did. None of them was so perfect; none of them belonged to him or was meant to give him an heir.

After drawing a long breath to subdue the forceful fury of his racing heart, he entered her body. She trembled at first, but her initial whimpers of discomfort soon turned into deep and quickening breaths. Her legs pressed tightly on his hips; her fingers dug into the skin of his shoulders.

As soon as she arched her back and moved her body together with his, the release came instantly. He let out an intense moan. It felt as good as victory on the field of battle.

Exhausted, he moved away from her and lay on his back. Staring at the intricate and colourful patterns embroidered on the bed canopy, he slowly caught his breath. He turned towards her.

She was looking at the fireplace on the opposite side of the room, quietly but with a smile still playing faintly in the corner of her mouth.

Sándor propped himself up on his elbow. "I'm glad that you enjoyed it as much as I did."

Margit sucked her lower lip.

"I must warn you," he continued. "I shall not leave you in peace until I have ten sons."

She looked at him with wide eyes and mouth agape. "Ten?"

He chuckled. "I jest. Three would be enough."

As soon as he lay his head back on the pillow, a wave of sweet lethargy swept over him. He closed his eyes and fell asleep.

***

Leaning on the stone parapet at the end of the small terrace, Sándor took a deep breath, soaking up the beauty of nature that surrounded him. It was that time between darkness and light, a magic-like moment when night and day exist together. Straight ahead, beyond the fields, the bronze colour of dawn had just appeared on the horizon while behind him and the lofty towers of the castle, the dark cloak of night was gradually receding.

Margit stood by his side, wrapped in a blanket but still shivering in the cool morning breeze.

"This is my land. I am home," he said.

How had that calm and peaceful place been the scene of so much destruction and death only two days earlier?

At the foot of the hill, below the fortress and its walls, stood the small town of Szentimre, still quiet in a grey haze, with only a faint light here and there in the houses. At its centre, the steeple of the church of Saint Imre towered above the surrounding buildings. And beyond the town's defences, the seven villages and hamlets of the estate's tenants lay scattered across the vast farmland.

The dark mass of a mountain range protected Sasfészek from behind like a giant shield. Pine and fir trees clung to its steep slopes, which extended as high as the eye could see. Real treasures lay hidden in its heart: gold and silver. Some fifty men worked the mine, their village nestled on the side of a narrow valley along a rocky, babbling stream.

Within its walls, the fortress included several buildings: the four-storied old stone keep, which now served as the family residence; the long, rectangular great hall attached to the side of the keep; the warehouse and armoury, the timber-framed chapel, the smithy, the stables and the barracks.

Even though five years had passed, on the surface nothing had changed – everything was exactly as he remembered. But at the same time, everything was different. The future was uncertain, and he was completely unprepared for it. If only he had paid more attention to his father's wise advice and instructions all those years earlier...

Margit withdrew her hand from inside the blanket and rested it on his shoulder. "Are you pleased to be home again, my lord?"

Sándor stood up straight, gazing far into the distance. "I don't know. I have been absent for so long that I now feel like a stranger."

"You are the new master of the estate. You must rule and protect these people."

"Yes, but I am not sure how. I am a soldier, not a landlord."

She ran her hand consolingly down his arm. "It will not be easy. But if you listen to your people and you respect them, they will respect you too. You must show them that you are not a haughty eagle, perched on this eyrie of a castle and preying upon the fruits of their labour, but a fair and compassionate master, who cares for them and values them. And I promise I shall always stand by your side. I am prepared to give you any assistance you may require."

He turned to her in surprise. "You?"

"Yes. I learned from your father. He was eager to teach me as one day I would become the mistress of the estate."

"No, *angyalom*, you need not trouble yourself with this. I shall take care of it henceforth. You only look after the household and the servants and leave the rest to me."

He spoke reassuringly, but his heart quivered at the thought. Although he would have counsellors at his disposal, he would still be the one to make the important decisions – decisions that would even make the difference between life and death, survival and destruction.

He stood in silence, absently trailing his hand along the hard surface of the parapet wall. The banners with his family coat of arms were flapping in the wind on top of the gatehouse and the watchtowers: a black mountain goat emerging from the flames against an image of three snow-capped peaks symbolising Szentimre, and the sun and moon representing the Székely side of the family. It was the emblem he wore and carried in battle – the only thing that reminded him of home when he was far away.

"It's still early," he said. "Let us go back to bed."

Until then, the two of them had been complete strangers, whose first intimate encounter had been a little awkward. But when they made love again, it was different. Margit gave herself to him so eagerly that all those other women he had been with before her quickly faded into distant memory.

4
From Soldier to Leader

Sándor, together with his brother, entered the great hall to meet his counsellors. He wore his best and most expensive clothes to make a good impression: loose-fitting linen trousers tucked into brown riding boots and, over his shirt, a short-sleeved, knee-length blue silk tunic decorated with golden embroidery on its front and hem. He had wrapped a red sash around his waist and carried a dagger in his leather belt. His attire would have been frowned upon at the king's court, but he preferred its comfort to the more fashionable tight-fitting hose and doublet. And he needed to feel comfortable.

His heart raced in anticipation of this meeting. Would he, at just over twenty-three years of age, be able to command the respect and obedience of those experienced older men who had counselled his father for many years?

At least, his brother's presence provided some encouragement. Despite their previous argument, Sándor needed a family member beside him as he was about to face the challenges that lay ahead.

The counsellors arrived and sat down at the long oak table. Even though he remembered most of them, he permitted them to reintroduce themselves and remind him of the positions they held.

In addition to being the castellan, László Balog was also the commander of the castle garrison. Although new in his post, he had served in the retinue of other noble landlords for twenty years.

Péter Havasi, a small and gaunt older gentleman, was the steward. He administered the estate's financial and legal matters as well as its provisions and the collection of taxes and dues.

Gábor Sipos, a big and strong bear of a man with a thick brown beard, was the forest warden, who also advised on agriculture and livestock matters.

The elegantly dressed paunchy blonde-haired counsellor sitting next to him was Josef Roth, a Saxon. He represented the craftsmen of the town: blacksmiths, goldsmiths, tailors, jewellers, as well as builders, stonemasons and the like.

The next official to introduce himself was Lajos Kendi, another strong and fierce-looking man with a smallpox-scarred face. He was in charge of the mine.

The small assembly also included the Hungarian Catholic priest and the Wallachian *preot* of the Greek rite, who looked after the spiritual needs of the population.

For over two hours, Sándor listened to the countless issues his counsellors raised. Each one drew his attention to different problems, but one concern appeared to be held in common: the destruction caused to Szentimre and the neighbouring estates by the Ottoman attacks, which had become more frequent during the past two years. The perpetrators of the recent raid had been a small unit of Akinjis – irregular light horsemen from Anatolia, who struck terror in the Hungarian southern border lands. Even though they were repelled, they had succeeded in destroying some of the farmland and stealing animals and supplies. The attack had cost six lives, including Sándor's father, who had the misfortune of falling off his horse and receiving a lethal hit from the spear of a retreating Ottoman while he lay on the ground before help had arrived.

At times, Sándor caught himself drifting away and gazing at the masterfully carved vaulted ceiling, the vividly coloured tapestries hanging on the walls, or the large marble slab with his family coat of arms above the fireplace.

A lot of the financial, agricultural, trading and religious matters brought up at the meeting were beyond his understanding. He postponed making any important decisions on these until he had obtained more information from his counsellors. But the need to strengthen the defence of the estate was something that he could address forthwith.

"We must be able to protect ourselves first and foremost. I propose that we employ our builders to enhance the fortifications and erect more defensive structures in the valley near the mine and perhaps around the more exposed villages. Also, all men over the age of sixteen must receive combat training so that they can turn into additional soldiers if needed. Only after we have addressed this matter, can we look at everything else."

"My lord, you must not forget that all these works are costly. The coffers are all but empty," the steward noted. "We were spared the worst of the peasant revolt of '37, but the frequent Ottoman raids have caused disruption. During the big attack in '38, most of the crops were destroyed. The estate has not recovered yet."

Sándor shifted nervously in his seat. His father had written to him about the raids. But why on earth had he not informed him of the real extent of the damage? Still, the Ottoman threat was his most immediate worry.

"Our protection is a priority. See what you can do, Master Havasi," he said, impatiently. He rose to indicate that the meeting had ended. "Thank you, gentlemen. Let us meet again same day and time next week."

The days which followed were difficult. Not only did Sándor have to supervise the works on the re-organisation of the estate's defence and the training of the civilian population, but he also had to deal with a multitude of other issues, most of which arose from his public audiences. People were complaining about this and that; some had arguments with their neighbours; others owed money and were not able to pay; the priests, concerned for the spreading of immorality among the population, wanted to have the one and only brothel closed; the steward kept saying money was short; trade agreements had to be signed so that gold and silver from the mine could be sold and bring some income. All those duties kept him occupied from dawn till dusk.

***

Margit's keys and gilded girdle prayer book jingled as she hurried back from church along the colonnaded portico of the great hall. The morning mass always felt too long to her, and she was looking forward to breaking her fast. But that would have to wait. Lajos

Kendi stood at the entrance to the keep. His flushed and sweaty face, dishevelled eyebrows and raspy breath indicated that something was amiss.

He took his hat off and bowed to her. "I've bad news, my lady. I must speak with your husband, but I can't find him anywhere. Was he in church with you? Is he still in the chapel?"

"No. I have not seen him." Margit pondered. "Perhaps he is in the armoury building, practising with the soldiers. Let us go and look for him."

She sent her maid to the house to supervise the preparation of the breakfast table and followed Kendi to the exercise hall. Their arrival did not alert the soldiers and knights for the thick layer of hay on the floor muffled their footsteps.

In the middle of the hall, Sándor, venturing to teach his brother how to defend himself with a sword and shield against multiple attackers, was engaging in a fight against not one, but three opponents.

He was wearing only his joined hose and a shirt, unlaced at the front and with the sleeves rolled up. Despite his height, he moved with the nimbleness of a lynx, shouting instructions at his training partners and showing off his combat skills and physical strength.

Margit's jaw dropped. Her pulse quickened, and her breath became short and shallow. How could she forget that women were not allowed in the training hall? As it was a warm day, her husband was not the only one who had stripped down to his undergarments. Although the men did not seem troubled by her presence, she flushed and dropped her gaze to the floor.

"My lord!" Lajos called out.

Sándor stopped, and so did the soldiers. He tossed down the wooden sword and shield and approached Kendi and Margit. "What's the matter?"

Kendi glanced about to make sure that no one else was listening. He spoke in a whisper. "We've a problem at the mine."

Sándor leaned in closer. "What kind of problem?"

"The miners are refusing to work. They haven't been paid for over three months."

"Three months?" Sándor's raised voice caused a sudden hush in the hall.

Kendi's face turned scarlet. "Aye, my lord. This is the way the mine operates. The men do the work, the metals are sold or exchanged, the men receive their wages. The process takes two months at most. But with your sire's illness, his death and the Ottoman raids all over the southern parts of the province, everything was delayed."

"I didn't know. Why did you not tell me before?"

"I believed I had it all in hand, and I didn't wish to trouble you. I requested the money from Master Havasi. The men agreed to wait another two weeks, but these have passed now. They can't wait any longer. The steward said he followed your orders and spent money on fortifying two of the villages instead. Until we've the payment for the latest trade agreement, he's nothing to give me. But the agreement won't be fulfilled if the miners stop working."

Sándor looked away and remained silent for some time.

"My lord, you need to speak to the workers," Margit intervened.

"The lady's right," Lajos agreed. "You're the only one to resolve this before we've a riot on our hands."

"Very well. Tell them I shall meet them at Nones... As for you, Master Kendi, never withhold such important information from me again."

***

The inhabitants of the miners' village had gathered around the stone water fountain in the square when Sándor arrived, accompanied by Margit, Miklós, Kendi and ten soldiers. The atmosphere was tense, but the crowd of workers and their families kept calm and did not make any threatening moves. Even the children stayed quiet, with mouths agape, staring at their new lord on his big horse.

A man of middle age with a stern, dirt-stained face took a step forward. He removed his straw hat, revealing a filthy linen coif underneath, and bowed his head.

"Lord Szilágyi, I represent the workers. We are aggrieved for weeks now," he said in good Hungarian, but with a heavy Saxon accent.

A group of younger miners, who had lined up at the front of the crowd, folded their arms, all at the same time as if they had received a signal. They made sure that the hammers, pickaxes and chisels that they carried in their belts could easily be seen.

Sándor held his breath for a moment and instinctively gripped the hilt of his sword. If they wanted a fight, he would give them one.

Margit leaned towards him from her saddle, touched his arm and said in a low voice, "Apologise and tell them they will be paid in three days."

"How? We don't know if –"

"Do it!"

How dare she give him orders in front of everyone? Following her intervention, some of the miners gazed at him with arched eyebrows while others lowered their heads, smiling to themselves.

But there was no time to argue. He released his grip on the sword and cleared his throat. "I have just been informed of the situation. I understand your distress and your anger. And I regret that you have not received your wages for so long."

The older miner squeezed the hat in his hands and spoke slowly but confidently, "With all due respect, lord, we can't work with empty bellies. Our families need feeding too. And the shops don't sell to us on credit anymore."

"I promise that you will be paid within three days. I shall instruct the shops to continue with the credit until then. Return to work now."

"Three days," the miner said, boldly lifting his eyes to meet Sándor's. "And we want to be trained in combat like the other men of the estate to protect our homes."

"You will be trained. I shall personally see to that."

The miner took a quick bow and stepped back. He turned to his fellow workers and said a few words in the Saxon language and then in Wallachian. The crowd slowly dispersed.

Despite his frustration with his wife's interference, Sándor had bought some time. But would he be able to keep his promise?

When they returned to Sasfészek, he pulled Margit into his bedchamber. "I told you not to meddle with the administration of the estate."

"I only tried to help. You were ready to attack them, not talk to them."

"Don't do that again! You make me look weak in front of my people."

"You need to start dealing with these issues, my lord. And I am here to support you. Accepting help from a woman does not make you any less of a man. The most important thing is to make the right decision. Whether you like it or not, you are the leader of people now. You must behave like one. I understand you spent many years among soldiers, and you feel more at ease with a sword in your hand. But not every problem in life can be resolved with the sword."

Sándor exhaled sharply. She was right. He had a weakness, and he needed to work hard to overcome it. Margit had behaved much more wisely than him, even when surrounded by dozens of disgruntled miners out there.

At length, he smiled. "Not only beautiful but proud, strong-willed and fearless too. Like a fiery mare."

Margit gasped. "You compare your wife to a horse?"

"My wife and horses are what I love. Riding is my favourite sport... Come!" He took her by the hand and led her to the bed.

A little later, they ended up lying side by side and out of breath.

He raised himself on his elbow and caressed her cheek with the back of his hand. "It was bold of you to enter the exercise hall when it was full of half-clad men."

Her mouth opened wide, but she regained her composure swiftly. "Oh, do not fear, my lord. My eyes were on you only."

"Did I look so handsome?"

"What mightier spectacle to behold than a half-naked warrior in battle?"

He burst out laughing. "Very well, my lady. Next time you are in the exercise hall, I shall lead you to a dark storeroom and take you there and then. Would that please you?"

"My lord!" Margit's face turned the colour of beetroot as she covered her mouth with her hand, trying to suppress a fit of giggles. She stood up and smoothed down her skirts.

"I have this matter of the miners to attend to first," Sándor said. He got out of the bed and pulled up his hose. "I only have three days to find the money and pay them. You did not give me much choice."

Kneeling in front of him, Margit tied the points of his hose to the doublet with deft hands. "Do not fret, my lord. We can pay them."

"How?"

She rose and looked him in the eye. "We can sell or pawn some of my jewels. I know there is no moneylender in the estate who could pay such a high price, but we can take them to Déva early in the morning and return by sundown."

Sándor's muscles tensed. "No! I shall not take your possessions to cover my own debts."

"Why not? You are my husband, and I wish to help you."

He dismissed her with an abrupt movement of his hand. "I don't want to hear that! I shall find another way."

***

The counsellors arrived on time for the urgent evening meeting.

Sándor turned to the steward. "What is the situation with the farmers' rents?"

"All paid for now, but we may have trouble henceforth because some of their land and animals were destroyed in the attack."

"Taxes?"

"Already collected and sent to the king."

"What about the contract with the Segesvár guilds for gold and silver that I signed a few days ago? When are they paying us?"

"At the end of the month, when they come to collect the goods."

"So, the question is: do we have enough money to pay the miners' wages now?"

Havasi examined his papers. "We have already spent a lot on repairing the damage caused by the Ottoman raid. I reckon we can pay them for a month but not for the three they ask for until we are paid by the guild."

"We need to find this money now," Sándor said. "If they are not satisfied, our agreement with the guild will fail. We depend on them."

No response was forthcoming.

"Gentlemen! I am sure we can all contribute a little to help us out of the crisis. You will be reimbursed at the end of the month."

"Er... we have our own expenses," Josef Roth said, and the others nodded in agreement.

Sándor exhaled forcefully. He could not tarry. Perhaps the problem required a different approach. He stood up and spoke in a clear and determined voice. "This has been the land of my family for several generations. But it is also where you earn your living and feed your families. You are all able to live a comfortable life because I give you employment and protection. If you wish for all this to continue, you must do what I ask. I do not wish to take extreme measures, such as confiscating everything valuable you have. Do you understand me?"

A deathly silence chilled the room. The counsellors glanced at each other, astonished.

"Of course, my lord. I'll oblige to your request," Kendi was the first to speak.

The others mumbled similar promises.

Two members of the small assembly, however, had not said a word yet: the two priests, representing the two religions in the estate. Sándor turned to them and waited, but they still did not speak.

"What about the Church?" he said.

"No," Miklós whispered. "Leave the Church alone."

"Why?"

"You must not anger the bishops."

Sándor dismissed him with an angry look. He approached the priests. "Fathers, you collect tithes from the estate, which you hand over to your bishops. A part of the tithes is in coin. I am sure your superiors will understand if you delay paying them this one time."

"This is not our money," the Wallachian priest protested.

"We don't have the authority to use it for other than its intended purpose," the Hungarian one continued.

"Then, tell your bishops that you need to perform a charity. The miners are your flock too, and they have fallen on hard times."

"It is the duty of the landlord and not of the Church to pay them," the Hungarian priest countered.

"I am merely looking for a loan, which I shall repay at the end of the month."

Sándor waited until they promised to contribute.

He smiled to himself for he had won his battle. "Thank you, gentlemen. You have done your duty to your lord and to your people. I shall not forget this. Let us meet again here tomorrow at Sext to put together the sums we need."

The counsellors and Miklós walked out of the great hall in silence.

However, Balog did not follow the others but turned around to Sándor. "May I offer some friendly advice, sir?"

"You may."

"Please do not be offended by what I'm going to say because it's important that I say it. What happened here today must not happen again."

The blood rose to Sándor's head. "Whatever do you mean?"

"With all due respect, sir, you cannot intimidate or threaten your counsellors because you have military power, and they don't. They are not your servants or your tenants. They may be of a lower standing than you, but they are still noblemen, and they serve you of their own free will. Their sons, brothers and cousins are the knights and soldiers who will fight under your banner in case of war. If you try to extort money from them like this, they will abandon you and work for someone else."

Sándor pointed at the door. "Leave!"

His sharp tone startled Balog, who bowed and departed in haste.

Sándor looked down. His hands were shaking badly. His heart was pounding.

"Not every problem in life can be resolved with the sword," Margit had told him, only a few hours earlier. Perhaps it would be wise to seek her advice more often. But no, that was not a good idea. He was a strong man and a powerful landlord. He would not resort to taking orders from a woman. He lacked experience, indeed, but he had to learn the hard way.

5
The Attack

Sándor shook hands with the Saxon merchant, who represented the Segesvár jewellers' guild. "Safe journey home."

At last, he could breathe freely. Having received his payment, he could reimburse his counsellors. He sat down at the writing desk to complete the recording of the transaction.

But his client remained standing. "Lord Szilágyi?"

"Yes?" Sándor answered without looking at him.

"Your family has been our supplier for many a year. Out of courtesy, I would like to warn you about something."

Sándor inclined his head towards the man. "What is it?"

"The Ottomans have resumed their raids recently. My guards and I barely escaped a large band of them on our way here. You must be prepared. We are going to leave during the night to avoid any unpleasant encounters."

Sándor rose before first light. Sooner or later, the Ottomans would come. Even if they did not use their full force to raid the estate, they would be capable of causing extensive damage. The defensive works had not yet been completed, and the male population was not fully trained. He had only thirty foot-soldiers, twenty archers, three sergeants, ten castle guards, seven armoured knights, the garrison commander and himself to rely on – seventy-two men in total.

It was time for action. He put the whole estate on the watch and dispatched scouts to trace the movements of the enemy. The scouts returned, looking troubled. The Ottomans were dangerously close. And with winter approaching, they would likely wish to raid before the harsh coldness set in. They could attack at any moment.

Despite the farmers' reluctance to abandon their homes, Sándor ordered them to bring their families, their most valuable possessions and as many of their animals as they could within the walls of the town or the wooden palisades of the two villages that had already been fortified. The area of the farmland was vast and the settlements so scattered that it was impossible to protect every part of the estate. The only defence was stopping the Ottomans before they entered his land through the mountain pass. This was where he had to concentrate most of his forces.

The pass was wider than he would have liked. He instructed the soldiers and the miners to dig trenches at the narrowest point and cover them with straw and grass. They would not be able to dig deep in the hard mountain ground, but at least the shallow ditches would hinder the advance of the enemy's horses.

He had to use all the knights and most of the soldiers to defend the pass. He left only the tower guards in the castle and another five men plus the garrison commander in the town in case the Ottomans managed to reach that far. The best-trained and strongest men of the estate joined Balog's team while the miners readied themselves to protect their village.

But even if his people were able to fight, would it be enough? Sándor needed to look for help elsewhere.

He summoned Miklós and Margit to his study. "I wish I could ask Lord Jankó, but I don't know where he is presently. It would take our messenger too long to find him."

Margit gazed intently at his face. "Who is he?"

"János Hunyadi, commander of the armies of the South. My men and I have served under him in battle. His wife, Erzsébet Szilágyi of Horogszeg, is my third cousin."

"I see," she said. "And what of our neighbours?"

Sándor pondered. There was someone, but even the thought of asking him for help turned his stomach. "Rudolf Holman."

Miklós's face flushed. "No! Do not beg that snake!"

Startled by his outburst, Margit spun around to him. "Why not?"

"That accursed Saxon is the most deceitful and scheming man."

She turned to Sándor. "You must do it, my lord. He is the only one who can help us now, and –"

"Don't listen to her!" Miklós interrupted. "Father always said that he would rather die than ask Holman for help."

"And so he did," Margit retorted, glaring at her brother-in-law. "He died and together with him some of our people. We cannot face this force on our own. We cannot afford to lose more lives."

Sándor slammed his fist on the desk. "Enough!" The two of them were arguing about the fate of the estate as though he were not there. He was the one who had to make the decision. "I shall do it. If the Turks raid our land, Holman is next. So, it's in his interest as well to assist us."

"You will regret this," Miklós insisted.

"Perhaps. But at this moment I have no choice. And I shall send you to his residence to convince him that it's for his own good that he has to help us. If he asks for payment, do not promise anything. I shall speak with him when the danger has passed."

Miklós folded his arms and looked away. "No. I refuse."

"I would do this personally, but I must stay here and defend my land," Sándor said, sternly. "So, I am giving you the chance to prove your worth. It's time you did something useful for our family."

"Very well," Miklós, at length, conceded, "but don't blame me if this fails."

Sándor ignored this remark. "Take Master Roth with you. Holman is more likely to listen to a fellow Saxon. Go now. We don't have much time."

As Miklós stamped out of the room, Sándor turned to Margit. "I wish you to go too. It will be dangerous here."

"No. My place is here with my husband." Drawing nearer to him, she rested her hand on his arm. "I have lived through raids before."

Why was everybody contradicting his orders? But there was no point trying to convince her. "Since you prefer to stay, I must show you something important."

He led her to his bedchamber, which used to be his father's before. He went to the side of the fireplace and ran his hand along the frame of the wood panelling on the wall until he found the right spot. He pressed on it. With a creaking sound, the whole frame slowly projected away from him.

Margit's jaw dropped. "What is this?"

"A secret passage, leading outside the walls. Its exit is in a cave, at the back of the hill, hidden by thick bushes. If the enemy ever breaches the defences and enters the castle, this is your way out. One of my ancestors had it built and connected it to the natural cave underneath when he renovated the keep. It's a secret that only the lord of the castle is privy to. My father told me years ago. No one else, not even Miklós, knows this. So, please keep it to yourself."

***

Sándor was at the mountain pass, supervising the defensive works in the light of lanterns and open fires, when Balog came to him. "The scouts are back, sir. A unit of three hundred Akinjis has camped one hour from here. It's a moonless night, thanks be to God. I think they'll wait until sunrise before attacking."

"This is good news. It will give us a little more time."

"You should rest, sir. I can take charge now."

Sándor patted his castellan on the arm. "Thank you. I must stay here so that the men do not lose faith. I am going to lie on one of the carts. Wake me up at the start of the fourth watch."

All through the night, the people of Szentimre worked hard to finish the trenches and then took a brief rest as the raiders had not yet appeared. A dozen villagers and as many miners came to the pass to join the soldiers. Balog returned to the town while Sándor gathered the knights and gave them instructions where to position the men.

Ideally, he would have liked to place soldiers at both ends of the mountain pass – to attack the Ottomans from both sides. He not only wanted to repel them, but also kill as many as he could to deter them from raiding his estate again. But he did not have enough men to spare. He could afford only ten of them to stay hidden halfway up the pass. Perhaps the element of surprise would be enough to confound the enemy when those soldiers attacked from the back. Then, he placed six archers on each flank of the pass and the remaining ones at the second line of defence, behind an earthen rampart a hundred paces inside the estate land.

It was time to prepare. "Bring my armour now," he ordered his squire. "I must not be taken by surprise when they come."

The Akinjis arrived just after dawn. They did not see the defenders, who were hiding behind trees, bushes and rocks on both sides of the pass. As they galloped through, their front line stumbled into the ditches. The ones coming from behind crashed into their fallen comrades. At the same time, the soldiers of Szentimre surrounded them while the archers came out of their hiding places and provided support from a distance. A fierce battle ensued. They were up against two or three opponents each. The villagers and miners helped as much as they could, but they eventually had to retreat to protect their homes.

Sándor was still on his horse, striking with his axe incessantly. Perceiving his enemies' weaknesses had become a strength of his. He aimed to kill with the first blow. The Ottomans had slain his father and his people. He was not going to show them any mercy.

In a close-quarter fight like that, he was grateful that he could afford good quality armour and, above all, a fine, highly trained destrier like Vihar.

"Up!" he shouted and tugged at the reins. The dapple-grey stallion reared. At the sight of this big and strong beast, some of the raiders cowered. The ones who did not, found themselves kicked on the head or in the face.

However, this was not enough. His men had held out for some time, but they had now been overpowered and were retreating to save themselves. Sándor glanced about him. It was only he, the knights and a handful of soldiers left fighting. Could this be the end? He had cheated death so many times in battle. But perhaps this was for a reason: that he would come to die protecting his home, just like his father. Everything around him became distant and distorted. The whole world slowed down for a few moments, and then, time speeded up again.

He was not going to stand there and wait for death to come. He was going to leave this world fighting and taking as many enemy men with him as he could. The axe had gone blunt from too much hitting on bodies and armour. He threw it to the ground and drew his sword. He spurred on his horse, screaming an order at him to attack.

**

The previous night, Miklós and Josef Roth waited in Rudolf Holman's study. The Saxon landlord did not even have the courtesy to offer them a seat. He stood upright, tapping his fingers on the desk and staring at the open door.

The intoxicating scent of lavender filled the room. Airy footsteps approached with the rustling of a silk garment. Miklós turned his head. A young woman brushed past him as she went to sit near Holman. Wearing no headdress or veil, she displayed her flowing nutbrown hair to the delight of the visitors. She casually twisted a lock around her fingers and then flicked it over her shoulder. She beamed a sweet smile at Miklós. His heartbeat quickened, and he could not take his eyes off her shapely bosom.

"My beloved daughter, Anna," Holman introduced her. He finally sat down but still left his guests standing. "What is the purpose of your visit at this advanced hour?"

A sneer appeared on his face as he listened to his neighbour's plea for assistance. "No, I shall not help you. Why would I? Your sire humiliated me and my daughter not only by rejecting the marriage between her and your brother, but also by spreading malicious rumours about us to the rest of the Hungarian nobility."

Puckering her lips, Anna cast a disapproving glance at Miklós.

His face heated. "I... apologise to you, lady..." He turned to Holman. "And sir." He cleared his throat. "I wish... I could do something to change that. But my father is dead, and I ask for your assistance as your fellow nobleman, your neighbour. If the Turks destroy us, you are next. We must unite against a common enemy."

"It took me years to restore my reputation by building a strong unit of cavalry mercenaries, famed for their skills and success on the battlefield. Now everyone wishes to hire them, and I'm making a fortune." Holman paused and scratched his chin. "I'll tell you what I can do. Because I can see the danger of the Turks, I shall lend you my soldiers only for this time. But you must be prepared to pay a high price."

"My brother did not authorise me to negotiate any price. He is asking for help. I'm sure he will be willing to repay the favour. Are we in agreement?"

"Then, there is no agreement."

Miklós rubbed his brow. There was one last thing left to try before admitting defeat. He nudged Roth. The latter made a desperate effort to convince Holman, by speaking to him in the Saxon language. The discussion went on for a short time. Anna watched and listened carefully, arching her eyebrows every now and then.

Roth looked at Miklós and shook his head. They had failed.

Holman was about to throw them out when his daughter stood up and said in excellent Hungarian, "Father, I hope you are not sending these good people away in the dead of night?" Although soft-spoken and elegant, she had an air of confidence about her.

"Why?"

"What kind of a host are you? Let them sleep here, and they can leave in the morning."

Holman looked askance at her.

"Please, Father. Do it for me," she insisted, her tone mellifluous.

She had kept her eyes fixed on Miklós all this time, their

expression communicating something mysterious but alluring.

"Very well," Holman said and signalled to his servant to show the visitors to their chambers.

***

Miklós was woken up by the sound of the door opening and closing. He jumped out of the bed and reached for his sword.

"Do not fear, good sir," a woman's voice whispered. "It is only I."

The figure standing in front of him and holding a candle was Anna.

"What are you doing here, lady?"

"I think I can help you."

"In what way?"

"I know my father refused, but I am sure I can convince him to lend his soldiers to you."

"We can't pay him."

"Shh." She came closer to him. "He will do it if I ask him. But you must give me something in return."

She placed the candle on the bedside table and wrapped her arms around his neck. Before he even knew it, she planted her lips on his. Her tongue slipped into his mouth so eagerly that he felt the blood flow fast and warm, almost bursting his veins. The flowery smell of her skin sent his head into a spin. He had little experience with women, and this one would charm the moon out of the sky.

Anna pulled away, leaving him craving for more. He put his

arm around her waist, grabbing her chemise, and drew her towards him. Their bodies touched again. "No. Not yet," she said as she freed herself from his passionate embrace. "I shall speak with my father first."

It was not yet dawn when Holman called Miklós into his study.

"I have decided to provide the assistance that you requested. I have ordered a hundred of my cavalry soldiers to accompany you. And I shall not demand monetary compensation."

Miklós heaved a sigh of relief. "Thank you, sir. You are most generous."

Holman smirked. "However, you will need to make a different kind of agreement with me in order to repay this favour; an agreement that your brother is not to be informed about until I tell him myself when the time is right."

***

Sándor had begun his desperate final charge at the enemy when shouts echoed in the distance. The Ottomans stopped fighting and turned their backs to him. He screamed at his soldiers to chase them. As soon as he came out of the narrow pass, he found the enemy under attack by horsemen, who had charged from the opposite side. Trapped between Holman's cavalry and the Szentimre defenders, the raiders were cut down, and those who were not slaughtered surrendered immediately.

He saw his brother among the mercenaries. "Well done! I'm proud of you."

A crooked smile formed on Miklós's face. He just nodded but did not say a word.

Sándor's men cheered at the mercenaries, who had tied the prisoners in a long row behind their horses. The captain, a fierce-looking Croatian warrior who spoke broken Hungarian, dismounted and approached.

"Borislav Gradić. At your service, m'lord."

Sándor shook his hand. "Thank you for your assistance."

"Master Holman comes Sunday... Celebration dinner."

That was unexpected! "Oh... very well. Umm, tell him... he will be welcome."

The mercenary saluted and returned to his soldiers. They departed, taking all the Ottoman prisoners with them. Holman was going to make a fortune by ransoming them, but Sándor was too tired to make any demands on keeping some of the captives for himself. Leaving one of his knights in charge of bringing the wounded and the dead to the town, he rode towards the castle.

The town gates were open as the peasants who had sought refuge there were returning to their homes. He arrived at the castle, dismounted and left the horse with the groom. He burst into the house, looking for Margit.

"My lord!" she shouted and ran to embrace him. "Thank God, you are well. I was so worried."

Yes, he was safe; but this was not so for some of his people. He had to take care of their families. He should be out there with them.

Holding Margit by the arm, he rushed her up the stairs and

into his bedchamber. With her help, he took off his armour, piece by piece. There was blood and dirt all over it and on his face too. But it was enemy blood. He had escaped with only chafes and bruises, some of them painful, nevertheless.

"Let me take care of you," she said on seeing the injuries when he removed his tattered and stained shirt.

He could not waste any more time. "Not now. I must go out again. I only came here to make sure you are well and to change clothes."

Margit shook her head. "No. You are hurt. You need tending."

She reached towards him, but he gripped her wrist and held it firmly, making her shriek.

"I am a soldier, Margit. I have received worse injuries than these. I only need a clean shirt."

She wrested her hand free and pursed her lips. "At least, let me wipe the blood from your face. You will scare the women and children."

Why was she not listening to him? "How many times must I say this? Bring me a shirt, woman!"

***

Late in the evening, after he had assessed the damage caused by the attack and consoled the families of the dead and wounded, Sándor allowed himself to rest in a warm bath. Then he lay on the bed while Margit tended to his injuries with herbal remedies. Her soft, caring and motherly touch transported him back to the safety of his childhood. He was at peace.

The flickering flame of the candles cast dancing shadows across her face. He brushed her cheek with the back of his hand. "Today was the first time I went out to fight since my return home. There was a moment, just before help arrived, when I thought the end had come. But that is not an excuse for my shameful behaviour towards you. I apologise and beg your forgiveness."

Margit sucked her lower lip and looked at him with narrowed eyes, rubbing her wrist. She spoke with a calmness that sounded menacing. "Never treat me in that manner again. My hand still hurts."

He nodded. "It will not happen again. I give you my word."

"Then, I forgive you." She smiled briefly and continued dispensing her loving attentions to him.

Sándor touched her arm, gently this time. "Margit, stop. You have looked after my injuries, and I feel much better. We have more important matters to attend to now."

She placed the wet cloth and bowl of warm water and herbs on the bedside table and turned to face him. "Which matters, my lord?"

He sat up and leaned towards her. He lifted her chin and nuzzled the side of her face, whispering, "I could have died today. I cannot die without an heir. I must have a son. You must give me a son."

His body was still sore, but this did not prevent him from offering his wife all the attention and pleasure she deserved. When finished, he kissed her tenderly on the forehead and fell asleep in her arms.

6
An Unwanted Alliance
and a Dark Secret

Dressed in the finest clothes and pointy-toed leather shoes, Rudolf Holman exuded confidence and vanity as he entered the keep.

"Welcome, sir," Sándor said, bowing slightly.

The Saxon snorted and strutted past him and Margit into the great hall.

Sándor quickly examined himself. The buttons of his doublet were done, the points of his hose laced, his boots clean, his hair neatly tied back. There was nothing amiss with the way he looked. Such contempt was uncalled-for.

He kept his eye on his guest as they sat at the table. Although the aroma of freshly baked bread, spiced roast meat and sugared apples would make anyone's mouth water, Holman only nibbled at the venison and spent most of the time drinking the sweet Hungarian wine and jesting in the Saxon language with his five knights while ignoring his hosts.

Why was this man so arrogant? Coughing for attention, Sándor raised his cup. "To our neighbour, Rudolf Holman. Thank you for helping us."

The Saxon nodded and smiled as he watched everyone drink to his health. He waited for a few moments before standing up. "Thank you for being such generous hosts. I, too, have an announcement to make."

Sándor looked at Margit. She was as surprised as he was.

"I am proud to announce the betrothal of my beloved daughter Anna to Miklós Szilágyi."

Sándor sprang upright in his chair. "What? I did not agree to this." He turned to Miklós. "Is it true?"

His brother nodded nervously and fixed his gaze to the plate in front of him.

Of course. Holman's behaviour now began to make sense. Still, how could Miklós dare agree to something so important behind his back and never tell him about it? Sándor cursed under his breath and tried to stand up, but Holman put his hand on his shoulder and forced him to stay seated. "Did you think that I would lend you my soldiers for nothing? I know you don't have the money to pay me, so I thought this would be the best manner to receive my compensation."

Sándor banged his fist on the table, making plates, cups and cutlery rattle. "No! I do not give my permission."

"Well then, sir," Holman continued calmly, "you will be indebted to me for a very long time. I shall take every single florin of the revenue your mine produces until I have my payment. Or perhaps I shall take some of your land. Your brother gave me his word of honour that he would marry my daughter in return for my assistance. He was negotiating on your behalf. It would be an insult not to honour the agreement."

The veins in Sándor's neck were about to burst. But there was no way out. "Very well," he conceded and then turned towards his brother. "A word, Miklós."

He stood up and walked out of the hall with his brother following him. When they were out of earshot of the others, he grabbed Miklós by the throat and pushed him against the wall. "You said that Holman is a snake and that I should not beg him. I gave you clear instructions not to promise anything to him. Why did you agree to this?"

"You should thank me." His brother's voice quavered. "I saw that you were in great peril when we arrived."

"I'd rather die than let this viper's daughter into my family."

"And what about your wife and your people? Would you have led them all to slaughter or slavery? Besides, I love Anna, and I wish to marry her."

"You love her? Have you even met her?"

"Yes. We embraced each other and kissed."

"You mean she seduced you? Foolish boy!" Sándor tightened his grip on his brother's throat. "You betrayed your family for a scheming whore. That witch had two husbands murdered so that she and her father could take their money and their estates. And now you want to bring her into my house. She will not hesitate to poison both of us to take Szentimre."

"She won't do that. She loves me too."

"You are so ignorant." Sándor finally released Miklós's neck. "I was going to give you a quarter of the estate as a wedding gift if you were to take a bride that I approved of. But now that you are marrying her, you will have nothing from me."

Coughing loudly, Miklós rubbed his neck, which had the red

marks of his brother's grip. Shaking and staggering, he retired to his bedchamber.

Sándor returned to the great hall and sat down.

"Let us drink to the blessed union of our families," Holman said, his eyes gleaming with imperious triumph.

Sándor clenched his fists. He wanted to rip the Saxon's head off, but he gulped down his wine instead and poured some more from the flagon.

Holman and his men departed shortly afterwards.

"Good riddance. May you fall off your horse and break your neck," Sándor muttered under his breath. He reached for the flagon again.

"Too much wine has loosened your tongue," Margit rebuked him like a mother addressing a bold child.

The last thing he needed was a lecture. "Leave me in peace!"

She glared at him and then walked out of the great hall.

***

A frightening dream awoke Margit. Her heart was pounding, her mind heavy with worry about her husband. She needed to make sure that all was well with him.

She had just turned into the corridor leading to his quarters when the door of his chamber opened and closed. She collided with a young woman in her underclothes. They both had a fright, but Margit acted quickly and gripped the other's arms, making her drop the shoes, kirtle and cloak that she was holding.

"Who are you? What were you doing in my husband's

bedchamber?"

The stranger tried to free her arms from Margit's hold. "Please, lady. Only done wha' I been ashkt tae do."

Margit shuddered at the woman's vulgar accent. She let her go and watched her pick her things from the floor and disappear around the corner.

She stood outside Sándor's room. Her hands were shaking, her knees about to buckle. But whatever was happening in there, she had to face it. At length, she drew a deep breath and opened the door.

The chamber was in darkness but for a single candle and the silver light of the moon, streaming through the arched window. Her husband was sitting on the edge of the bed, clothes off and with his back to her, while a naked young woman was on her knees in front of him with her head between his legs and her hands tied behind her back. A second woman, also unclothed, had her arms around him from behind and was kissing his neck and shoulders. The smell of wine and sweat pervaded the air.

The contents of Margit's stomach rose to her throat. She forced herself to swallow them back down. "What are you doing?" She could hardly recognise the hoarse sound of her own voice.

They all stopped and turned towards her.

"Leave!" Sándor ordered the women.

The one who was behind him leapt off the bed, untied the other, and then they gathered their clothes and hastened out of the room.

The heartbeat pounded in Margit's ears. She approached him,

picked his shirt from the floor and flung it at him. "How can you disrespect your wife and shame our marriage?"

"Do not raise your voice to your husband!" he growled like a cornered animal. He grabbed her arm, forcing her to sit beside him.

She wrested herself from his grip.

"I'm sorry you saw this," Sándor said as he put his shirt on. "Please, calm yourself. I shall explain." Although still abrupt, his voice had become a little subdued by now.

"Explain what? That you pretend to care about me, but you do all this behind my back?"

"I do this because... because I care about you."

Margit looked at him in disbelief. "You are not even making sense!"

He leaned towards her. "You are my wife. You will be the mother of my children. And you are a devout woman. You always say your prayers and never miss church. I would never degrade you or make you do unnatural and sinful things to satisfy me in bed."

Margit jumped to her feet, her heart thumping like a heavy hammer. "Why would you do unnatural and sinful things at all?"

Sándor lowered his head and stared at the floor. "It's a long story."

She folded her arms. "I would like to hear it."

"Very well." He cleared his throat. "During my time in Buda, the noblemen and knights of the royal court frowned upon me and my companions because we came from Transylvania. They called us 'provincial savages'. They thought we were too loud, unrefined and as wild as the wolves that roam our forests. But some of their ladies fancied us. One of them took me on as her lover. She was the wife of a foreign ambassador. Her husband did not care for her but was more interested in corrupting adolescent boys instead. Wanting to pay him back in his own coin, she introduced me to a world beyond my wildest dreams – a world of ultimate pleasure, where everything was allowed."

Margit clenched her fists so tight that the muscles of her hands hurt. How little did she know about her own husband, the man she had given her heart to!

Sándor stood up, walked towards the window and leaned on the sill, his body a shadow against the moonlight that shone through the glass pane.

His voice trembled as he continued, "And she invited other noble ladies to join us. It was not long before it went to my head. I could have all those women pleasing me and, more importantly, I knew many ways to enjoy myself without getting them with child."

An awful tightness gripped Margit's body and kept her pinned in her position.

"There is more," Sándor said.

A heavy groan escaped her mouth. How much more of this humiliation could she take?

He lowered his head and covered his face with his hand, muffling his voice a little. "After leaving the court a year later, I fought as a mercenary in Northern Italy and then, upon my return to Hungary, with the king's army in Bohemia and Serbia. I constantly faced death on the battlefield. I did not know if I would be alive the next day, so I sought to escape awhile – escape into this world of pleasure and gratification, where I was in charge, and no one could threaten me." He finally turned around to face her. "But I swear to God, I have never forced myself upon anyone. Those women either enjoyed being with me, or they were paid to accept me."

Margit tugged at the front of her chemise, almost tearing it as she fought the urge to pounce on him like a feral cat. "Is this what you do on the nights you don't visit my chamber?"

"No! I swear. I did not wish to bring home the vices of my past life. But the events of the last few weeks have put a huge weight upon me. I feel I have failed my family and my people. So, after the humiliation of today's dinner, I could not bear it anymore."

Silent tears streamed down Margit's face.

"Oh, don't cry, *angyalom*," he whispered, reaching for her; but she recoiled as though burned by fire.

"Don't touch me!"

"I have wronged you, dear wife, and I beg your forgiveness."

She stepped back, panting and trembling, unable to look at him. "You have hidden all this from me. You... you are a... liar and an adulterer! Why should I forgive you?"

Sándor walked back to the bed, sat down and patted the mattress by his side. "Here, come sit with me. Take a breath."

She inhaled and exhaled heavily. Despite herself, she obeyed him – absently as if she were in a dream and exhausted as if all her strength and will had abandoned her. At a different time, his manly touch on her hand would have stirred her blood from excitement. But now she felt nothing. A single thought ran through her mind: was he worthy of forgiveness?

A long time passed without a word between them.

"I love you more than life itself," he broke the silence. "I admit it was your beauty and your purity that captivated me at first; but then I came to love your moral strength, your wisdom, your unwavering sense of loyalty, your fearlessness. What woman would dare confront her husband like you did?" He held her by both arms and looked into her eyes. "I stand in awe of you, dear wife. You must not call me 'my lord' again. Because the truth is, I see you as my... equal."

Margit let out a deep sigh and lowered her head. His impassioned words had breached her defences, reaching deep into her heart. He was a strong man on the surface, but he had lost his way. Perhaps he deserved another chance... Perhaps it was her duty as a wife to guide him back to the path of righteousness.

Pressing her lips together, she lifted her eyes and held his gaze. If she were to forgive him, she had to make sure that what he had done was not to happen again. "Will you swear to me in the eyes of God that you will not lie with another woman as long as I am alive?"

"Yes, of course, *angyalom*."

"And that you will let me share your burden by accepting my help with the estate?"

He nodded.

"I promise I shall give you the best counsel. You must trust me.

I endured a difficult time while you were away. Your father shunned me in the beginning. In his eyes, I was only a weak little girl. But I am a Bátori. My family is one of the most powerful in Hungary. I would not sit in my chamber all day, doing embroidery and waiting for my lord's return. I decided to fight; to show him that he should respect and trust me. I would hide in the great hall and listen when he had meetings with his council. I wished to learn about everything that was happening in Szentimre. He eventually discovered me and rebuked me severely. But I did it again and again until he finally accepted me as his partner in the administration of the estate."

Sándor took her hand and kissed it softly.

She raised the forefinger of her other hand at him. "Make sure you keep your word, husband. Next time, I may not be so forgiving."

7
János Hunyadi

The carriage travelled through ancient forests, valleys and mountain passes – all cloaked in soft snow and gleaming brilliant white in the sunshine – but Sándor was only interested in one sight: that of his wife as she slept peacefully in the seat opposite him despite the jolting, bumpy ride. His love, respect and admiration for her kept growing with each passing day. Letting her assist him with the administration of the estate was the best decision he had ever made. She was present in all the meetings with his counsellors, supported and even substituted him as a judge and arbitrator in the disputes among the people of the area. She offered her advice and opinions on various subjects. The officials did not object to her making decisions and giving orders because they knew her well from the time when she would help her father-in-law. She had a talent for leadership, and Sándor was eager to learn from her.

Their trip had been her suggestion. János Hunyadi had returned to his castle after a long time fighting in the civil war. Margit had convinced Sándor to visit his acquaintance and ask for assistance.

Although tired from the long journey and the icy weather, they were keen to speak with him as soon as they arrived at the castle of Hunyadvár.

János received them in his quarters, where a large masonry stove – decorated with yellow figures of armed horsemen on its glazed green tiles – spread its warmth about the room. The remains of a delicious meal lay on a low trestle table, along with a glass beaker half-filled with sweet-smelling wine.

"Thank you for seeing us, sir," Sándor said loudly, trying to cover the sound of his grumbling stomach. He held Margit's hand, and they both knelt in respect.

"Stand up! We are all friends here," Hunyadi jested. After eyeing Margit for a few moments, he stared at him until recognition flickered on his face. "Szilágyi of Szentimre? 'Red Sándor'?"

Margit chuckled.

Sándor frowned at her. "Something amuses you?"

"Did they call you that because of the enemy blood you spilled or because of the colour of your hair?"

His face heated, but he became at ease as soon as János cracked a smile.

"It was both," Hunyadi said. "Dear lady, you are fortunate to have this man by your side. I fought with him many a time, and I can tell you he is one of the most formidable knights in the kingdom. He was born to fight. Look at him: towering by a whole head over the rest of us. This is what good 'cross-breeding' creates. Hungarian noble blood, complemented by impressive Saxon appearance and Székely warrior spirit."

"I agree, my lord. But he is also fortunate to have me as his wife."

"How so?"

"I shall let him explain. I'd better keep quiet now."

Hunyadi turned to him. "Well? You still haven't properly introduced us."

"I apologise, sir. This is my beloved wife, Margit Bátori. We wed five years ago while I was still training as a knight in Buda. She is also my best counsellor and an excellent negotiator."

Hunyadi nodded in admiration. "So," he said, his eyes fixed on her, "not only beautiful, but also clever, witty and fearless if I dare say. You have done well, *barátom*, despite your ugly face."

"Sir! I am not that ugly," Sándor objected.

János raised his eyebrows.

Sándor turned to Margit. "Am I?"

She could not reply for she had both hands over her mouth, struggling to contain her giggles.

Hunyadi patted him on the arm. "I'm only teasing. You surely turned quite a few ladies' heads when you were at the court. Still, out of the three of us here, you are the ugliest one."

Sándor raised his hand. "Very well, I accept that."

"My dear," János addressed Margit, "you are a Bátori. Where from?"

She hurriedly adjusted her veil, which had gone askew following her earlier laughing outburst. "Szatmár County, my lord. We are related to the Ecsed branch of the family. My father was Lord András Bátori. He died six years ago, fighting the heretics in

Bohemia."

"And your mother?"

"Anna Wójcik of Kraków. She died of grief, only three months after my father. My uncle, János Bátori, became my guardian and arranged my marriage."

"So, you are half-Polish. Then, I trust you are supporters of King Władysław. The civil war is still raging in Hungary, and I need as many nobles as possible on our side here in Transylvania. I bear no grudge against King Albert's widow for trying to put her boy on the throne. But the simple truth is that a woman and a little baby cannot defend us against the Ottomans on the battlefield. That is why we offered the crown to Władysław instead even though he is a foreigner."

"Yes," Sándor said. "We are at the king's service any time he needs us."

"I'm pleased to hear that. I can assure you that the king is also committed to helping his loyal subjects against the Turkish aggression. By the way, I heard about the raid on your estate. People say you fought like a Spartan warrior and slew hundreds of Ottomans completely on your own."

Sándor inhaled deeply, his chest filling with pride at Hunyadi's praise. "Did they also say that I breathed fire out of my nose? I am honoured, but I only did my duty. And the truth is that we would have been defeated but for Rudolf Holman's help."

"Not a good person to be indebted to. I hear that your brother is to wed Holman's daughter. I would be careful if I were you. He has a reputation. No one trusts him."

Sándor's jaw clenched. Without a doubt, the Saxon had spread the news far and wide, bragging about his family's ascent to a higher rank of nobility. "Believe me, sir, I did not wish to request his assistance, but he was the only one close enough and capable enough to help. Which leads me to another matter and the reason of my visit." He cleared his throat. "I did not come here, sir, seeking an office to advance myself. I only wish to protect my land and my people."

Hunyadi motioned the two of them to sit on a cushioned wooden bench. He sank in his own high-backed chair. "I am listening."

Fighting his pride, Sándor described the difficult situation he was in. He held his hat in his hands and tapped his fingers on it as he admitted that he needed help. Otherwise, he was in danger of losing everything his ancestors had achieved.

János listened intently. He apologised that he was not available at the time to offer military assistance but promised that he would not abandon his old comrade in the future. He offered immediate financial support to help restore the damage the Ottomans had inflicted on Szentimre. He was also willing to send a unit of soldiers and knights to protect the estate against future raids.

Sándor's pulse quickened. What price would he have to pay for such 'generosity'?

"Tell me about that mine of yours," Hunyadi said. "How does it operate?"

Sándor twitched. Of course. That was the price.

"One of my Székely ancestors saved the life of King Károly

Róbert in a battle, more than a century ago. The king ennobled him, granted him Szentimre and permission to mine for gold and silver. My ancestor would pay the workers and operate the mine. He was obliged to exchange only two thirds of the precious metals at the royal mint. As for the remaining one third, he was free to sell to whomever offered the highest price, provided he was not a foreign buyer. King Zsigmond re-confirmed this agreement with a new charter to my Szilágyi grandfather."

Hunyadi pressed his lips together and stroked his chin. Any trace of friendliness and compassion had disappeared from his face like the sun during an eclipse. "Hmm, these are very favourable terms. But we live in perilous times. We must all do our duty to protect our homeland. Your mine is valuable to the realm. So, I suggest that you place it fully at the king's disposal. I shall send my own people to operate it. The king will compensate you with a fair rent, enough to pay the workers and allow you a steady revenue. And with those soldiers and equipment that I promised to give you, your estate will be defended in the case of another attack."

Sándor became lost in thought. With Hunyadi's proposal, he would not be able to sell the precious metals or exchange them at the mint for coins. His revenue would reduce significantly. But he did not have a choice. Amidst the turbulence of the times, it was safer to keep his family, his land and his people protected.

"Yes, sir. I accept."

"I have but one more request," János added. "You must pledge yourself, all the mercenaries that I shall give you and as many of your own soldiers as you can afford to my command. Hungary is at war, and I'm building an army to defend her. You are an experienced fighter. I'm sure you will make an excellent officer, too. I need you to make yourself available whenever I call upon you and your men. I understand that you have a young wife and your land to look after, so I shall not demand a permanent commitment from you. But you must be at the ready at all times in case you are called."

Instinctively, Sándor turned to Margit. Her face darkened, but she did not speak. It was a decision that he had to make. "Of course, sir. I swear to serve the king whenever I am needed."

"Thank you." Hunyadi shook his hand. "And now, go have a rest. I'm sure you are tired and hungry. My people will look after you."

***

They returned home in high spirits.

"I'm proud of you," Margit said. "You can now rule this land as your father did and his father before him. And you don't need my help anymore. So, I can return to my embroidery."

"Embroidery? I shall not believe it until I see it."

They burst out laughing.

Margit cleared her throat. "I have something for you, dear husband. I think you deserve a reward."

"A reward? What is it?"

She did not reply but took him by the hand and led him to her bedchamber. She wrapped her arms around his neck, gazed up into his eyes and smiled. "You have proven to the world that you are the master of this place. Now prove it to me too. I shall surrender my body to you to do as you please."

He freed himself from her embrace and looked at her with both wonder and suspicion. "Are you willing? I do not wish to force you into anything you would not like."

"I have given it much deliberation since that horrible night, and now I am ready to submit to all your desires."

Sándor's face lit up brighter than the sun on a summer's day as he drew her into his arms.

With trembling hands and shivering with anticipation, they undressed each other. After they had removed all their clothes, he took her hand, kissed it and placed it on his chest. Margit's mouth opened wide as she felt his heart beat like a horse's gallop against her palm.

"Look what you are doing to me," he whispered in her ear.

He made her kneel at the end of the bed and tied her hands to the bedpost with his belt. She groaned as the leather tightened around her wrists. But the pain melted into a warm stream of pleasure that ran through her body when he glided his hand along the line of her spine, from the nape of her neck to the small of her back.

He gave her a playful slap on the backside, and she let out a surprised shriek – not from discomfort but from pure delight. "Saucy vixen!" he jested. "Making fun of me in front of Lord Jankó? You need to know your place, woman. You need to know who the master is here."

She could not wait a moment longer. "Of course, my lord. Please, show me."

"Do you think what we do is sinful?" Sándor looked hard at Margit's face after the wild fire of their passion had subsided. "When you go to confession, will you tell the priest?"

"We are married, we are trying to have children, and we cause no harm to anyone with what we do. Still, lust is a sin and must be confessed."

She giggled and buried her face in the pillow. Her skin tingled at the touch of his fingertips on her bare shoulder.

"Why are you hiding, dear wife? Are you ashamed?"

She let out a sigh and turned around to him. "A little. That is why I am not going to recount all the details to the priest. If I did, he would make both of us do penance for the rest of our lives. We have broken so many rules."

Sándor chuckled. "With the danger of sounding like a heretic, I certainly do not agree. Why should the Church tell me which days of the week I can lie with my wife, what to do or not do with her and even how to feel about her? We are surrounded by misery, disease, war, death and destruction. Why should we also be miserable in our most intimate moments? If we can make each other happy with material things, like jewellery, clothes and gold, why can we not give each other happiness through non-material means, such as love and pleasure of the flesh?"

Margit shook her head. "What a strange and dangerous theory! Perhaps, I can accept what you say as far as it concerns husband

and wife. But you sound like you are trying to justify adultery."

"I am not," he protested, slightly embarrassed. "If my woman makes me happy, why would I desire another one?"

"And if she doesn't?"

He winked at her. "You need not fret about that."

Margit smiled to herself. Like Anna Holman, she was using her body to control her man. But unlike Anna, who wanted to bend Miklós to her will and use him in her devious plans, she was trying to raise Sándor's confidence and make him believe in his abilities. She had guided him through a difficult adjustment period while he turned from a soldier to a landlord. She had disputed his orders, argued against his decisions and sometimes even made him look inadequate in front of other people. But this was a lesson for him. He had learned to fight back, use his intelligence to solve problems, not be afraid to ask for help, compromise when needed. All these actions made him a better leader; someone who would be much more respected by his people.

By agreeing to satisfy all his desires in bed, she was in a way rewarding him for the man he had become. And equally importantly, while other noblemen had mistresses and fathered illegitimate children, she was making sure that her husband would never stray from the marriage bed.

8
What God Gives He Can Take Away

February 1441

Margit's cheeks flushed as soon as she heard the news. The fact that she had not bled for two months had not made her suspect anything – it was something that had happened before. But when she felt extremely nauseous in the mornings, her maid called the midwife, who officially confirmed it. After six months of frustration, her husband's constant nagging and countless prayers to God, the Virgin Mary and all the saints, it had finally happened.

She jumped up and down and clapped her hands.

Erzsi tapped her on the shoulder. "Calm now, my lady! I know you're excited, but you must watch yourself."

Margit grasped her maid's arms and squeezed them. "My dear husband will be so pleased. I must tell him forthwith."

"You should wait for a few weeks to make sure all's well," Erzsi still ventured to calm her down, but Margit flew out of the bedchamber, completely ignoring her. "At least, put some clothes on!" the maid shouted after her.

Sándor was in his study with the steward when she burst in like a madwoman, breathless, in her bare feet, cheeks ablaze, her hair loose and uncovered and, worst of all, in her undergarments.

Both men leapt to their feet. Havasi's face reddened. He bowed his head and hastened out of the room while Sándor expressed his disapproval with a big frown. "Have you lost your mind?"

"God has finally blessed us. I am with child."

She flung herself into his arms with such enthusiasm that she nearly knocked him to the floor. Yet, he did not complain, only stared at her with mouth agape. "Are you... s... sure?"

"Yes!"

He touched his forehead with his palm, struggling to find the words. "We must... tell everyone... We... we... must... have a... feast..." He raised his gaze upwards. "Dear God, let it be a son."

"It will be, *szerelmem*. I feel it."

He lifted her off her feet and spun around with her in his arms until they were both lightheaded and giggling like little children.

And then, for the first time, she saw him cry tears of joy and relief.

But the happiness did not last for long.

"The Lord gave, and the Lord has taken away." The priest had said this phrase many times in church. Margit had never thought it would be relevant to her one day. It was barely a week later when joy turned into tragedy. The pain and the blood were only physical symptoms. They would be forgotten very soon. What worried her most was how she was going to face her husband. How was she going to tell him that his long-awaited heir did not exist anymore?

***

Notified by the servants that his wife had been taken ill, Sándor dropped everything he was doing and ran to her.

The women were standing at her bedside with sad faces.

His whole body went numb.

Margit dissolved into tears. "I'm sorry. I'm so sorry!"

"What happened?"

"She lost the baby," Erzsi replied, and before he even opened his mouth to say anything, she continued, "Please, my lord, be kind to her. She's been in so much pain."

His only reaction was an involuntary facial twitch. Then, he dismissed the women with an abrupt movement of his hand.

Margit was still sobbing, even louder now.

What could he say to her? No words would make the sorrow go away. He sat on the bed and held her quivering body against his chest, letting her cry for as long as she needed. When she finally stopped, he brushed away the tears on her face. "Do not weep, *angyalom*," he said quietly. "All will be well next time. You must rest now."

He helped her lie down, pulled the bed covers over her and kissed her on the forehead. She closed her eyes and, overwhelmed by exhaustion, fell asleep.

When Sándor walked out of her bedchamber, he could not hold back any longer. He banged his fist on the wall and cursed.

"My lord," Erzsi called him from behind. "I beg of you, don't be angry with her! It wasn't her fault. It was God's will."

He turned around and glared at her. "I am not angry with Margit. I am angry with God. Why did He take my child away?"

"Perhaps you should go to church more often. We rarely see you there."

"Perhaps you should shut your mouth and mind your own affairs!"

Erzsi pressed her lips together and looked away.

Sándor raised his hand apologetically. "You must go to her now. She needs you."

9
Scheming

The wedding of Miklós and Anna took place on Easter Day in the chapel at Sasfészek. Rudolf Holman took on all the expenses, and it was no small event.

The following morning, he strode into Sándor's study as if he were its owner. "I must talk to you. Now!"

Sándor eyed him with some wonder and motioned him to sit down. "What's the matter?"

"How much of the estate and the mine did your father bequeath to Miklós? And don't tell me this is none of my concern. I must make sure that my daughter will be looked after well and live a comfortable life."

Sándor folded his arms. He had been tricked into an unpleasant situation, but now he was about to reciprocate in kind. "Miklós has inherited three hundred acres in the north-western corner of the estate. This includes a hamlet, an apple orchard, arable and forested land and a large hunting lodge. He can reside in the castle of Sasfészek for as long as he wishes; but if he decides to leave, he cannot return." He forced himself to suppress a smirk as he watched Holman writhe in his chair. "I do not understand why you fret about your daughter's welfare. You already hold, on her behalf, the landed properties of her first two husbands because they had no heirs: the one where you live and the other near Szeben."

Holman jumped to his feet. "Three hundred acres? Out of an estate of twenty thousand? And you forgot to mention this to me before?"

"You never asked."

"I did not ask because the Hungarian custom is that a nobleman's land must be divided equally among his male heirs. Did your sire lose his mind?"

Sándor shrugged. "Don't complain to me. That was my father's will, and my brother has accepted the arrangement."

"And what about the mine?"

"I have placed it at the king's disposal in exchange for an annual rent."

Holman's face changed several colours, but he did not utter a further word of complaint or displeasure. "Could I have the title deeds of this plot of land?" he begged.

Sándor drew a deep breath. He savoured the moment for as long as he could. Now, it was time to thrust the knife even deeper into the wound. "The deeds? Absolutely not."

"Why not?"

"Even though my brother is wed to your daughter, you have no authority over him. I am still his guardian until he comes of full age and becomes entitled to hold land in his own right. I shall give him the document then."

Holman turned around and left with his tail between his legs.

***

On the small terrace atop the keep, Anna closed her eyes, soaking up the seductive warmth of the midday summer sun. This was the kind of life she had dreamed of since she was a little girl: being the mistress of a spectacular hilltop fortress, in an estate that extended as far as the eye could see. Of course, she thought, 'Sasfészek' meant 'Eyrie' in Hungarian, and the castle certainly lived up to its name. Although not palatial, it was still much more beautiful and comfortable than her second husband's damp, draughty and dark manor house. But things had not worked out so well. Despite her father's scheming, their plans to take over half of Szentimre had come to naught. And she was now tied to Miklós. He was young, good-looking, noble and madly enamoured with her; but when it came to lovemaking, the poor boy could not last. Even her father's rough-mannered mercenaries had given her more pleasure.

The only way to put her hands on the estate and mine was to get rid of her brother-in-law. How was she going to do that though? Murder was out of the question. She and her father had escaped punishment twice. They had been fortunate. She was not willing to tempt fate again. And if she waited for Sándor to die in battle, she could be waiting for a long time. She had to hatch a plan as soon as possible; before he managed to produce an heir and complicate things even more.

She walked back into the house. After descending to the second floor, she ran into Margit, who had just come out of Sándor's study, accompanied by Erzsi and holding a letter in her hands.

Anna's curiosity was piqued. "What's the news?"

"It's the contract that Sándor agreed with the king about the mine. The charter is signed by János Hunyadi as Voivode of Transylvania."

"Oh! I'm sure your husband will be pleased to hear that his good friend has become one of the highest-ranking men in the kingdom." Too bad for her, though. Now she would have the voivode himself against her if she tried to harm Sándor. She forced a smile.

Margit dropped the letter and staggered towards the wall. The maid held her as she was about to collapse. "My lady!"

"I... feel so... weak," Margit stammered. She turned to the other side and threw up.

"Lady Anna, please, let's take her upstairs to her chamber," Erzsi said.

"Of course."

They helped Margit lie on the bed.

Anna regarded her sister-in-law with feigned concern. "Shall we call the physician?

Erzsi smiled. "I don't think it's necessary." She turned to Margit. "You've felt like this before, my lady, haven't you? And you've missed your monthly bleeding twice. You never told me, but I knew it."

Margit nodded. She was out of breath. "Yes, I am with child."

Anna's face dropped. Things were going from bad to worse.

"I wish to speak with my husband," Margit said.

"I'll fetch him, my lady."

"No, Erzsi. I need you with me. Anna, can you find him and ask him to come here forthwith?"

"Now I am her little errand boy," Anna mumbled to herself as she stepped into the courtyard. A guard pointed her in the direction of the exercise hall.

She entered the building, her vexation augmenting with each stride, but stopped when she saw Sándor. He was fighting with a sword and shield; but for some reason, he threw both to the floor and ended up in a grapple. Within a few moments, he lifted his surprised opponent – a well-built and strong man – off the ground and tossed him into a large bale of straw in the corner.

"You need to be prepared for everything," he jested, helping the man to his feet. "That's enough training for today." He took off his helmet, gambeson and shirt and dried his face and chest with a clean cloth.

Anna gasped. Damn István Szilágyi! Why had the old man rejected her father's proposition to arrange a marriage between her and Sándor seven years ago?

He must have heard her footsteps behind him because he spun around and glared at her. "What?"

She grasped his arm while she placed her other hand on his bare chest. The hardness of his muscles alone was enough to light a fire inside her – a fire so fierce that could consume her in a heartbeat. Her gaze slowly shifted down his body. She gulped. Scheming aside, she would sell her soul to the Devil to have this man in her bed. "We can all rest easy knowing that we have warriors like you to defend us."

The colour on Sándor's face matched that of his hair. He

stepped away from her and quickly put his shirt on. "What do you want?"

She blurted out the first thing that came to her mind. "Hunyadi is now the Voivode of Transylvania."

"You came here to tell me this? Could you not have waited until I was back in the house?"

"No... no." She was lost for words. "I came here... because... your wife has asked that you go to her immediately."

His eyes narrowed. "Why? What's the matter?"

"She has been unwell, but there is no cause for al –"

Sándor pushed her out of his way and ran out of the exercise hall.

"I know that you hate me, but it won't kill you to be a little more civilised," she muttered.

***

Anna quickened her pace along the corridor. Margit was late for mass, which was unusual. Perhaps something bad had befallen her. Her sister-in-law had lost a baby before. If only she would lose this one too...

But there was nothing wrong with Margit. Anna bit her lip as the hand of jealousy pinched her heart.

Sándor stood in the doorway, kissing his wife while he stroked her round belly. "I shall see you at supper."

"Yes, *szerelmem*. Have a good day and remember my instructions."

Anna deliberately brushed against him as he turned around to leave.

He grunted and made a face at her before walking away and mumbling in disgust.

She entered the bedchamber. "Margit! You are not even dressed. Shall I summon Erzsi? We are already late for church."

"No, I cannot attend today. I was... busy and didn't notice the time go by. Let us sit here and read from the Holy Book instead."

Anna closed the door. She stood with hands on her hips, frowning at her sister-in-law. "Do you still let your husband sleep in your bed? You know it's not allowed when you are with child. It's a sin."

"No! It's not what you think." Margit blushed. "I cannot be out there with him because I feel weak and dizzy all the time; so, he comes to me for advice about the estate. Sometimes, he spends the night here. But we do nothing more than kissing and holding each other."

"You are like a sister to me, and my only concern is your well-being. You should keep him away from you completely until after you have given birth. Not only because the Church forbids it but for another reason as well. He is a young man in his prime. One of these nights, he will become too 'excited' and have his way with you. This could harm your baby."

Margit's face darkened. She slumped on the bed and remained silent for a long time.

Anna sat down and put her arm around her shoulder. "I understand, dear. You fear that if you keep him at a distance, he might seek to fulfil his needs elsewhere."

Margit sighed.

Anna made her voice as sweet and as friendly as possible. "That will be his test, my dear sister. If he truly loves and respects you, he will not betray you."

The lord of Sasfészek was as strong and as impregnable as his fortress. But she had finally discovered a crack. It was only a tiny one, but she could make it bigger, much bigger.

***

Daylight was all but gone. Sándor rubbed his stinging eyes and sighed. He stood up to stretch his legs and light a few more candles. There was still a lot of work to do. His steward's accounting method was disorganised and difficult to follow. He had to examine every record and every entry to make sure that the taxes had been calculated correctly before they were sent to the king.

A knock on the door. Whoever that was, they would be a welcome distraction from all those lists and numbers. He took a deep breath. "Enter!"

Yes, anyone would be welcome – except for her!

Anna covered her mouth with her hand. "I apologise. I did not intend to disturb you."

He frowned. Of course she did. Why else would she come into his private space?

She approached and placed her candle on his desk. The scent of lavender enveloped him, bringing back a distant memory: that of his former noble lover in Buda. The thought was dangerous. He had to dismiss it immediately. "What do you want?"

His abruptness made her raise her eyebrows. "I only wish to borrow a book."

"Take whatever you like," Sándor said, shrugging indifferently.

She tapped her finger on her lips as she examined the items in the bookcase. "Mmm... Everything here is in Latin. Do you have anything in Hungarian? So that I can practice the language?"

"I don't see the need. You speak it perfectly."

Anna turned towards him, her grey-blue eyes sparkling with amusement. "Good sir! This is the first compliment to me that has come from your mouth."

She did speak the language fluently, albeit with a slight, enchanting foreign accent that he had never noticed before. He had never spent more than a few moments with her, and this was probably the longest conversation they had had. She had always been an evil presence; he had never seen her as a flesh-and-blood woman.

Even though she did not have Margit's virginal beauty or statuesque body, all her movements were graceful and fluid and, at the same time, full of arrogance. She twisted one of her long plaits around her fingers. "So, what do you recommend?"

Sándor pulled out a book and gave it to her. "This was my father's favourite."

Anna slid her hand across the cover, a motion as sensual as caressing a lover's face. "*The Romance of Alexander.*" She giggled. "Did your father name you after Alexander the Great?"

"Yes."

"The name suits you. You are a warrior and a leader. You may not have conquered lands, but I am sure you have 'conquered' many ladies."

She twisted her plait again in a slow, hypnotising manner. An invisible string drew him towards her. Their bodies touched. As if having a mind of its own, his hand traced the line of her spine, from the curve of her lower back to the middle of her shoulders. She let out a barely audible moan. Her bosom moved up and down. All his muscles tensed. He would push her against the wall, lift her skirts and...

One of the candles flickered and went out with a hissing noise. Sándor blinked and stepped away from Anna. "You should leave. I have work to do."

She furrowed her brow. "Why do you hate me so much? Is it because I married your brother? I had to obey my father's wish. Did you not do the same when you wed Margit? This is the fate of us nobles."

He snorted. "You are not noble. You and your father climbed into nobility. Over dead bodies. Two of them."

"Both my husbands were old. It was their time to go. I had nothing to do with that."

He shook his head.

"You and I are not that different," she continued. "I know your history. Not all your ancestors were born noble. One was a Székely warrior, ennobled by the king for his service. And you had a Saxon grandfather."

"Not a grandfather. My maternal grandmother."

"Oh, yes. I apologise... I bet you inherited the red hair from her, didn't you?"

He folded his arms. Why wouldn't she go away and leave him in peace?

Anna threw the book on the desk. "I have lost my appetite for reading." With that, she turned her back and walked out.

Sándor slowly raised his hand to his forehead. The veins in his temples were throbbing. His throat was so dry that it hurt. That was an unforgivable slip. It was not to be repeated.

10

Betrayal

The sumptuous Christmas evening meal in the great hall had been Margit's idea to bring the family together. Sándor would not oppose his wife's wishes, especially now that she was just a few weeks away from delivering his heir. But he was the only one at the table who was not enjoying himself.

After that almost fateful night, he had avoided Anna like the plague. And now, she was there, sitting opposite him, staring at him and making the hairs stand up on the back of his neck. She was undoubtedly a witch. Perhaps not one using magic potions and spells but one who had perfected the art of seduction: playing with her hair, touching her breasts and licking her lips in a way he had never seen before. And the things she was doing to a spoon with her mouth and tongue made even an experienced man like him blush. How had nobody else noticed all this? Why was he the only one?

He gulped some more of that sweet wine and looked away. His heart was beating at a frantic rate. Damn her!

His drunken brother raised his cup. "Let's sing a song! Lalalala..."

"No! Let's play a game," Sándor burst out. "Find the whore. It's easy. There is only one at this table."

Margit kicked his leg.

Miklós jumped to his feet, screaming incomprehensible words.

"Let us go, husband. The air smells foul in here," Anna hissed as she rose and held him by the hand.

Sándor swept his arm dismissively towards the two of them. "Yes, yes, go to bed, little boy."

"And I thought Christmas would bring us peace," Margit said to Erzsi and stood up.

Sándor gripped her wrist. "Please, stay with me. Now that they have left, we can enjoy our evening."

"I am tired, and I feel unwell. I should retire." She pulled her hand away and quit the great hall, with her maid behind her.

Sándor emptied his cup so fast that streaks of wine dribbled down his chin. He cursed. His head was about to burst. Without a doubt, he had distressed his wife. Would he forgive himself if anything bad befell her because of his shameful behaviour? He had to make sure all was well.

After stumbling up the stairs, he tried to enter Margit's bedchamber, but her maid stood in his way.

"Get lost, woman!" he shouted, slurring his words. "I wish to speak with my wife."

"No, my lord. I know what you intend to do, and I won't let you in. You must keep away from her until after she's given birth."

"This is none of your concern. Get out of my way!"

Despite her small size, Erzsi did not flinch but let him bark like an angry dog.

"Margit!" he screamed through the door.

"Leave! I beg of you. I am unwell."

He called her name a dozen times until she finally came to him. She waved Erzsi away and then stood behind the door, keeping it slightly ajar to prevent him from entering.

"Let me in, Margit."

"No."

"I promise I shall behave. I only wish to lie by your side and hold you in my arms."

"Did you not hear a word I said? I am in pain, and I feel ill. Show some respect!"

He bobbed his head a few times. "Very well... I apologise... I shall go now."

"Good!" She slammed the door in his face.

Sándor held on to the wall, trying to steady himself. Why on earth had he drunk all that wine? It took him an eternity to stagger to his bedchamber. He undressed with slow, fumbling movements while letting each item of clothing drop to the floor.

He only had his shirt left on when footsteps from behind made him jump. He turned around. Anna stood in front of him. The only thing she was wearing was a gold necklace.

"*Úristen*! What are you doing here like... like... this?"

"I am here for you," she replied in the sweetest voice. "Your wife is big and heavy, and she cannot give you what you desire. But I can."

He raised his hand. "Stay away from me. I know what you are trying to do."

"I only wish to give you the pleasure you deserve, and which Margit has deprived you of for so long."

"No, no. You want to have a child with me so that you can get your hands on my land."

Anna paused for a moment but did not give up. "You are wrong. I don't need your child or your land. What I desire is you. My husband is inadequate. He is only a boy. I want a real man."

Her hand between his legs made all his muscles tense in an instant.

She smiled like a mischievous child. "Good sir! Your body speaks a completely different language from your mouth." She lowered herself and lifted his shirt.

Sándor's heart raced at the touch of her lips on his bare stomach. His knees turned to water. Anna was the Devil personified, bent on destroying him. But she was also a beautiful, strong-willed woman begging to be dominated – the kind of woman he had always liked.

All sense of self-restraint escaped from him like a slippery eel. He hauled her to her feet, his fingers digging into the soft flesh of her arms. He raised her chin with his hand and stared down into her lustful eyes. "On the bed, whore! I shall give you what you wish for," he said, his voice hoarse and trembling. "But I shall make sure that you do not conceive a child tonight."

***

Margit was getting dressed the next morning with Erzsi's help when Anna burst the door open.

"Out!" Anna ordered the maid.

Erzsi turned to Margit. "My lady?"

"Yes, you can leave us."

Erzsi walked out of the room with a perplexed look on her face.

"What can I say!" Anna exclaimed. "You have a beast of a husband."

"What do you mean?"

"Look here." There were red marks around her wrists and bruises on her neck. "I could also show you other parts of my body."

Margit shuddered. "What happened? Who did this to you?"

"Who do you think? Your 'beloved' spouse. Because you could not lie with him, he came to me. And he was like a wild animal."

Margit's face went cold. Her stomach tumbled. She clung to the bedpost. "You are lying!"

"No, I am not. Ask him. Although he will surely deny it."

"Shut your mouth! Begone!"

"As you wish." Anna shrugged and left as quickly as she had come in.

Margit slumped on the bed and stared at the wall. This was the last thing she needed. The sharp, tearing pain came back. She pressed her hand against her belly. The baby was going to come before its time. But she could not let it go like this. She had to find out if Anna was telling the truth. Her sister-in-law's behaviour was strange. Why did Anna boast about what had happened instead of feeling shame and regret?

Pulling herself together, she stood up and ran out of her

bedchamber. She hurried down the stairs. People were shouting. She stopped and listened, holding her breath for a few heartbeats. Sándor and Miklós were screaming at each other in the entrance hall.

"I'll kill you!"

"How dare you? I did not force myself upon her. She is a liar."

Margit advanced slowly towards the top of the stairs and looked down.

"No! You are the liar," Miklós said. "She showed me the marks and bruises on her body."

Sándor stepped back as if pushed by an invisible force. "Marks and... What?... I did not hurt her."

"Were you so drunk that you don't remember?"

"No! I swear I did not hurt her. She must have bruised herself to make me look like a monster. I have told you since the beginning that she was trouble. She wants to make us fight. She wants to destroy me and take my land."

"Nonsense! You hurt her, and you must pay."

"This was her evil plot. She seduced you into marrying her, she came to lodge in our house, and last night she came to my chamber unclothed and begged me to take her. She is a shameless whore."

"How dare you?"

"Only a whore would offer herself in that manner to a man who is not her husband. You should have heard how much she enjoyed having me inside her."

Miklós pounced on his brother like a wildcat on its prey. They started wrestling.

"It's... all... true." Margit felt the ground move under her feet. She staggered towards the safety of the wall.

***

Sándor punched Miklós in the face, knocking him to the floor. His whole body shook as he stood over him. "You two deserve each other. I want you out of my house. Now! If I ever see you again, I'll kill you!"

A bloodcurdling scream made him stop. He looked up towards the top of the stairs. His wife collapsed on the floor, holding her belly.

"Margit!"

He jumped over Miklós and ran to her. He sat down and lifted the upper part of her body into his arms. Red stains had formed on her kirtle. "Margit... Margit... talk to me!"

"Fetch the midwife, now! And the physician!" Erzsi ordered one of the servants who had come to help. She knelt near her mistress. The stains on Margit's clothes were expanding slowly. "Her water broke. But she shouldn't be bleeding. Something's wrong."

Sándor sat there, holding his wife. Everything around him became a blur except for her pale face.

Someone pulled her from him and took her away. Somebody else tried to lift him up. He struggled to rise to his feet.

"Sir!"

László Balog's voice jerked him back to reality. Four servants were carrying Margit, with the midwife following them and shouting orders.

"I must go to her," Sándor whispered, hurrying after them.

During his time in the army, he had faced horrific scenes: decapitations, amputations, disembowelments, impalements – everything that a soldier would see on a battlefield. And yet, all those paled in comparison to the sight of his beloved wife lying in bed, bleeding and screaming in so much pain.

The midwife lifted Margit's skirts and placed both hands on her belly, feeling at different spots. "The baby is in the wrong position. The birth will be difficult and long." She turned to Sándor. "My lord, I shall do my best to help her, but if things don't go well..."

"You make sure they do go well! If she dies, I'll kill you with my own hands!"

The woman shrank in fear at his threat, but then pulled herself together and went back to attend to Margit.

Old and painful memories flashed before Sándor's eyes, from the time when his mother had died after giving birth to Miklós. A shiver ran through him. All this time, he had taken Margit for granted. She had always been there for him, helping and supporting him, seeing him through good and bad times. He had never thought what would happen if she died.

The physician arrived in the meantime and quickly assessed the situation. "You should leave, my lord," he suggested and nodded to Balog. The latter put his hand on Sándor's shoulder and said in a low, calming voice, "Let's go, sir. We can wait outside and pray for her."

Sándor followed the castellan in a daze. The whole world became distorted, like it was moving farther away from him. As soon as they left the room, he sat on the floor with his back against the wall and covered his face with his hands. He could still hear her screams.

Balog knelt beside him. "Come, sir. The church is the best place to go in this difficult hour."

Still numb, Sándor allowed himself to be led away.

They went into the chapel, where he and Margit had married. A chill ran down his spine. Apart from the meagre light of a few candles, the chapel was dark. Balog was about to open the window.

"No, don't. Please leave me. I wish to be alone."

After the castellan departed, Sándor fell to his knees on the cold stone floor. Although he believed in God, he had never been a devout or pious man. For many years, he kept missing church because he was either fighting, drunk or in some woman's bed. He always lived so fast that he did not even think about his soul. But in this hour of despair, he had to look for help somewhere. He could not remember when it was the last time he prayed. And now he needed to. He wanted something to give him hope, and at the same time, he wanted to unburden his own sins.

The hundreds of men he had killed and wounded when he was in the army did not weigh too heavily on his conscience. That was war, and all soldiers were given absolution by the priests before going into battle against the enemies of the Catholic faith. As he reflected on his life until then, he realised that his biggest sin was his arrogance. He thought that he could get away with anything as long as he could justify his actions. He bedded those married ladies in Buda because they were neglected by their husbands, and he was doing them a favour. It was his prerogative as a male to reassure himself of his manliness by using women for his pleasure because they enjoyed being with him or they tolerated him for the right price. He could live a life of sin because he was a soldier, and death could come to him at any moment. And he could treat his brother with contempt because Miklós was weak and easily influenced. But all his past transgressions had finally caught up with him, and he was punished for them by losing the people that he loved. First, his father and now, possibly, his wife.

He wept and prayed to God and begged Him not to let Margit die. She was the only innocent person around him. She had never hurt anyone. He was the guilty one. He should be in her place, dying and paying for what he did to her. In a moment of weakness, he had broken his promise and had betrayed her by lying with another woman; the very woman who was trying to destroy him; the one that he hated so much.

He stayed there for hours, praying and taking a vow that if Margit was spared, he would never hurt her again, he would never get drunk again and lose his judgement, and he would never again be with another woman until the end of his life.

***

On the way to Holman's estate, Anna sat in the carriage silently, preparing herself to endure the forthcoming 'storm'.

"You lay with my own brother!" Miklós shouted. "How could

you do that? All this love that you said you had for me – where did it go?"

She turned away in disgust. An ungrateful child in a fit of temper. Not worthy of a response.

"Did you cause all those marks and bruises to yourself on purpose?"

She could barely restrain herself from slapping him.

"Well? Answer me, woman!"

He was not going to leave her in peace unless she put him back in his place.

"You, craven fool! You allow your brother to do whatever he wills. He can dishonour your wife, and you still won't fight back. Look at us now. Running away, scared."

"He beat me and threatened to kill me. Both of us. And the way he is now, it was not an idle threat."

Anna shook her head. "You should have stood up to him a long time ago. Your father's will was unfair. You should have fought for your rightful share of the estate instead of letting your brother take advantage of you. Fortunately, we still have a good chance."

"What do you mean?"

"I watched from around the corner as Margit swooned, bleeding. This is not a good sign for her. She could lose the baby; perhaps die as well. And even if she survives, she may never be able to have a child again. So, there will be no heir to Szentimre."

Miklós dismissed her with an abrupt gesture. "Sándor can take another woman. It would not be difficult for him to have another child."

"This would take time. Presently he is distraught and full of guilt. So, you should march to the castle with my father's men to arrest him and punish him for what he did to me. I am sure that he will not surrender. He will choose to fight instead. But his mind will be distracted, and you will kill him. And it will not be cold-blooded murder but only a chance event, a death in battle."

His eyes opened wide. "You want me to kill my brother!"

"He never loved you as a brother. He thinks of you as inferior and weak, not worthy of inheriting your father's land. I have seen how he treats you; like a little boy, incapable of making his own decisions and running his own life."

Miklós crinkled his nose like a scorned child. "This is true. Father resented my existence. He always believed it was my fault that Mother died when she gave birth to me. Sándor thought the same. He did not even play with me when we were children. 'Milksop' and 'dull boy' is what he called me. He has nothing but contempt for me."

"So, here is your chance to take revenge; to show that you are not a child but a strong man."

He nodded. "You are right. There is nothing else I desire more than prove to the world and to you that I am worthy of being the lord of Szentimre and Sasfészek."

Anna smiled to herself. Whatever the outcome of the fight between the two brothers, she would be the real victor. If Sándor died, she and Miklós would take his estate. And if Miklós died, then she would be free to seek a more advantageous marriage.

11

Regret

The chapel was now in complete darkness. The candles had gone out a long time ago, but Sándor was still there, sitting on a wooden bench, still praying for his wife's life. No one had come to look for him. Perhaps something terrible had happened, and they were afraid to tell him. But he would not leave and return to the house either. The image of Margit's pale face, the blood on her clothes, her screams... It all kept coming back again and again into his head, like a nightmare without end.

The door creaked open. Someone entered, holding a torch. The light cast an eerie gleam on the large bronze crucifix above the altar and reflected on the whitewashed wall, blinding Sándor. He covered his eyes with his hand.

"Sir! You must come, quickly!"

Balog's voice.

Sándor stood up with his back to the castellan. What if the man's face betrayed the bad news he might be bringing?

"You have a son."

Now he turned round. There was only one thing he wanted to know. "Is she alive? Tell me!"

"Thanks be to God, yes. But the physician says she's still in great peril."

Sándor hurried past Balog and ran out of the chapel. His heart was racing, his breathing ragged. There was this terrible pressure on his chest. Despite his shaking legs, he hastened up the stairs to the third floor of the keep and then down the corridor towards Margit's bedchamber.

At the same time, Erzsi came out of an adjacent room, holding the newborn baby. "My lord!" She grabbed him by the arm just as he was about to walk past her. "Your son. We've cleaned him. Look. So precious. Here, hold him."

The boy was so small and so light. How could such a tiny little thing be alive and breathing? He looked more like a toy than a person. He looked so fragile. Sándor became afraid of doing any damage to his son even just by holding him. He gave him back to Erzsi.

"His name?" she asked.

"István, after my father."

He entered his wife's bedchamber, and Erszi followed.

Margit was lying in bed with her eyes closed, looking paler than ever. The midwife had left, but the physician was still there, washing blood off his hands in a small copper basin. "My lord, she is such a brave soul. All she kept asking us was to save her child. She suffered so much. It was a difficult birth. We did the best we could. The baby is small and weak. I hope he will survive. At least, Erzsi has found a wet nurse for him."

"And Margit?" Sándor asked in a faint voice.

"She is in God's hands now."

Sándor approached the bed and touched her forehead. She was

as cold as stone. He knelt on the floor beside her. "*Angyalom*," he whispered, "please, don't leave me."

She mumbled something incomprehensible before opening her eyes, slowly as if their lids weighed a ton. She looked at him, and then her eyes searched around the room. "My baby." Her face winced with pain.

Sándor rose and let Erzsi bring the child to his wife.

"Here, my lady. Little István."

Margit made a big effort to smile but gave up halfway. "Please look after my little prince." Moments later, she lost consciousness again.

"I shall stay with her," Sándor told the physician. "You should have a rest. Thank you for what you have done."

"My lord, I shall pray for her and the child. Please call for me if you need anything." He picked up his bag of medical instruments and left with Erzsi.

Sándor lay on the bed, next to his wife. He kept himself close to her and put his arm around her. He could not do anything to save her, but at least he would try to keep her warm. The feeling of coldness when he touched her scared him. It was as if she were already dead.

***

Erzsi did her best for the welfare of the newborn baby. She made sure that he was always swaddled well and kept warm. She also found a healthy young woman from the town, who had recently given birth, and asked her to stay in the castle with her family to look after and nurse little István. The child did not react so well in the beginning. He cried and kept refusing the milk of the woman as if he knew that she was not his mother. They were all worried that he would not survive, but eventually his fighting spirit prevailed, and little by little, he started feeding.

On the other hand, Margit's situation worsened. She developed a fever the day after the birth. Her whole body seemed to be in a terrible state. One moment she was shivering, the next sweating. She constantly drifted in and out of consciousness, and the only thing she could take was water.

Sándor sat by her side all day and lay beside her at night. He barely slept, just napping for a short while here and there. His heart ached at the thought that he could lose her; that she could die while he was not there or while he was asleep. He so much wanted to protect her and save her. If only Death were not a sly and elusive shadow, but a man like him, so that he could fight him and keep him away from her.

***

On the third day after the baby's birth, Balog called Sándor for an emergency.

"What's the matter?"

"There is a band of horsemen outside the town gates."

"Turkish?"

"No, sir. Holman's mercenaries. Your brother is with them."

"Miklós? Why?"

Something was not right. Sándor did not have enough time to

arm himself properly. He quickly put on a gambeson and an open-face helmet and mounted his horse, carrying his sword and axe. He rode through the town, followed by Balog and ten soldiers. The big wooden gate of the fortification wall opened, to let him and his men exit. In the open field, his brother and about fifty of Holman's soldiers stood fully armed.

"What do you want, Miklós?"

"I'm here to arrest you."

"What for?"

"For what you did to my wife. Her father wants to put you in front of a judge."

"I did not do anything to her against her will. Do you still believe her lies?"

"If you don't come with us, we shall take you by force."

Miklós signalled to Holman's men. They formed a circle around Sándor and his soldiers.

There was no time to call for reinforcements. "Damn!" Sándor growled. He was too tired and not thinking straight. He had fallen into a trap.

Both sides drew their swords.

He had to find a way out. "Stop! Stand down, all of you! This is between my brother and me. There is no need for bloodshed." He then addressed Holman's men. "You are highly trained professional soldiers. You are more useful fighting the Ottomans than dying to settle a personal matter for someone who is not even your master."

The men looked at each other. Some even bobbed their heads

in agreement. They sheathed their swords and re-formed behind Miklós.

"Cowards!" the latter shouted at them.

"Let us settle this between us, like men," Sándor challenged him.

Miklós hesitated.

"Go on! Be brave!" his soldiers egged him on.

"Very well," he said, at length, and drew his sword. "Let us do that."

A spell of dizziness overcame Sándor, making him regret the challenge. He had barely slept during the last three days. He could hardly hang on to his horse, let alone fight a duel.

His brother came straight at him. Instinctively, Sándor raised his sword and deflected the blow. The metallic sound of the two weapons clashing echoed in the silence, and a spark flew at the point where the blades met.

Sándor had no notion of how he managed to stay in the saddle. His last meal gushed violently from his mouth. He blinked a few times, but the flashes of light in front of his eyes did not clear.

Miklós turned around swiftly and attacked again. Sándor bent forward, swinging his sword blindly.

The bang came from an unexpected direction: the back of his own head. Everything froze for a moment. Then, the ground came at him at an incredible speed.

"I have humiliated my 'warrior' brother. Time to finish this," Miklós bragged to his men.

The world spun around Sándor.

But Balog's voice brought him back to reality. "Stand up, sir! For your family's sake, defend yourself!"

He was a sitting target, and he had to react. Grunting, he pushed himself up on all fours. As Miklós galloped towards him with his arm extended holding the sword, Sándor jumped up. He frantically reached for the axe that hung from his belt, drew it and struck his brother on the breastplate. Miklós's horse continued forward while its rider flew backwards and hit the ground with a thud, the brutal force of the blow leaving him gasping for air.

Sándor put his foot on his brother's chest and raised the axe.

"Mercy!" Miklós shouted.

"Why should I spare you? A few moments ago, you were ready to cut my head off."

Miklós closed his eyes, mumbling a prayer.

Sándor tossed the axe to the ground and stepped away. "I know I am going to regret this, but you are my blood, damn you! Get out of my sight and never come near me and my family again, or I'll take your head next time."

Two of Holman's men helped Miklós to his feet and then hoisted him onto his horse.

"I truly regret what happened with Anna," Sándor continued addressing his brother. "But she is as guilty as I am. Perhaps even more so because she tempted me."

Still dazed, Miklós said nothing, but rode away with the others.

Sándor let himself fall to the ground, exhausted. His heart was beating fast and loud as if it wanted to leap out of his chest. His arms and hands began to shake.

Balog hurried to help him stand up. "Sir! You are unharmed, thanks be to God. Come. Let's go back."

***

On the same day, Erzsi decided to ask for help from a Wallachian woman called Marina, who was known for her knowledge of medicinal herbs and concoctions. This woman lived outside the castle walls, near the village of the miners. Some people claimed that she was a witch, and the truth is that she looked like one. When Erzsi visited her, the strangest things hung from her kitchen ceiling or were mixed in pots.

Marina gave Erzsi infusion herbs for internal healing and for the pain, a kind of paste that she was to put on Margit's forehead to reduce the fever, and another one that would help heal the wounds caused by the birth.

By the next day, Margit's health improved. Her temperature dropped, and she finally woke from her long, deep but disturbed sleep. She was still in pain, though, and a little dazed and confused. Erzsi gave her more herbs to drink, and Margit finally found the strength to sit up in her bed and hold her child.

Baby István, who had been uneasy and grumpy during the time he was with his nurse, became quiet and peaceful immediately, cosying up to his mother.

Margit smiled. She stroked his face and kissed the top of his head. "My little prince. You are so small and yet so brave. You survived without your mother all this time. I must start feeding you before my milk dries up."

"Yes, my lady. You should do that promptly. It'll help you feel better as well."

Someone knocked on the door. Margit nodded to Erzsi. "See who it is."

A few moments later, the maid came back. "It's your husband."

Margit rolled her eyes. "Tell him to leave."

"My lady! I know he did a terrible thing, but I can assure you he's regretted it. He was by your side all the time. He wept and prayed for you. He's barely slept. Please, give him a chance."

"Very well. Let him in. But only so that I can give him a piece of my mind."

Erzsi was about to head for the door but hesitated. She went back to Margit and tidied her lady's hair.

"What are you doing?" Margit scolded her. "Trying to make me beautiful for him? He does not deserve this. Go! Let him in."

When Sándor entered the bedchamber, his face lit up. "This is the happiest day of my life. To see the two people that I love most in the world."

He approached the bed and was about to embrace her, but she stopped him with an abrupt movement of her arm. "Don't touch me!"

His face flushed. "Margit, what's the matter?"

She handed the baby back to Erzsi and waved her out of the room. "What's the matter? How do you even dare ask me that?"

"Margit, please. I'm so sorry. Truly."

"The physician told me it would be too dangerous for me to have another child. I may not be so fortunate next time. Do you understand that? I am not even twenty-one yet. I should have at least another twenty fertile years in my life, but instead I am useless as a woman now. And all this because of what you did with that hateful viper."

Sándor winced. "I swear I did not force her. She tricked me and took advantage of me. And I did not hurt her... I swear... I did not hit or bruise her."

His words – his excuses – made the anger swell inside her. "Is this supposed to make me feel better? I forgave your indiscretions at the king's court. You were on your own in a faraway place, and we had not consummated our marriage yet. I forgave you when I found you with those prostitutes. You promised you would be faithful from then on, and I did everything you wished to please you. But this was not enough for you. You could not restrain yourself!"

Sándor sat down on the bed. He reached for her hand, but she snatched it away before he even touched it.

"I don't know what else to say, Margit. I have regretted this, time and time again. I have sworn to God that I shall never touch another woman for the rest of my life. And I am willing to confess and do whatever penance is required of me, no matter how harsh."

"I pray God will forgive you because there will be no forgiveness from me. Anna is not any woman. You have committed a sin as vile as incest. You have brought shame upon yourself and your family. You should thank the Almighty that your father is not alive to see this. Now, begone! Leave me in peace!"

He did not reply but stood up and left, banging the door

behind him.

Margit raised her hand to her mouth and bit the side of her forefinger, desperately trying to prevent herself from bursting into tears. She did not know if the distress she experienced after finding out what he had done was the reason she had gone into labour prematurely, or why she had nearly died. Still, she wanted to make him think that it was. He had betrayed her, and she was going to make him suffer as much and for as long as possible.

12

The Ottoman Invasion

March 1442

The messenger's face was flushed and his breathing laboured. Water dripped from his clothes, forming small pools on the floor.

Sándor frowned at him. The mess this man had made in his study!

"Speak!"

The messenger cleared his throat, and then the words gushed from his mouth like a torrent. "Call to arms, m'lord. The Ottomans have returned. The Prince of Wallachia let Mezid Bey pass through his land with thousands of troops and enter Transylvania. They're pillaging, burning and killing. The voivode is away, and Bishop Lépes is in charge for now. He's called all able-bodied men to gather in Gyulafehérvár."

Sándor summoned Balog. "Order our men to prepare to march. I shall lead them. They must wear most of their armour. We can only take four or five packhorses with us. A full baggage train would be too slow on the mountain paths. Send word to the lords of the surrounding estates to assemble their forces and meet us in Gyulafehérvár." He motioned towards the messenger with a jerk of his head. "And see that this man changes into dry clothes."

Since the day he met Hunyadi, Sándor had been dreading the moment when he would have to return to the battlefield. But now that he had finally received the call to arms, it was a great opportunity for redemption. In addition to genuine contrition, prayer, fasting and abstinence, fighting the infidels would increase his chances of having his sins absolved much sooner. And equally importantly, by being away from Margit he hoped to make her miss him and possibly forgive him, eventually.

He made ready to depart with a unit of forty soldiers and knights under his family's banner. He left Balog in charge of the defence of the estate and requested his counsellors to obey and report to Margit.

Before leaving, he went to say farewell to his wife and son. Erzsi led him into Margit's bedchamber. She brought little István to him. Sándor held the boy in his arms, talked to him and kissed him.

Smiling, Erzsi nudged Margit. "Oh look, my lady! A tall and strong man in steel armour, holding a tiny two-and-a-half-month-old baby with such affection. It warms your heart, doesn't it?"

But her words had absolutely no effect on Margit, who just looked on stone-faced.

Sándor handed the child back to Erzsi and approached his wife. He embraced her, but it was like hugging a statue.

"So, it is time for you to do your noble duty while I shall do mine by looking after the estate in your absence," she said.

Her bitterness stung him like a venomous serpent. "Balog,

Kendi and the other officials will do all the work; do not fret. You only need to keep an eye on –"

"Yes, yes!" She dismissed him with an abrupt hand gesture and turned her back to him.

Sándor stood and waited while she looked out of the window, staring at the rain tumbling down. Any moment now, perhaps, she would turn around, run to him and kiss him farewell; or something like that. But this did not happen. Although she had her back to him, she knew that he was still there. "Off you go!" she said impatiently. "God be with you."

He walked out of the room with his head down, feeling like he had been kicked in the stomach. But he had only himself to blame. His actions alone had turned his beloved's heart to ice.

***

The sky was dark and sorrowful, and thunder rumbled above. Sheets of rain came down on Sándor and his men as they rode through treacherous mountain passes and narrow valleys. The horses slipped on wet rocky ground in one place and plodded through thick mud in the next. They baulked at the sight of raging streams. The men had to dismount, blindfold the beasts and guide them across by hand, wading waist-deep in the freezing water and weighed down by their armour. And in many places along the way to Guylafehérvár, frightened locals struggled up the forested hills with nothing but the clothes on their backs, cursing both the infidels who had raided their villages and the king who had failed to protect them.

When the high walls of the town finally appeared in the distance, Sándor and his soldiers ran into long columns of local troops retreating to the safety of the fortress. The battle was already over.

Sándor approached one of the mounted archers and rode alongside him. "What happened?"

"Disaster, sir. The Turks waited for us in the valley near a small village."

"Valley? It was a trap, wasn't it?"

"Aye, sir. But the bishop didn't see it. He ordered us to charge head-on. The heathens had hidden their reserves in the village. Those attacked us from behind. The Turks killed the bishop and many men and took hundreds prisoner."

Sándor shook his head. The Transylvanians had already suffered a defeat and Hunyadi was still a long way away. Surely, the voivode would not let that go unpunished. There would be another battle soon.

But when Lord Jankó arrived, he still did not have enough forces at his disposal to face the Ottomans forthwith. The bad weather, the Turkish raiding parties and the mountainous terrain of Transylvania had delayed the arrival of reinforcements by a few days. And even as those finally came, most of them were ill-armed peasants and serfs, and Saxon townspeople. Hunyadi ordered them to march together with his experienced soldiers to attack the Ottomans before they left the province with plunder and prisoners.

"It's about time we dealt with their countless and costly raids on our land," the voivode told the officers. "And the only way to do that is to teach them a lesson they will never forget."

***

The cavalry troops waited, hidden in the woods. Men mumbled prayers and whispered words of encouragement to themselves and to each other. Their steeds snorted impatiently, blowing steam from their nostrils. Muffled clanks of armour and weapons echoed in the distance. The Ottomans were already engaging with the Saxon and Székely forces.

Sándor breathed in the refreshing smell of wet grass. He could hardly restrain himself or his horse. The anticipation made him giddy and lightheaded. It was as if he were suspended by a thread as thin as a spider's web, which was just about to break and set him free – as free as the little bird that chirped cheerfully and hopped from branch to branch above him.

The command finally came. "Attack!"

They hit the enemy like a whirlwind. One unit pounced on the Ottoman supply train, creating mayhem among the non-combatant support crews and the wounded soldiers, and freeing the Hungarian prisoners of the previous battle. The latter picked up weapons and joined the fray.

Sándor and his men fell on the Turkish rear guard. His brand-new axe drew first blood by breaking the back of an Akinji. Then he attacked a group of Azap foot-soldiers, leaving none alive. He was in his element. He could not understand why a few days earlier he was so worried about returning to the battlefield.

Hunyadi's pincer movement paid off. Seeing that his army was losing, Mezid ordered a retreat. But it was not a tidy one. Crushed from all sides, the Ottomans fled in panic, with the Hungarian cavalry in hot pursuit and continuing the slaughter even after darkness fell.

Many hours later, Sándor rushed into Hunyadi's tent, oblivious to the blood spattered all over his armour.

"I would not like to be on the wrong side of you," the voivode said in jest.

"Forgive my appearance, sir, but I have just returned. We chased them all the way to the Wallachian border. Both Mezid and his son are dead. One of the captains will bring their heads to you in a moment."

But Lord Jankó's face hardened, and he furrowed his brow. "Let us not be fooled, *barátom*. The Ottomans have been knocking on our door for some time now. They are not going to give up until they have devoured every last piece of land that dares to stand in their way."

***

Sándor and his soldiers returned to Guylafehérvár. They needed to rest before making their way home. Some of the men were wounded and required treatment.

They celebrated the victory together with the locals. There was a lot of drinking and having a good time with the young women of the town, who were all too grateful to their 'saviours'. But Sándor did not participate in that. He was dreading the return home. The battle had been a distraction. Soon he would have to face the grim reality of going back to a broken marriage and a wife who did not even wish to speak with him. Would his absence have softened her cold and hostile attitude towards him?

As he stood on the town's battlements, looking at the setting sun, a hand touched his shoulder. It was an old friend and comrade-in-arms: a bearded, brown-haired, ruddy-faced and heavily inebriated knight called Imre Gerendi.

"Aren't you proud of our victory, sir?" he said, offering Sándor a pitcher.

"Of course I am, Imre." Sándor sniffed the ale and grimaced. "But I shall not drink this. It smells like piss." He turned his gaze towards the distant horizon.

"Why, it's no worse than the piss... umm... the ale we used to drink in the whorehouses of Milano," Gerendi protested.

As he received no response, he shrugged and threw the pitcher to the ground, spilling its contents everywhere. "You look like you have the weight of the world on your shoulders," he slurred.

Sándor laughed. "Is that your drunken wisdom talking, *barátom*?"

Imre let out a loud belch. "Me, drunk? Naaah. I'm only merry. And I got lucky with a comely local wench."

"Oh, that explains it."

"Sir, you don't know what you're missing. These girls are so delightful that I think I'll move here myself. With your permission, of course."

"You rascal! You will desert me for a pretty face?"

Imre grabbed him by the arm and led him towards another part of the wall, which overlooked the town square. He pointed at a gaggle of young women, who were laughing and jesting with the soldiers. "Look at the big-breasted redhead. She's your perfect match."

"Why? Do I also have big breasts?"

Imre quickly measured him with his eyes. "Naah… but you have the same colour hair."

Sándor slapped his forehead. "Of course! Why did I not think of that?"

"Don't move. I'll fetch her. I'm sure she'll love being courted on top of the castle walls."

Sándor shook his head. "No, Imre. I am not interested. My whoring days are in the past."

"Nonsense," his friend dismissed him, but as he turned around to leave in haste, he bumped his head against the low doorway which led back down the turret stairs. He fell to the ground with a thud.

Sándor knelt and shook him by the shoulders.

Imre mumbled something and then passed out.

"I'm glad I did not have any of that ale. It certainly turns men into clumsy fools," Sándor said to himself, chuckling.

***

Upon arriving home, Sándor was welcomed by Balog, who informed him that all went well during his absence, apart from an issue relating to the mine. The Saxon merchants, with whom Sándor used to trade before he signed the agreement with Hunyadi and the king, had paid them an unexpected visit a few days earlier.

"They talked with Master Kendi and your wife for hours," the castellan said. "I'm not sure what the result was, but they looked angry when they left."

"Call the officials for a meeting presently."

Sándor went into the house. He did not have much time to rest as he needed to attend to this matter first and foremost.

He called one of the servants. "Where is my wife?" She had not turned up to welcome him.

"In her chamber, my lord."

He hurried up the stairs and straight into her room without even knocking.

Margit was sitting on the bed, feeding István while Erzsi was tidying up around her. Her husband's sudden entrance startled her.

"What in the name of God are you doing, bursting in here like this?" She moved the baby away and covered her breast. The little boy whined, still hungry. Margit handed him over to Erzsi, who took him out of the room.

"How about, 'Welcome home, dear husband. I have missed you very much'?" he said in an overly mordant way.

She rolled her eyes. "Very well. Welcome. I'm glad you are back safe. Now tell me, what troubles you?"

"What happened with the merchants?"

"They are vexed because you stopped trading with them."

"Did you explain about the contract I have with the king?"

"Yes. But they still want compensation for the business they lost because it took them a long time to find another supplier."

"Damn them! I have called a meeting with the officials. Will you attend?"

"No."

"Why not?"

"You are well capable of dealing with this on your own."

Sándor sat on the bed and put his hand on her knee. "I need you there. You always bring out the best in me."

Margit pushed his hand away. "Did you think that by walking back here after a few weeks' absence everything would be different? Well... No, it will not."

He let out an exasperated sigh and stood up. "I accept that you do not wish to lie with me because you are still hurt. But can you forgive me at least? I have admitted that I wronged you. I bitterly regret what I did, and I have sworn to you that it will not happen again. What else do you need?"

She did not answer.

The silence became unbearable. Sándor shook his head and hastily quit her chamber. He was the only one among his war comrades who was not glad to be home.

The discussion over the issue of the Saxon merchants was heated. Josef Roth and Péter Havasi believed that Sándor should offer some kind of compensation to his former trading partners.

Kendi, Balog and Gábor Sipos did not agree. Given that the mine was under the protection of Hunyadi and the king, no compensation should be paid. The arguments were coming in thick and fast from both sides.

"The merchants have a lot of influence," Havasi noted. "They may turn other noblemen against you."

"I can't break my contract. Lord Jankó saved my estate from ruin. We may not be receiving the same high price for the silver and gold, but we have a stable revenue. And all the soldiers who have moved here will protect us from future Ottoman raids."

The counsellors scratched their heads and stroked their beards, keen to find a solution that would suit both parties. They needed the merchants to continue buying their other products, so they had to do something to keep the trade alive.

"Why don't you consult with Lord Jankó?" Kendi proposed. "He's the voivode. He has power and influence."

"This is good advice. I shall visit him forthwith."

**

The voivode's manservant led Sándor to his master's quarters through a secret corridor. "The Wallachian and Moldavian ambassadors are in the great hall, waiting to see Lord Jankó. He's trying to convince their princes to stop paying tribute to the Sultan and switch their allegiance to Hungary. But he has agreed to see you first. So, you must be quick."

Under pressure for time, Sándor explained the situation he was in.

"Do not fret," Hunyadi reassured him. "I'll take care of the Saxons. Give me their names and leave the rest to me."

"You, sir? Why would you pay them on my account?"

"I always help the ones who are loyal to me and to the king. The merchants' only allegiance is to money. Besides, I'm not going to pay them. I'll just send them a 'strong' letter, which will put the fear of God into them."

"I have no words to thank you, sir! How can I repay your kindness?"

"Continue to provide your services to Hungary. Your military experience and your soldiers are the most valuable thing to me. I'm sure I shall need you again soon."

13
Blood on the Ialomiţa

September 1442

The new call to arms came at the end of the summer. The Ottomans had returned with a larger army, determined to take revenge on the voivode for inflicting such a humiliating defeat on Mezid's troops.

Sándor crossed into Wallachia together with a few thousand men under Hunyadi's command. All around him, the camp near the valley of the Ialomiţa River, bustling with soldiers and support crews, sounded like the biblical Tower of Babel.

Here, German mercenaries sat together, diligently polishing their splendid suits of armour. Farther down, the Polish ones, gathered around a steaming cauldron of sharp-smelling cabbage soup, recounted the heroic deeds of their ancestors. At the perimeter of the camp, the Bohemian gunners rolled out sleeping blankets within a circular wooden fort of war wagons. In their own areas, the Serbian and Wallachian light cavalrymen – valuable allies of the voivode – were grooming their horses, while the Saxon foot soldiers persisted drilling in the last light of the day. The levies of the Transylvanian nobility shared jokes and cups of ale.

And true to their reputation as men of few words, the Székelys were sharpening their swords and arrowheads, stern-faced and barely exchanging a phrase in their distinct dialect of Hungarian.

Sándor left the camp and went to sit on the edge of a ridge overlooking the valley and river. Leaning back, legs outstretched and eyes closed, he savoured the peace and quiet. Only the distant murmur of the flowing water and the flapping of wings – as the birds came to perch among the trees for the night – intruded upon the silence. The air was still warm and filled with all kinds of smells from the camp yonder, wafting on the light breeze.

According to the scouts, after burning and looting its way across the Wallachian countryside and capital, the enemy was set to ford the Ialomiţa and then, continue its destructive path into Transylvania. At the point where the waters are the shallowest, Hunyadi had predicted. The Ottomans had to be stopped there.

It was good to be back on the battlefield beside trusted comrades. Sándor always welcomed a good fight. After his alienation from Margit, the battle had become a substitute for lovemaking. The excitement and anticipation before the start, when all senses are heightened and the world seems unreal, was, in a strange way, similar to being enchanted by a beautiful woman. The initial skirmishes were like courtship while the main battle was the act itself. At the end came exhaustion, but also the sweet satisfaction of victory – because victory was the only outcome; defeat was not an option.

***

While the men returned to their units after the early-morning prayer, Sándor prepared for battle in a different manner, away from everybody else. Wearing his full harness of plate armour, helmet in hand, and sitting on his horse, he spent a few moments with closed eyes. His sole thoughts were the orders Hunyadi had given him and the way he was going to fight. And as if knowing that, Vihar stood perfectly still so as not to disturb his master's concentration.

The moment Sándor opened his eyes, the stallion tossed his flaxen mane, snorted and scraped the ground impatiently with his front right hoof. Sándor took a deep breath. After tying his hair back, pulling up the padded hood and securing the helmet in place, he moved to join the mounted men-at-arms. His knights rode beside him while his soldiers joined the light cavalry and infantry units as they marched out to meet the enemy.

News had arrived that the Ottomans were crossing the Ialomița, laden with loot and unaware of the voivode's men, who waited for them, hidden among the trees of the nearby hills.

It was still early in the day, but the sun shone bright. Heated by the rays and flushed with eagerness, Sándor lifted the visor of his sallet to wipe the sweat from his face.

"I hope we move soon, or we'll start to melt," Imre jested.

"We must wait until most of their army has crossed hither," Sándor explained. "For if they are still on the other side of the river when we attack, they will simply run away."

He had barely spoken his words when the signal was given. "Make ready!"

Sándor smiled. "Lord Jankó has chosen the best place to have his battle."

Along the banks of the river, extended a valley with grassy slopes of moderate steepness, which served as the perfect vantage point; a terrain that a smaller army could take advantage of. All that remained now was for the soldiers to do their job.

"We have had enough of the shame!" Hunyadi's speech still echoed in Sándor's ears. "We have had enough of them ravaging our lands, killing the elderly and the weak, dishonouring and enslaving our women and children. I know that there is not one amongst us in Transylvania and Wallachia, who has not suffered the loss of a loved one at the hands of the infidels. But we shall not tolerate this any longer! Today, we are here to fight in Christ's name. With His help, we shall all fight as one, and we shall put an end to this!"

Sándor thought of his father and his people who had died, not long ago, during the Ottoman raids on his land. He could not bring them back, but at least he had his chance for revenge.

"Formation!" he ordered the men under his command. The three hundred knights and men-at-arms that Hunyadi had given him were the toughest and most efficient professional warriors. Covered in plate armour and riding fully barded horses to magnify the power of their attack, they had a special mission. They formed the shape of an arrowhead, ready to charge down the slope.

"The Turks fear our steel wall. They call us devils. Let us prove them right. Let us send them all to Hell!"

The men cheered at his words and banged their weapons

against their shields, creating an almighty clang that echoed across the valley.

Facing them were thousands of Akinji and renegade Wallachian riders, who – albeit surprised – had swiftly assembled for battle after wading across the river. Although heavy in numbers, they were light in armour and weapons. The enemy bows and arrows, the sabres and small axes were no match for the mighty double-edged swords, the heavy war hammers and flanged maces, and the accelerating power of that mass of metal crashing into them.

Dead bodies and severed body parts were flung in all directions; a red mist of blood spread in the air before spattering on the ground and on the soldiers' armour. But that was by no means the decisive moment. When the Ottoman light cavalry faltered and split, the Janissary infantry stepped in its place. Those were the best soldiers the Sultan had at his disposal. They were tough, well-disciplined and ruthless; and there were hundreds of them, supported by thousands of foot-soldiers. Despite its efforts, the heavy cavalry encountered severe resistance and could not break the Ottoman lines. The latter took significant losses, but their sheer numbers managed to stall the attack.

Sándor lifted his visor and turned back to check on his comrades. Spread along the riverbank, units of Turkish riders had regrouped and were now launching a counter-attack against Hunyadi's light cavalry, which covered the flanks of the Hungarian formation. At the same time, the Janissaries surrounded the knights and men-at-arms, isolating them from the rest of their army. Sándor stood his ground, fighting off the blows of the enemy. The arrows were flying around him. They were bouncing off his armour and his horse's barding, the hits painful but not damaging. So far so good. How long would he last though? Farther ahead, more and more Ottomans had crossed the river and joined the fray.

The battlefield was so densely packed now that Vihar had no space to move. He tried to lift his front legs off the ground several times. Sándor moved his body forward on the saddle and leaned into Vihar's neck. "Stay down!" The last thing he needed was having his horse rear and expose his belly to the weapons of the enemy. But Vihar struggled against his master's orders. He neighed, snorted, kicked and even butted men and animals. Sándor, notwithstanding, held the reins tight, exerting his all to steady the beast.

Something sharp and heavy struck his hip from behind. The pain shot through him, leaving him out of breath. A second Ottoman grabbed his right leg. He lost his grip on the reins and just managed to hold on by hooking his arm around Vihar's neck. If he fell, it would be the end of him. He swung the axe towards the Ottoman who was pulling his leg, but the latter stepped aside and avoided the hit. Another strike from behind, on his lower back this time, made him scream. The two of them were working together to bring him down. As a nobleman and an officer, he would be a great prize to them, dead or alive. He could not move away from them because the second man was still tugging at his leg. He kept sliding downwards, a little bit at a time. He managed to grab the reins again and somewhat slow down his descent towards certain death, but he was still trapped and was struck from behind once more.

Suddenly, Vihar spun around so fast that he sent the second man crashing to the ground. Sándor's leg was finally free. He ended up facing the first soldier. Although still precariously hanging on to his horse, he brought the axe down on the Ottoman's head with such force that both helmet and skull broke. Breathing a sigh of relief, he lifted himself back into the saddle.

"We're stuck!" Imre shouted while desperately trying to push back the Janissaries who had surrounded him. "What are we going to do?"

Sándor looked up towards the higher ground. He saw movement. It was time. "Turn your horse around! We must protect each other's back!"

The command was passed down the line. Each rider was now facing the opposite direction from the comrade next to him. They were in the right position to execute the rest of the battle plan safely.

"Retreat but keep fighting!" Sándor bellowed his command.

Stepping on and, at times, stumbling over the dead and the wounded, the cavalry fell back. The Ottomans had won many battles using that tactic of 'feigned retreat' and then returning to trap their unsuspecting enemy. And yet, on that day Lord Jankó beat them at their own game. When they realised that they had been lured further upriver where the valley narrowed and the waters ran deeper, it was too late.

A loud bang cracked and then another and another. Hunyadi's

war wagons, now in position on the slope, took action. The gunners used small cannons and handheld firearms – weapons that took the enemy by surprise. Smoke covered the valley. It blinded and choked the soldiers of both armies, but the firearms continued unleashing their deadly load. Attacked from three sides now, the Ottomans' only way out was to retreat. This was not possible though, as they fell backwards on their own troops, who were coming from behind, or into the river and drowned. Their large numbers did not matter anymore.

***

After the thirst for vengeance had been quenched and the rush of battle had subsided, Sándor sat down and silently surveyed the world around him: the horror in the eyes of the departed, the gravely wounded begging for a quick death, the prisoners pleading for mercy, the victors squabbling over the spoils. It was a grim and grey world that left him cold and lonely inside. Had it all been in vain? No matter how sweet revenge felt, it had only lasted for a fleeting moment. It would never bring his father back. And no matter how satisfying victory was, it would never replace the fervour of his wife's kisses or the thrill of her touch. But he had to become accustomed to this world because such was his life going to be thenceforth.

14
It's Good to be Home

February 1444

The familiar view of his castle and surrounding land was the most welcome sight. Even though Sándor lately preferred the battlefield to his estate, he heaved a sigh of relief when he arrived home safe after spending the most part of the last two years on campaign. He had fought in the valleys of Transylvania and Wallachia, in the forests of Serbia, and in the mountains of Bulgaria. He had fought in the day and at night, in sunshine and under cloudy skies, in the rain and hail, in knee-deep snow and on thick ice. He had gained a lot of experience and even learned to communicate in a few different languages, but the continuous marching and fighting had taken their toll. Although he was only twenty-seven, the physical exhaustion and injuries made him feel ten years older. He needed a good rest.

During his absence, the population of Szentimre had grown. More people had come to live and work there. The relative peace and security of the last couple of years attracted farmers, traders, craftsmen and miners from other areas that were less stable. It was good for the estate because more rents and taxes were collected, and the newcomers brought their skills and knowledge with them, which benefited the local economy.

But the most pleasant surprise was waiting for Sándor in his own home. As soon as he entered the keep, his son welcomed him with a few good hits as he tried to show off his new toy: a little wooden sword.

"Oh! Oh!" Sándor pretended he was defenceless against his 'assailer'. "People help me! This knight is so strong. He smote me so hard. He has a great sword."

The boy screamed triumphantly and continued the attack.

"Yes, yes, you beat me. Please, stop! I surrender." He knelt in front of his son. "Now give me a hug."

István wavered. Erzsi, who was standing nearby watching, encouraged him, "Go on, István. Hug your daddy."

The boy dropped his sword and obeyed.

"And what did I tell you to say?" Erzsi asked.

"Wuv you, Daddy."

"I love you," the maid corrected him. "Say it again."

"Wuv you."

Sándor's chest swelled with pride. "You can talk already? You are such a clever boy."

The tiredness and bad memories of the battlefield had disappeared. He lifted István up and seated him on his shoulders. The boy clapped with excitement. Everyone and everything must have looked so small from up there. "Mama! Look! Yiant!"

Margit was standing at the top of the stairs. Sándor did not know how long she had been there, but as soon as he looked up towards her, she descended the stairs and approached him. The smile on her face made hope flutter in his heart.

"You finally found your way home."

There was no embrace. She only put her hand on his arm for a few moments and then withdrew it, stood and regarded him as if waiting for his reaction.

Sándor lifted István off his shoulders and set him back on the floor. Erzsi took the boy by the hand and led him away.

"I'm glad you are safe," Margit said. "You have never been absent for so long. All this fighting so far from home... And I did not receive any messages from you. I was sick with worry."

"So, you do care about me."

"You are my husband and the father of my child. Of course I care."

"I am your husband, yet you still refuse to lie with me. Even God has absolved me, Margit. But you –"

"Keep your voice down!"

She took him by the arm and led him to the great hall. She looked about to make sure no servants were listening. "This is different. The thought of you doing what you did with that... viper still turns my stomach."

"It has been more than two years. If the situation were reversed, I would have forgiven you by now."

"I would never be unfaithful to you. I am not of that disposition. But you always liked a bit of 'adventure'."

"Dear wife, I swore to you that I would not lie with another woman again, and I have kept my promise all this time. I cannot bear this distance between us any longer. I miss the softness of your touch and the warmth of your body beside me."

He put his arms around her waist and drew her towards him. Her slap made him see flashes of light. "For the love of God, woman!"

"Go find some prostitute if you are that desperate!" she blurted out, leaving him speechless.

Footsteps approached. It was Balog. Margit turned around and walked away in haste.

Sándor tried to cover the red mark on his face with his hand.

"I'm sorry, sir," the castellan mumbled.

"Can it wait?"

"Yes, of course. I'll come back later."

Sándor slumped on a chair and let out a deep sigh. Would this torture ever end? He had done all he could, but it was not enough.

The needs of his body he had learned to control: a cold bath, a run in the forest or any type of vigorous exercise, some sparring or even a fistfight with Imre or another one of the knights. His soul, though, was heavy as lead and restless as if waiting for its final judgement in Purgatory. He could not find peace until Margit allowed him; until she said the words that would release him from this hellish nightmare: *I forgive you.*

He prayed to God for a sign, for something to happen; something so powerful that would finally melt the ice in her heart.

***

Margit breathed in the sweet scent of lavender and the other herbs mixed in the warm water. She always enjoyed a good chat with Erzsi about the events of the past few days while she took her bath before going to bed. But that night, she was not in the mood, something that her maid could not help but notice. "My lady, why are you torturing yourself so much?"

"Whatever do you mean?"

"You're a sensible woman. You know what's best for yourself and your family. Don't you think it's time you forgave your husband and accepted him back into your bed?"

Margit clenched her fingers around the rim of the tub. There was a fight within her that she could not subdue.

"And so that you know," Erzsi continued, "I spoke with his mate, Imre Gerendi. He assured me that your husband is telling the truth. He didn't have any women during the time he was away."

Margit let her hand drop into the water with a splash. "I would have forgiven him if it concerned anyone else. But he knew very well how deceitful Anna is. He destroyed his sacred family bond with Miklós. He broke the oath he swore to me in the eyes of God. He gave me so much pain."

"I'm sure he's regretted this more than anything else. You're both still young. Don't waste your time away from each other when there's so much violence and fighting around us. He may go to war again and never come back."

Margit felt her cheeks heating up. Erzsi was right in that, but... "I know. I admit I truly miss our intimacy and the safety of having him by my side. Yet every time he touches me, I think of what he did with her, and it sickens me. And I cannot forget that the physician told me I must not have any more children. I fear what may befall me if I become pregnant again."

"I'm sure the wise woman will have something for you to take so that you don't conceive."

She shook her head. "Thank you Erzsi, but I don't think it would change anything. I am still in pain. I am not ready to forgive him until I have made sure that he deserves it... You can go now. I need to be alone."

"As you wish."

The maid placed a clean towel on the edge of the tub and left.

Margit leaned back and stayed there for a while, staring at the ceiling. How could she love someone so much and hate him so much at the same time? While he was away, she was praying for him to come back safe; and yet, when he returned, she did not wish to be with him.

She cried herself to sleep that night, and many nights thereafter.

15
God's Soldiers

Autumn 1444

Just after dawn on a foggy September morning, Margit stood on the steps of the keep while the preparations were in full swing. The castle courtyard was bustling with soldiers, servants and horses. Sándor and his men – sixty in total, including armoured knights and their squires, light cavalry and archers – had been called to offer their services once again.

She gathered her skirts in one hand, negotiating her way around the puddles of water and the foul-smelling animal droppings, which dotted the uneven cobblestoned ground. With the other, she pushed through a group of men and rushed towards her husband as he was about to mount his horse.

Sándor smiled. "I thought you would not come to see me off. But I'm glad that you did."

"If you think that the king and Hunyadi were wrong to break the treaty with the Sultan, why must you go?"

"I must do my duty. We have lost the army of Despot Branković. He is now angry because he will never recover the parts of Serbia promised to him according to the terms of the treaty. So,

Lord Jankó needs all the experienced men he can muster. He has given me command of more soldiers, in addition to my own. Also, my cousin, Mihály Szilágyi, is going, and he has asked for my help."

She shook her head. Why was he so fascinated with war? She had spent so much time and effort to make him a strong and competent master of his estate, but he always ended up running away to fight. It was as if his heart belonged to the army and not to his home and family. "Very well," she conceded. "Do as you wish. I cannot stop you."

Sándor's face twitched. He turned his gaze away from her. "I have left instructions with Master Havasi on what is to happen in case I do not return."

She gasped. "Why do you say this? You always come back."

"I don't know. It feels a little different this time. It feels like right is not on our side."

Unable to hold back any longer, Margit flung herself into his arms. She held him tight awhile and then, standing on the tips of her toes, whispered in his ear, "May God protect you. I shall pray for you." She reluctantly moved away from him and wiped her tears.

"Remember, I have always loved you." His voice was hoarse with emotion.

She nodded. "I know."

Sándor took her hand in his. She let out a sigh. Was it the cold metal of his mail gloves or the warmth of his kiss on her fingers that made her shiver?

He got on his horse and rode away, followed by his men.

A lump rose in Margit's throat. What if he never came back? What if she did not see him again? She only had herself to blame. Her anger and selfishness had kept her apart from the man she loved most in the world.

When she called the priest to the castle chapel for confession, she tried to unburden all the guilt that had accumulated inside her. But even after she had received absolution, her soul was still in such turmoil that she was not sure if she would ever be able to find peace again.

***

On the first night they made camp on their way to meet Hunyadi's forces, Sándor could not sleep. He left his tent and went to sit by the fire that still burned outside. There was something about Margit's behaviour that morning. She had shown signs of softening her attitude towards him before, which had resulted in giving him false hope. But this time things were different. The manner she embraced him, looked at him and talked to him had been much warmer and gentler than before. He could not forget the tears in her eyes and the effort she made to hold them back. Something had truly changed in her this time. He would bet his life on it.

And that made his mission even more difficult. Contrary to the previous campaigns, when he was glad to be away from her and her unbearable attitude and even did not mind dying in battle, he was now already homesick. If only he could just turn around and return to Sasfészek. But this was not an option. He had given his word to both the voivode and his kinsman, Mihály Szilágyi. He could not recant and drag his family's name through the mud.

"I've said it before: you look like you're carrying the weight of the world on your shoulders," a familiar voice said.

Sándor laughed. "Imre! You still remember saying this to me. You were so drunk that night."

His friend sat beside him and stretched his legs towards the fire. "Yes, I was. But tell me, what's troubling you now?"

Sándor took some time to answer. He did not wish to talk about his marriage with Imre. But he could discuss the upcoming campaign. "Have you ever doubted our purpose? Have you ever thought that perhaps what we are doing is not right?"

"Why, sir, I've known you for fifteen years. I've never seen you waver like this when it comes to fighting the infidels."

"Our duty is to protect our homeland and our families. The king signed a truce with the Sultan, which could give us a chance to live in peace. And yet, the Pope and this Cardinal Cesarini have forced us to go to war again. We are not defending any longer; we are attacking now."

Imre gave him a surprised look. "We're defending Christendom, sir. All these Christian lands that are enslaved by the heathen must be liberated."

Sándor picked up a stick from the ground and poked the fire. "I suppose you are right. We are fighting for the Faith. We are God's soldiers."

"That's the spirit!" Imre slapped him on the back. His hearty laugh echoed in the quietness of the night. He rose to make his way back to the tent.

"Hey!" Sándor said. "Please keep this conversation between you and me. I am responsible for these men, and I don't want them to think that I have had a moment of weakness."

Imre winked at him. "Not a word. I've had a few of those moments myself."

***

Hunyadi slammed his fist on the table. "We have been abandoned by our allies. Branković has made every effort to stop any Serbian forces from joining us. The Emperor of Constantinople changed his mind because he thought he would leave his city undefended if he sent us assistance. And now, the Sultan is here in Varna with his whole army."

Sándor shifted the weight of his body from one leg to the other as he attended the war council in the early hours of the tenth of November. The king's tent was packed with officers and noblemen; and yet, he could hear a pin drop. Even King Władysław was unable to utter a word. The only sound that disturbed the silence was Hunyadi's booming voice. "We are outnumbered three to one and trapped from all directions. Does anyone know why the papal fleet did nothing to stop the enemy crossing the Bosporus strait?"

"We don't know," Cardinal Cesarini replied. "Perhaps the ships are on their way here. I propose that we fortify ourselves behind the war wagons and wait until the reinforcements arrive."

Most of the commanders seconded this proposition by nodding and mumbling words of agreement.

János shook his head. "No, no. If our allies have not arrived by now, they are not going to come at all. Waiting will only strengthen the enemy's position."

There was deathly silence again. And then, Hunyadi's stark declaration sent a chill down Sándor's spine. "There is no way out and no way back. We shall stay here and fight with honour and dignity."

"Let it be so," the king agreed. "You have the command. Prepare the troops for battle."

With furrowed brow, János looked at the map spread before him and at the notes he had made on its margin, based on the reports of his scouts. The officers huddled around him, waiting anxiously.

Hunyadi drew a line in the shape of an outward-facing crescent between the lake and the marshes on the left and the high ground on the right. He divided the army into twelve *banderia* and placed each one of them on the map.

"Left flank: Mihály Szilágyi at the edge." He drew the first square.

Lord Jankó's brother-in-law punched the air with his fist.

"Next will stand the four Transylvanian *banderia*: Hungarian, Székely, Saxon and my mercenaries. Mihály will have the overall command of the left flank." Hunyadi added those four squares to the map and continued, "In the centre, two *banderia*: the royal mercenaries and Hungarian nobles in the first; the king's personal guard in the second. They will be under my command."

Gasps and whispers all around. The Cardinal and most of the noblemen turned to the king with a worried expression on their faces.

"Of course," Mihály whispered to Sándor. "They don't like Jankó. How dare he place the king's guard under his command? To them, it's an insult."

But the king did not seem concerned about that. He hushed everyone with a wave of his hand.

"On the right flank: Bishop of Bosnia, Bishop of Eger, the Croatians and the Cardinal with the remaining allied mercenaries and knights. At the end, slightly behind the formation and facing northeast, there will be the men of Bishop de Dominis. He will have the overall command."

Finally, at the back of the army formation he positioned the Wallachian light cavalry, who were the reserves. Behind them and near the Black Sea coast, stood the crusader camp with the war wagons and the Bohemian infantry soldiers.

"And now return to your men and encourage them," the commander-in-chief concluded the meeting. "We may be fewer, but one of us is worth five of them. All we need to do is trust in God and in ourselves."

"It will be hell out there," Sándor said to his cousin when they were leaving the king's tent. "But it will be an honour to fight with you, sir."

"Likewise," Mihály responded and patted him on the arm.

Sándor would prefer to serve under Hunyadi's command.

However, the voivode had placed him and his men in Szilágyi's *banderium*. Perhaps Lord Jankó thought that it would be more honourable for him to fight alongside his kinsman. But then Sándor remembered the battle formation. Szilágyi's banner was to stand at the edge of the left flank. They would be the first ones to face and bear the brunt of an attack by the Sipahi heavy cavalry. Quite a dangerous position to be in. Therefore, that unit needed to have stronger and more experienced soldiers to repel the attack and even fight back.

The *banderium* numbered about a thousand men, split into smaller teams with their own captains. In addition to his own soldiers, Sándor commanded another two hundred men-at-arms. Most of them were Holman's mercenaries. The crafty Saxon had seized the opportunity to make more money by selling the services of his soldiers to the Hungarians. Sándor was worried that he would have discipline problems commanding those men, but his fears were put to rest after he talked to Borislav Gradić. They were professional soldiers, they obeyed their orders no matter who gave them, and they did not care about the issues between Holman and Sándor.

"How is my brother?" Sándor asked.

"Well, but sad," the Croatian officer replied, in his broken Hungarian. "The woman took his man parts."

"What?"

"She commands him... like he's a stable boy."

Sándor shook his head. Anna was a terrible woman, well-taught by her father to take advantage of everything and everyone.

Even though he had banished Miklós, he still cared about his brother. He would try to reach out to him when the battle was over, and he was back home.

Home... It felt farther away than ever before. In the eerie silence of the chilly night, he knelt on the ground, closed his eyes and tried to give himself some hope. He was responsible for the men under his command. He had a duty to his superiors, to the king, to Hungary and to the Christian faith. He crossed himself, prayed for victory and, in case victory did not come, for a quick and honourable death. The only thing he did not wish for was to be taken prisoner. Torture and slavery scared him more than death.

A few moments later, he rose and looked ahead. The fires at the sixty-thousand-strong enemy camp flickered in the distance. He could smell the upcoming battle in the air.

16

Fields of Death

10 November 1444

The Christian army had been waiting for a full three hours in formation. The Ottomans had not made a move yet.

With the taste of Communion wine still lingering in his mouth, Sándor fiddled with every leather strap of his armour that was within his reach as he sat on his horse. He was always composed and able to keep a level head in the previous campaigns. He always trusted his skills in battle. But things were different now. The longer he had to wait, the more doubt and uncertainty crept into his heart.

Even when defending Sasfészek four years earlier, fighting with a handful of his men against a sea of enemies and saved at the last moment by Holman's mercenaries, he was willing to die protecting his home. And yet now, amidst thousands of comrades, he had been seized body and soul by a new, invisible enemy: fear. But why?

It was not the first time he had been part of an outnumbered and worse-positioned army, nor the first time he had to fight so far away from home. He was well prepared and experienced, and he had embraced the idea of ridding Europe of the Ottoman danger.

He closed his eyes for a moment. A powerful shudder went through his body. It was his wife. Her behaviour at the time of his departure had given him hope that reconciliation was possible; that there was a greater chance than ever for them to become a proper married couple again. All he wished now was to return to her and make up for the time they had lost by being apart. Dying on foreign soil, miles and miles away from home and without seeing her face again: this consideration made his blood run cold.

His thoughts were interrupted by a vicious storm, sweeping across the battlefield like the Devil's deadly breath. Ferocious winds and clouds of dust battered the standing army, blowing away their banners, reducing visibility and startling the horses. The whole formation started to shake.

And then, hell unleashed its hounds.

Using the cover of the storm, the Ottoman Akinji and Azap skirmish units that were hiding on higher ground attacked the right flank of the Christian army.

"It has begun!" Imre shouted and crossed himself. "God help us."

Sándor squinted, but the distance and the cloud of dust that the heavy cavalry had raised obscured his vision. They must have succeeded though because the Ottomans retreated in haste.

Waiting for their turn to join the battle, the Transylvanian troops on the left flank erupted into a cheer so loud that it would echo in the mountains and valleys of home.

The dust had barely settled when the Sultan sent the Anatolian

Sipahi cavalry to support the Akinjis, who were now chased by the men of the Bishops of Eger and Várad. The Croatians joined in, and the fighting spread to involve the remaining two *banderia* on the right.

At the same time, the Rumelian Sipahis prepared to attack the left wing of the Christian army. Sándor's unit was the first one in their path. The mass of enemy riders surged like an angry wave, screaming and chanting their battle cry while hundreds of arrows rained from the sky.

"All yours. Make sure they don't fall into the lake," Mihály said in jest and rode away to inspect the rest of the front line.

"Hold the formation! Wait!" Sándor ordered the men. He had to keep the line of defence united. Any premature move would create gaps. They all had to act as one, if they wanted any chance of success.

In the distance, his cousin signalled to him to go ahead.

"Lances ready!" Sándor shouted.

The densely packed front line of knights and mounted men-at-arms held their lances couched, tilted them upwards and stood still.

The enemy was now in plain sight.

"For *Erdély*! For Hungary! *Szent László!*" The rest of the captains repeated Sándor's words, one after the other like an echo. But when the battle cry reached the Székely *banderium*, it turned into another, more ancient one: "*Huj! Huj! Hajrá!*"

Sándor took his position alongside the knights, holding his lance at the ready. He pulled the visor of his sallet shut, raised his left arm, and as soon as he moved it downwards, the booming sound of the war horns gave the signal to attack.

The two cavalry forces galloped from the opposite sides of the battlefield at breakneck speed. When they collided, the clanking of metal was deafening. But the Hungarian lines held. The lances ripped through the enemy riders and horses, and the Ottomans were repelled.

"Kill the infidels!" Mihály's voice thundered over the noise of the battle.

Now they were fighting at close quarters. The lances were no longer of any use. The knights and men-at-arms opened their formation to allow the more flexible light cavalry take over. Hit for hit, the swords, maces, axes and war hammers clashed; dust covered the men; horses neighed and snorted. Ottomans and Christians were all in one big tangle.

The Hungarians gained the upper hand at first. The Sipahis faltered after the initial attack and were in disarray. But things changed rapidly when thousands of additional riders came from the back of the Ottoman army to replace their fallen and wounded comrades.

This new wave crashed into Sándor's unit. An enemy spear found its way through to his lower left side. It did not penetrate the plate armour, mail and padding underneath; but the force of the hit and the sharp pain that came with it nearly unhorsed him. He felt Imre's strong hand support and steady him just at the right moment.

Sándor did not have time to thank his friend as three enemy

riders set upon him. Vihar stood on his rear legs and scared one of their horses off. The Sipahi fell to the ground only to be trampled by Vihar and the other horses. Sándor lifted the visor. He needed full vision. The other two men came at him from both sides. He let out a horrifying scream, not so much to frighten the Turks but to encourage himself. With a sideways blow of his sword, he struck the opponent attacking from the right. Although the blade did not cut through the man's mail aventail, the sheer force of the hit broke his neck. The third Ottoman charged from the left side with a mace. Sándor instinctively raised the shield strapped to his upper arm. His muscles almost tore absorbing the force of the strike. Gritting his teeth, he pushed the weapon and enemy downwards. At the same time, he swung his right arm around and thrust the sword through the Sipahi's back.

"Forward, men!" Mihály shouted at the top of his lungs. "We can win!"

Win? That was something that defied reason. Was it even possible? Sándor quickly readjusted the shield and pulled down the visor again. He fought for the better part of an hour with the same intensity. His heart pounded; his arms were as heavy as lead; he struggled to breathe inside the closed helmet and under the pressure of his breastplate. But he could not stop. If there was even the slightest chance of victory, all the pain was worth it.

The Ottomans continued to come at him in waves, like demons from the bowels of the earth. He killed and wounded many until one of them hit him in the face with the spike of a war hammer. The pain stunned him. The front of his sallet broke, and the metal cut into his forehead. Blood trickled into his eyes. The whole world dimmed around him. Where was that accursed Sipahi?

"I got him, sir!" his squire screamed to his left.

Thank God for that!

Sándor pulled back from the front line. He took off helmet and gauntlets and wiped the blood with his hands. His eyesight was still affected. The concussion made everything spin. His horse was limping too; so, he rode towards the camp, followed by his squire.

"Tamás! Water! And look at Vihar's right foreleg."

The young man helped him off the horse and brought him a bucket of water.

Sándor washed the blood off his face and out of his eyes. Finally, he was able to see. He was still dizzy though and had to lean on his squire's shoulder. It took him a few moments to steady himself. He hastily wrapped a rag around his head to bind the wound and stop the bleeding.

"How is Vihar?" That horse was more valuable to him than the richest treasure on earth.

"It's only a cut, sir. Not too bad, but it's bleeding."

Tamás heated the blade of a knife in the fire. Sándor let Vihar drink some water and calm down a little. He then stroked his head and held the reins, keeping him steady while his squire cauterised the wound and bandaged it.

"Do you need a fresh horse, sir?"

"No. He will recover soon. He is strong and tough. Like me." Vihar neighed and scraped the ground with his hoof. "Do you see? He wants to fight."

Sándor unstrapped his breastplate and threw it to the ground. "I can't breathe in this. I need something more flexible." Tamás helped him remove the backplate, the faulds, and the skirt of mail, and then disappeared into a nearby tent.

While waiting for the young man, Sándor took a few moments to observe what was happening around him. It was a battle on a gigantic scale. There were men and beasts spread on the field as far as the eye could see. The multitude of colours from the clothes, armour, shields, banners and horses blended with those of nature, creating a massive moving tapestry. If it were not for the horrific loss of life, it would have looked beautiful.

The sudden, loud bursts coming out of the war wagons jolted him back to reality. Things must be bad, he thought. The wagons were at the front of the camp. If the enemy had reached that far, all hope was probably lost.

Indeed, the Christian army was in trouble. The right flank had all but disappeared. Groups of panicked horsemen galloped away behind the camp and towards the swampland. "*Úristen*! These are the bishops' men. What are they doing back here?"

"Look, sir!" Tamás pointed at the Anatolian riders pursuing the Hungarian, Polish, German and Croatian cavalry men, who had sought refuge behind the war wagons. The Bohemian gunners fired incessantly, killing dozens of Ottomans at the same time. The smell of burnt flesh turned Sándor's stomach.

"Time to go back, Tamás," he said faintly.

The squire handed him a new helmet and helped him put on a brigandine, which he laced tightly to the pauldrons. They both mounted their horses and galloped away.

Halfway there, they ran into Hunyadi's messenger. "Are you an officer?" the latter asked, panting and wheezing and desperately trying to steady his horse.

"Yes."

The young man – a Székely boy of about sixteen years of age – was in a miserable state. He had lost his helmet, and his head was covered in blood. The top part of his right ear was half-sliced and hanging against the side of his face. An arrow was stuck in his left shoulder. But he did not show any signs of being in pain.

"You must hold at all costs!" the messenger screamed. "The right flank is broken."

Sándor glanced about. The left wing was not in a better position either. "We need help!" he shouted at the boy as though it were his fault.

"No help, sir. Lord Jankó's gone to support the men of the bishops. The Wallachians did their part and left. You must hold. The voivode's orders."

The messenger wheeled his horse and disappeared into a cloud of dust.

When Sándor re-joined his men, the left flank was barely holding. Under heavy pressure from fresh Ottoman troops, who kept coming and coming amidst a hail of arrows, his comrades were suffering significant losses.

He had to pull them together. "Fight on! Show them what the men of *Erdély* are made of!"

A few paces away, the Croatian captain of Holman's

mercenaries screamed for help. Two Akinjis had unhorsed him and were hitting him with their spears. Sándor's blood boiled with rage. He drew the axe and tapped his legs on the horse's flanks. Vihar understood exactly what his master wanted and charged without being spurred on.

The force of his first blow smashed the head of one of the Ottoman soldiers. His frightened comrade desperately charged at Sándor. But Vihar stood on his rear legs, knocking the spear and the enemy rider to the ground. Still dazed, the Akinji tried to scramble back on his feet only to be struck on the neck by Sándor's axe. This time he fell to the ground and did not move.

Sándor rushed towards Gradić but realised at a glance that he was dead. More Ottoman soldiers penetrated the Hungarian formation, so he screamed at his horse to attack and set upon them with his mighty axe.

He had no notion of how much time had passed when the ground shook. Surprised, he turned around. Finally, help had arrived.

The sight of Hunyadi's personal banner – a raven holding a golden ring in its beak – created panic in the Ottoman forces. Lord Jankó's men-at-arms forced them back again and again. The Sultan's Rumelian riders retreated and kept running away as if the Devil himself were pursuing them.

Having eliminated the danger on the left side, Hunyadi and Szilágyi were now able to gather all their forces and return to assist the right flank. That move was also successful. They not only managed to repel the Turkish soldiers but also kill the Anatolian commander-in-chief.

The battle seemed to be going well, Sándor thought, but then...

"What happened to the king's guard?" Mihály exclaimed.

The whole of Władysław's five-hundred-strong Polish personal guard was missing.

Sándor glanced about, the breath catching in his throat. He turned to his cousin. "Where is the king?"

"There!" Mihály pointed far into the distance. Władysław's banner was barely visible among the sea of Janissaries, who were protecting the Sultan. "He went straight for Murad! Jankó told him to wait, but the young hotspur thought the battle would be won without him getting any of the glory."

"Shall we help him?"

"Too late."

The infinite mass of enemy troops had swallowed the king's banner. Wild screams of triumph came from the Janissaries when one of them raised Władysław's severed head on a high pole.

"*Krisztus*, have mercy," Mihály mumbled. "We are doomed."

Within a short time, the enemy cavalry troops that Sándor and his comrades had defeated and chased away returned to the battlefield. Had they heard the news of Władysław's death? Or perhaps it had been the usual 'feigned retreat' the Ottomans employed so often in battle. Sándor shivered. Was this the end? Had their struggle been for nothing?

All around him, thousands of men and horses were lying dead or gravely wounded on the battlefield. The smell of death hung everywhere. The screams of the dying and the cawing of the carrion birds echoed in the air, creating an otherworldly atmosphere. He could not tell who had won the battle, but his side was in a worse situation because it was a smaller army and its losses proportionally higher.

Under the brigandine and gambeson, his shirt had almost melted into his skin. The injury on his left side gave him terrible pain, and he still reeled from that blow to his head. He growled in anger. He could not show weakness. Spurring on his horse, he moved to assist Hunyadi and Szilágyi in re-organising the remainder of the troops.

But it was all in vain. There was no formation anymore, only small groups of soldiers here and there, fighting individually, trying to escape towards the north to find their way home, or running for cover behind the war wagons at the Christian camp.

Hunyadi gathered as many of the survivors as he could. It was better to save some of the men by leading them away rather than lose them all by remaining there. An escape route was hastily organised just as the shadows of the night began to fall on the battlefield.

"What about the men who are on the far side of the field and those who went back to the camp?" Sándor asked his cousin. "And the wounded? Are we going to let them all die?"

"Are you mad? Don't you see the chaos? It's every man for himself now."

Sándor clenched his teeth and cursed under his breath. Abandoning his comrades to a terrible fate felt like betrayal. But he could do nothing about it. His duty was to take care of his own men first and foremost. Those of his knights and soldiers who were still alive gathered around him. Only thirty-five of the sixty had survived.

"We shall cover the voivode and the other nobles as they leave," he explained to them. "Imre, you will lead our men. I shall stay at the back to make sure everyone has passed through safely."

"Why, sir? You should go with Lord Jankó and the commanders, and we'll be behind you."

"No! I promised these men's families to bring them home safe, and that is what I shall do. And I need you to look after them if I don't make it out of here alive. So, don't dispute my orders!"

***

While heading northwards through a forested area, they came across a small group of Azaps, who were returning to their camp. The size of the Hungarian force was too large for the Turkish to engage, so Hunyadi and the main body of his fleeing troops proceeded without a problem. Sándor's men, who formed the rear guard, were much fewer. The Ottomans took their chance.

Four of his soldiers were already in a skirmish. But, at least, the rest of them had to get away safely. "Continue!" he shouted to Imre. "I'll take care of this."

His sword was broken, but he still had his favourite and most reliable weapon: the horseman's axe. He turned Vihar around to face the enemy.

It was only five of them against twelve or thirteen Turks as he estimated quickly. The daylight was gone already. It was hard to see in the dark, let alone fight. Sándor and his men had removed most of their armour to lessen the weight carried both by them and their tired horses. Now, they were vulnerable.

They fought hard against multiple attackers. The Ottomans were on foot, and some of them carried bows and crossbows, so the two sides were not equally matched. His soldiers had the advantage of being on horseback and therefore moving faster while the Turkish were able to inflict damage to the horses and riders from a distance with their arrows and bolts. Three of the Transylvanians fell but only after taking down half of the enemy men.

The last one was his squire, who escaped on foot deeper into the forest, chased by a group of Ottomans. Sándor glanced around. He was alone. How many were chasing Tamás? Possibly three or four. He had killed three and his men another six. Twelve or thirteen in total. "That must be all of them." Relief washed over him. Both he and Vihar were unharmed.

As he turned to go to his squire's aid, sharp pain ripped through his right side. Then again, in his back and a third time in his right thigh. He screamed at his horse to run. Vihar took off like a fiend. He was going so fast that Sándor could barely hang on. They flew through forests, fields, bushland, more forests... He had no notion of where they were heading; everything was a blur.

All of a sudden, Vihar stopped. He fell to his knees, snorting and breathing heavily. Sándor rolled off the saddle. The contact with the ground shook him up. He reached towards the source of his pain. Damn arrows! There must have been more enemy soldiers hiding behind the trees back there. He tried to pull out the arrow from his side. The pain became even worse, so he left it there. The one on his back had snapped during his fall, its metal edge lodged deeper into his flesh.

"Vihar!" he gasped.

The poor stallion was dying, his body riddled with arrows. Yet, he had carried his master out of harm's way, over such a long distance.

Sándor stretched out his arm and stroked Vihar's head. "I'm sorry, *barátom*. We have been through so much together, but this is the end. I'm honoured to die here beside you."

The horse jerked his head up and down as if acknowledging his master's words and then remained still.

Tears flooded Sándor's eyes. He was bleeding now. His body throbbed with pain. It became harder and harder to breathe. He gasped for air as a wave of panic overwhelmed him. That was why he had a bad feeling before the battle. He was meant to die alone in a foreign land, far away from home, from Margit. Would she weep for him? Would she mourn him? A few months earlier, he had prayed to God for a sign, for a powerful event to end his misery. Perhaps that was it: his own death. Perhaps he had to pay the ultimate price to receive her forgiveness. He winced as he struggled to create an image of her in his mind. But he could not. He screamed. How could he not even remember her face in his last moments? His body numbed little by little as if affected by a powerful drug. The pain ebbed away.

He looked up towards the starry sky and stared at it until the little lights dissolved, and darkness covered everything.

17

Ghost

May 1445

He passed through the town gate as the shadows of twilight were enveloping Sasfészek and the land around it. After crossing the main square, he hurried along the narrow streets and then all the way up to the castle. No one noticed him. He knew exactly where to stand and walk, always in the shadows and keeping the hood of his cloak on. Avoiding the attention of the guards, he entered the family residence through the back door, straight into the kitchen.

"Good evening, my good people." He took the servants by surprise as he helped himself to a seat at their table. "Would you spare some scraps for a weary traveller?"

They looked at one another. "Where did he come from?"

He pulled down the hood. "Pardon my intrusion. I've come from far away. From eastern Hungary. My name is Jakab. I'm looking for a cousin of mine, Erzsi. I was told she works for the lady of the estate."

"Aye, she does," the head cook replied. She nodded to one of the younger servants to fetch Margit's maid. "Here's some pottage and bread whilst you wait."

"Thank you, my good woman. God bless you." He gorged on his delicious supper.

He had barely finished eating, when Erzsi entered, huffing and puffing at the servant girl for pulling her out of her warm bed.

He jumped to his feet and gave her a big hug. "Erzsi! I'm so glad to see you."

"Whoever you are, you stink really bad," she said in disgust.

She tried to push him away, but he held her tight. It was so good to embrace someone familiar. Someone he could trust. Someone from home. He was home at last. He could not pretend any longer. "It is I, Sándor," he whispered in her ear. "Please, don't give me away."

At length, he let her go. Erzsi stood there, frozen, and stared at him wide-eyed. It took her an eternity to respond. "Cousin! It's been so long."

Holding his hand, she led him out of the kitchen and into a corridor. "My lord! You're alive. It's a miracle." She crossed herself.

"Yes. I was gravely wounded, but some good people saved my life back in Bulgaria. Then, I had no money and no more help, so I had to make my way home on foot."

"We waited for three months, and then you were declared dead. You must have seen the black flags outside."

"Right. And I was wondering why."

"I'm sorry, my lord, I didn't recognise you at first." Erzsi covered her mouth with her hand, blushing. "Your face is black with dirt; your hair and beard so filthy that it's hard to tell what colour they are."

"Yes, I know. No one in the kitchen had any notion of who I was."

"Let me take you to my lady now. She'll be so pleased to see you."

She grabbed his hand again and pulled him along behind her, but he stopped her. "No! She cannot see me like this. Please help me make myself presentable. I do not remember when it was the last time I had a bath."

***

The warm water relaxed his sore and tired body, making him feel as if he were lying on a bed of clouds. He closed his eyes and let Erzsi take care of him. Finally, a woman's tender touch that he had missed so much. It took her a long time to scrub the filth off his body and hair. Then, she cleaned and shaved his face.

If only he could stay there forever. But he had important things to do, such as holding his son and his wife in his arms again. He stood up and stepped from the tub, dripping wet and oblivious to his nakedness.

Erzsi's face turned bright red. "For the love of God, my lord! Cover yourself." She handed him a towel and turned away. "I see you're back to your normal self. Well, you're too thin, but it's nothing that some good food, exercise and fresh mountain air can't fix."

"What has happened here during my absence?" Sándor asked while getting dressed.

"Oh, my lord, you won't believe it, but your brother's here. After the official declaration of your death, he came to the castle. He said he wanted to protect your wife and son until the boy comes of age. But my lady's troubled. She fears for her safety and that of little István."

The news did not surprise him. "I am sure his evil wife and her scheming father are behind this. They would probably devise a plan to get rid of the boy before he became a man."

"But now you're back, and all will be like before."

"Yes, I shall sort everything out. But please don't tell anyone yet that I am here. Especially not my brother or any of his men."

"Of course."

"I am ready now. Let us go."

He followed Erzsi to his son's bedchamber first.

"He kept asking for you every day, my lord. 'Where's my daddy? Where's my daddy?' We didn't have the heart to tell him that you weren't coming back."

They tiptoed into the room. Sándor knelt beside the boy, who was sleeping peacefully. It was so good to be home again. He had missed his son's laughter and the games they played together. Careful not to wake up the child, he stroked his hair gently and gave him a light kiss on the forehead.

"Come, my lord," Erzsi whispered. "It's time to see your wife."

Sándor followed her along the corridor. He stood at the side of the doorway, peeping through the narrow opening that the maid had left after walking into Margit's bedchamber. Dear God, he could finally see her in the flickering light of Erzsi's candle! At the sound of her sweet voice, he struggled to keep his quickening breath under control.

Margit sat up on the bed, rubbing her eyes. "Erzsi! What is it?"

"There's someone here to see you, my lady."

"In the middle of the night? Can he not wait until the morning?"

"He has information about your husband."

"What?" She jumped out of the bed. "Where is he?"

"Standing outside. I'll bring him in."

"Yes, yes!" Margit hastily put on a cloak over her chemise.

Erzsi lit a few more candles. She smiled and nodded as she walked past Sándor.

His knees were shaking when he entered. After what had happened between them, how would she react to seeing him?

At first, she froze. Then, she put her hand over her mouth, trying to stop herself from screaming. Silent tears rolled down her face. "Are you a ghost that has come to torment me?"

"I am no ghost. Although I probably look like one."

"We thought you were dead."

"So did I. But it seems I had a guardian angel."

"Oh, merciful God!"

Margit stood far apart from him as though she could not believe that he was there. Then, she threw off the cloak and stepped in front of him.

"I was unfair to you. I treated you so badly. Will you please forgive me?" She fell to her knees and raised her arms towards him with her hands joined at the wrists. "I have not done my duty to you as a wife. You can punish me in any way you wish."

His heart raced. A lump rose in his throat. "No, no... There is nothing to forgive." His voice trembled. "There will be no punishment... I shall never hurt you again. I swear... I am not that man anymore." Holding her by the wrists, he hauled her to her feet. "I wronged you. And you had every right to be angry at me. I am the one seeking forgiveness. Will you take me back?"

"Of course. Welcome home, dear husband. I have missed you so much."

"Thank God!" A huge weight had been lifted off his chest. He drew her into his arms and kissed her.

She pulled away, leaving him in doubt. But all she wanted to do was take off her chemise and let it drop on the floor. As she stepped towards him again, he could not wait any longer. He lifted her off her feet and carried her to the bed.

The few moments it took him to undress felt like an eternity. "Make haste, *szerelmem!*" she complained.

Sándor clambered across the bed to her. "We must be quiet, *angyalom*. To protect your reputation. Apart from Erzsi, nobody knows I have returned. I am sure you don't want them to think that you have a man in your bed so soon after your husband's 'death'."

Margit giggled.

He touched her lips with his forefinger. "Shhh."

They both struggled to suppress expressing their passion. He finished with a low groan while she stifled her moans by burying her face in his shoulder.

"I have missed this," Sándor said, trying to catch his breath. "I had forgotten how good it feels." He leaned on his elbow beside her and gently brushed aside the strands of hair that were stuck to her face. "And I have missed you, dear wife."

Margit fought back the tears. "*Szerelmem,* I was lost without you. When the men came home and you were not with them, I felt like the world had crashed around me. I spent countless sleepless nights, praying for your return. But the days passed, and you were still missing. Then they declared you dead. Even Hunyadi sent me a letter of condolences, praising your bravery in Varna. I could not bear it. I wished to die. If it were not for István, I would have jumped off the castle walls."

He traced the side of her face with his fingers. "Thank God you didn't. The battle was utter carnage. I shall never forget it. Why did the Almighty let all those young lives be lost? Some of them had not even grown a beard yet. They fought for Him and for all Christendom. Is He a fair God, who deserts His soldiers in their time of need?"

"Please, husband, do not say such words! Those men were His martyrs. They will have their reward in the next life; they will be with Him in Heaven for all eternity."

Sándor covered his face with his hand. He could not get those horrible images out of his head.

"But tell me now, what happened to you?"

"I was gravely wounded after the battle as we were leaving to return home. My horse fell and died, and I thought the end had come for me too. All I could think of in those moments was you. I was not afraid to die. I was afraid that I would not see you again. I woke up many days later in a local family's cottage. One of the villagers had served as an army surgeon's assistant in his younger years. Thanks to him, I survived. I did not realise that I spent five months there. I had lost... all sense of... time..."

His throat constricted, making his voice fade. He had never been so close to dying. The thought shook him to the core and took the air out of his lungs.

Margit's light touch on his face felt like a lifeline pulling him from the darkness.

He could breathe again. "Those people saved me despite the threat of a possible Ottoman reprisal. But they were poor, and when I decided to leave, they could not help me anymore. They gave me clothes and enough food for a few days, and then I had to make my way home by myself. Sometimes I was fortunate to get a ride on a passing cart. Otherwise, I had to walk, eat whatever I could find and sleep wherever I could get shelter. I don't know how I got back here. It feels like a bad dream."

"It's over now, *szerelmem*," Margit whispered, with the sweetest smile. "You are home."

He leaned over her. They surrendered to a long and ardent kiss. He was the first one to come back to reality. "I wish I could stay here and love you all night and all day, but there is something I must do." He got up, picked his clothes from the floor and started to dress.

Margit propped herself up on her elbow and watched him. A mixture of admiration and lustful desire lit her face, but then she darkened. "Do you know your brother is here?"

"Yes, this is what I must deal with. I was ready to make peace with him. But after hearing that he has tried to take my land again and possibly harm my family, I have changed my mind. He is going to receive what he deserves."

She sprang upright in the bed. "Sándor, I beg of you! Don't do anything foolish! He is your family too."

He did not answer but left the room in haste.

18

Blood is Thicker Than Water

Miklós woke up screaming as the cold steel of Sándor's sword touched his throat. "Don't kill me, please!" His eyes narrowed as he desperately tried to discern, in the faint light of dawn, who was standing over him. "What is this? Who are you?"

"You always make me break my promise."

Miklós gasped. "You are dead!"

"Obviously not if I am standing here."

"What are you talking about? What promise?"

"I told you many times that if you come near my estate and my family, I shall kill you. But I can never do it, so you always escape the punishment."

"We all thought you were dead. I came here to help your family."

"I don't believe you. I think you came here to steal what is mine. Now, rise and dress." Sándor moved the sword away from his brother's throat.

Miklós sat up on the bed, with both hands on his forehead. After a few moments, he stood up and put his clothes on.

Sándor opened the door and called two guards in. "Take him to the dungeon until I decide what to do with him." He left before

Miklós had time to put up any protest.

***

The servants and soldiers at Sasfészek were overjoyed to see that their lord had returned. There were embraces and tears all around. Imre cried as he held his dear friend in his arms. After all they had gone through in Varna, he had managed to lead the surviving men home without any more losses on the way. But since his return, Imre was not himself. The disaster at the battle, the deaths of so many comrades and the fact that he had to break the news of Sándor's self-sacrifice to Margit had deeply troubled him. So strong was his grief that he had sworn not to pick up a sword and fight again. But now his friend had come back alive, so Imre would not need to keep this promise.

The second happiest person to see him was Balog. The castellan was delighted, laughing and jesting – something which surprised everybody, given how serious and stern he always was.

After talking to the people in the castle, Sándor rode to the town. He spoke to the men, women and children who had gathered in the main square. He told them how happy he was to be home among them and promised that he would continue to work with them for the better future of the estate. Everyone was glad that their landlord had returned, and that the estate would not be taken over by Miklós or Holman.

Following a visit to the mine to reassure the workers there, Sándor returned to the castle. He had to do something about his brother.

He walked into the dungeon and found Miklós pacing up and down. "I want you to leave," he said coldly.

Miklós halted and turned to him. "Don't treat me like this! I came here to help."

"I do not believe you. You are merely a pawn in your wife's and her father's chess game. Now that the king is dead, they wish to take control of the mine. Master Kendi told me that you resumed trading with the Saxon merchants, and you removed the mine from Lord Jankó's protection. I am sure this was not your decision."

Miklós dropped his gaze to the floor. "No, it wasn't." He turned to his brother again with a distressed look on his face. "But please, don't send me back. I shall do whatever you want provided you let me stay."

"Why?"

"She said that she would kill me if I failed. She said I would not be worth being called a man."

"Did she?"

Sándor shook his head. He had his differences with his brother, but he would not allow anyone threaten Miklós's life like this. He had to take action. "Gather your things and prepare. I shall take you back to your wife, but I shall go with you and make sure you are safe."

"And what will happen after you leave me there?"

"Do not fret. After she sees me, she will be afraid to harm you."

Miklós gripped his arm, eyes wild with despair. "But I don't want to go back to her! You were right all along. She is using me to promote her father's plans. I was too blinded by love to see this. I don't care for her anymore. I wish to be as far away from her as I can."

Sándor pushed his brother's hand off him. "Miklós! When you married that woman, you cut off all bonds with this family. She is your family now. You will go back to her whether you like it or not."

Miklós let out a sigh of frustration and reluctantly followed him upstairs.

Holman's estate was about three hours' ride away, so they would be able to get there and back before midnight. Sándor took twenty soldiers with him as he escorted his brother home. He needed protection in case the Saxon tried any sly trick against him and Miklós.

When they arrived, it was that time between day and night when the evening shadows descend from the sky to give the land a sinister and eerie look. They stood in front of the fortified manor house, and Sándor demanded that Anna came out to talk to him.

The heavy gate opened, and she rode towards him, escorted by three guards. She came so close to him that he could hear her gasp and then clear her throat. "I'm glad you are alive. And I see you brought my husband back."

Miklós sneered.

"Go home!" Sándor ordered him. "I shall speak with her. Don't fret. You will be safe."

"I don't want to know you anymore. You are dead to me!" his

brother growled. He spurred on his horse and galloped away.

Sándor turned to Anna. "I must talk with you in private."

"Why don't you come in?"

"No, I don't have the time."

"Then, follow me." She gestured to her men not to accompany her and rode towards the ruins of an old house farther downhill.

Sándor went after her. They dismounted and walked until they hid from the view of the others behind a wall.

"Your plot failed. Miklós revealed everything to me. He is so afraid of you."

"He is so weak!" Anna scoffed. "I wish he were half the man that you are."

She slowly slid her hand down his arm.

He was not going be fooled this time. He grabbed her by the throat and shoved her against the wall. "If I hear that you did any harm to my brother, I shall kill you. I shall not bring an army but come on my own at night, steal into your home and your bedchamber and slit your throat while you sleep."

"Really? And what else are you going to do to me before you kill me?"

She breathed heavily and moaned under the pressure of his hand on her throat.

He was trying to scare her, but he had failed miserably. Instead, she had come so close to tempting him again. If it were five or six years earlier, he would have had her on her back forthwith. She was the kind of woman he used to like. But he was a different man now.

He released her, stepped back and wagged his finger in her face. "Stop! You are only making a fool of yourself."

She rubbed her neck and swallowed hard. "Very well. I shall not harm Miklós on one condition."

"Condition? You are not in a position to negotiate."

She looked him straight in the eye. "You will spend a night with me."

Her audacity knew no bounds! "Are you out of your mind? After all you did to me and my family? I hate you. Do you not understand this?"

Anna pressed her clenched fist against her mouth. "It's all my father's fault!" she burst out. "He used me to fulfil his ambition of becoming a landed gentleman and make as much money as he could. As if he will take it all with him when he dies. Do you think I enjoyed being married off at the age of fifteen and then again at seventeen to lecherous old men, who made my skin crawl every time they touched me? And if I dared to say anything, my father would beat me until I could not bear it any longer."

She was sobbing loudly now. Sándor took a deep breath and put his hand on her shoulder. If what she had said was true, she had definitely lived a terrible life. "I am sorry this happened to you. But look now, you are married to a handsome young man with a noble name, who loves you very much. Look after him. Give purpose to his life. Create a family with him so that all the land and wealth you have goes to your children when your father dies. Despite everything, I still care for my brother, and I wish to see him happy with the woman he married."

She gently pushed him away. "You are right. It's time to start living again."

He smiled, trying to cheer her up a little. "For what it's worth, I was flattered to have the attention of such a beautiful lady."

"Don't make it worse!" she snapped, then spun around and walked away.

19

Time to Rest

Wearing a long, dark cape with a hood covering her head, Margit followed Erzsi to the hut of the Wallachian wise woman. It was still early in the morning, and there was not a soul on the path that led there.

Surprised to see the landlady pay her a visit, Marina bowed and welcomed her to her humble house.

Margit's knowledge of the Wallachian language was limited, but Marina spoke reasonably good Hungarian. "What does the Lady of the Eyrie need?"

Margit covered her nose, offended by the strange and smelly things that lay about the place. She gathered herself together and asked the woman for something to prevent her from conceiving a child.

"The lady has lover?" Marina said with a broad smile on her face.

Margit blushed. "No! My husband has returned."

"Oh! Good news! You must be very happy."

"A little too happy. I lay with him last night, and I am worried now. I must not have another child after what befell me the first time."

"Fear not, lady, you come to right place."

Marina disappeared into the back room for a few moments and returned with a small vial, which contained a strangely coloured liquid. She handed it to Margit. "Drink it. It makes you bleed three days. Clears what the man left inside you."

Margit felt like vomiting. The way that woman talked turned her stomach. She nodded to Erzsi to take the vial and put it in her purse. "And I need something to stop me from conceiving in the future."

"Yes. Here, lady." Marina produced a glass jar full of a pulverised substance. "Secret recipe. I give to 'working girls' in town. They swear it's good. Chew a pinch of it on same day every week. When it finishes, come to me and I give you more."

The jar went straight into Erzsi's purse.

"And one more." Marina handed the maid another jar, containing a thick, yellowish transparent liquid. "Dip linen cloth in it. Spread inside you before you lie with man. It will stop the seed. Use the two, and you have no baby again."

"Thank you," Margit said, placing a silver coin in the woman's palm. "Please keep my visit a secret. I do not wish any gossip to reach the priest."

"Yes, lady," a beaming Marina promised and bowed as low as she could.

Margit hastened back to the castle, leaving Erzsi struggling to keep up with her. "I shall never set foot in that place again. It was disgusting!"

"Don't fret, my lady," the maid said, panting. "I can go on your behalf next time."

***

Margit tossed and turned in her bed. Her husband had gone to escort Miklós home. She could not bear the thought of him seeing Anna again. Surely, that woman would try some sly trick to tempt him.

She heaved a sigh of relief when Sándor knocked on the door and entered. Looking spent and without uttering a word, he took off his clothes and got into the bed. He leaned over to kiss her, but she stopped him by putting her hand over his mouth. "How did it go?"

"Well, I think."

She was dreading to ask the question, but she did anyway. "Did you see Anna?"

"Yes."

"I bet the evil wench tried to charm you, didn't she?"

"Yes. I did not respond, of course."

Margit smiled. Her husband had not fallen into the trap. But the smile froze on her face as soon as she heard his next words. "You know, she is not as evil as I thought."

Her heart leapt. "What do you mean?"

"She has had a difficult life. Her father not only forced her into marriage with old men so that he could take their land, but he also used to beat her badly when she was a girl."

"Really? Do you believe her? Perhaps she was trying to attract your sympathy."

"I don't know, but I have a feeling she was telling the truth."

"Perhaps... Still, I shall never forgive her for what she –"

He shut her mouth with a kiss. "Enough about Anna," he whispered as he nuzzled her hair and the side of her face. "So good to be home."

Margit trembled with anticipation while he slid his hand from the back of her neck down to her buttocks and then squeezed her body against his. But he did not continue. His eyelids drooped, his head lay on her shoulder, and he fell asleep at once.

She smiled as she watched him, peaceful at last, looking like he did not have a care in the world. She gently stroked his face and then touched the new scars on his body. He had done too much fighting in his life. It was about time he took a rest.

PART TWO

20

The Dark Clouds of War Gather Again

May / June 1456

The young man, wearing a hauberk and carrying a sword and a dagger in his belt, closed the door of Sándor's study.

Margit seized him by the arm.

He looked at her, surprised. "My lady?"

"Who sent you, soldier?"

"My lord, the Captain General."

"Hunyadi?"

"Aye. May I leave now? I've more messages to deliver."

She stood with folded arms and watched him as he descended the stairs. He was no ordinary courier. He was a military one; a type of messenger that she had not seen for a long time and hoped that she would not see ever again. She let out a deep sigh.

Following his narrow escape from death in Varna, her husband had decided to exercise his right as a nobleman not to go to war outside the borders of the kingdom. Nevertheless, he continued to provide soldiers for Lord Jankó's offensive campaigns, under the capable leadership of Imre Gerendi. Occupied with more important matters, such as governing the realm on behalf of the Habsburg boy-king, László V, Hunyadi did not try to persuade Sándor to return to the battlefield. As long as the taxes were paid and soldiers were available whenever needed, there was no issue at all.

All this had lulled Margit into a false sense of security for eleven years. Apart from occasionally taking up arms to fend off raids in the local area, Sándor had not left home to go on campaign. But now that Hunyadi's messenger had just been in her house, everything was about to change.

With a trembling hand, she opened the door and entered the study. Sándor was sitting at his writing desk and staring at a letter in front of him.

Anticipating the worst, Margit took a deep breath. "What's the news?"

"The old enemy has appeared again with a new face. It seems taking Constantinople was not enough for young Sultan Mehmed. He now wishes to conquer Hungary. He is planning an attack on Nándorfehérvár."

There was a trace of a smile on his face and a sparkle in his eyes.

Her heart sank. It was not the news of the impending invasion that frightened her but the fact that her husband could hardly contain his excitement.

She pointed at the letter. "This is a call to arms, isn't it? It could not have come at a worse time. The harvest will start soon. There is so much work to be done here..." She swallowed the lump that had risen in her throat.

"Things are bad, Margit. King László has gone to Vienna with his court and a large part of the army. Some say he went there to protect his Austrian lands, threatened by the Holy Roman Emperor. But others say that he is afraid of the Turks. Most of the nobles have refused to help Lord Jankó, either because they do not like him or because they need their tenant-soldiers home for the harvest. I am in a better position. I can take the mercenaries, the knights and levies from Szentimre and the neighbouring lands and still leave enough men here to tend the fields and protect the estate."

"I am so afraid," Margit whispered.

Sándor drew a deep breath and exhaled loudly. He stood up and walked towards her.

The slight limp in his right leg was the last straw. Tears were stinging her eyes. "Your leg hasn't healed yet, after the last raid."

"My leg is fine." By the way he spoke, she sensed that he was desperately trying to sound calm and reassuring.

He was about to embrace her, but she recoiled and raised her arms. "Don't treat me like a child! Hugs and kisses won't make me feel better."

After an awkward pause, Sándor's face hardened. "I am a nobleman, a landlord, a husband and a father. But you know very well that, above all, I am a soldier. Our homeland, our faith, our way of life and even our freedom are under threat. It's my duty to defend them. I know that you fear for me. So, I promise I shall be watchful. And God willing, I shall return to you safe."

Margit sucked her lower lip and smeared away her tears. As a soldier's daughter and a soldier's wife, she understood that duty all too well. She was fooling herself if she thought that she could keep her husband at home forever. And so, she did not say another word.

***

Sándor clenched his teeth and brought the sword down on his son's shoulder with great force.

István staggered backwards.

"Shield up! Close to the head! Don't leave gaps!"

The boy straightened himself, raised the shield and hit back at him with continuous strikes, forcing him to retreat towards the line of the tall fir trees.

His son was good, but he still had a lot to learn. It was time for another valuable lesson. He kicked István hard on the hip, bringing him to his knees and ending the fight immediately.

The boy took off his helmet and tossed it to the ground, revealing his flushed face. "Father! That is so unfair!"

"Why is it unfair?"

"You always win by tripping me, kicking me or throwing things at me."

Sándor helped István up. "Stop whining like a little child. Do you think that your enemy will abide by the laws of chivalry? He will ambush you, bring you down from your horse; he will try to kill you in any way that he can. War is not a knightly tournament with rules and regulations. It's a nasty affair."

The squires helped them out of their armour. Sándor embraced the boy and patted him on the back of the head. His heart fluttered with anxiety. Very soon he would have to say farewell to his family and go to war. Would he ever see them again?

They sat down to have a bite to eat near the fire. Darkness was falling. The coolness of the evening breeze was welcome after such a hot day. Sándor let out a sigh. "This is our last night together before I leave for Nándorfehérvár. I shall miss our fights. But it will be good for you to have a rest and apply yourself to your studies."

The boy snorted. "Studying is tedious. And I hate Latin. It's so difficult."

"*Mens sana in corpore sano,* the ancients used to say. A man who is both a warrior and a scholar is a rare man to find. As a nobleman, you will need your fighting skills to protect your land against invaders, and your education to ensure that no one takes advantage of you. And equally importantly, you may attract a beautiful, noble lady with your strong body, but you will keep her captivated forever with your good manners and intelligence."

István blushed. "Father, studying and training aside, don't you think it's time you talked to me about the ladies too?"

Sándor smiled. The boy was growing up so fast. He was already fourteen years old. It felt like yesterday when he had held him in his arms as a little newborn baby. And now, with his mother's blonde hair, blue eyes and fair skin and his father's height, István was already drawing the admiration and fancy of maidens and married women alike. "I promise I shall tell you all about the ladies when I return. Until then, stay away from them."

They both burst out laughing. But only a moment later, István's countenance altered. "Father?"

"Yes?"

"Take me with you tomorrow."

Sándor's back stiffened. "Out of the question."

"You have trained me well. I can be useful."

"You are too young."

"All knights take their pages to war, and most of those boys are twelve or thirteen years old."

"Those pages are not my sons, but you are. If I think it is too early for you, then it is."

"Oh, I beg you, Father! I wish to go."

Sándor shook his head. There was no way he would allow his son to put himself in such grave danger. Even if he were there with him, it would be impossible to watch over him constantly and protect him.

"Listen to me," he said with as much paternal authority as he could. "You are the heir to the estate. If I die out there, you will be needed here to take care of the land, the people and, above all, your mother. So, stop behaving like a child if you wish to be treated like a responsible man."

István grunted in frustration but did not continue the argument.

As the castellan, László Balog, had died, Sándor gave strict orders to his successor, Balog's son Pál, not to let the boy leave the estate under any circumstances.

The big plain in northern Serbia was crawling with people. Men, women and children, sweating heavily under the scorching summer sun; carrying their possessions on carts, wheelbarrows, on their own backs and on the backs of mules, donkeys, oxen and even goats. They raised a cloud of dust as they trudged along the dirt road, flanked by fields of wheat and barley.

"Refugees from Nándorfehérvár and the surrounding areas," Imre said to Sándor. "Lord Jankó commanded them to leave for their own safety. But the truth is he wants them out of the city to make more space for soldiers. And he fears too many civilians would be a drain on the supplies in the event of a siege."

The stream of people made itself narrower and stepped off the road entirely to allow the army of Szentimre and the other Transylvanian troops pass by as they marched in the opposite direction. Colourful company and noble banners flew proudly above the well-polished helmets of men lined up in perfect discipline. The tired and gloomy faces of the people lit up.

"Heroes!" an old man shouted, inciting a fervent response from the rest of them.

"God be with you!"

"Save us!"

"The army of Christ!"

Young women ran to embrace the foot-soldiers; some even stole a kiss or two before being pulled back by male members of their families.

Sándor rose in the stirrups, stretched his neck and peered into the distance. There was no end to the line of people. He exhaled sharply, sat back in the saddle, turned his horse around and stood between the two columns, which were moving in opposite directions. "We shall win!" he shouted in Serbian, at the top of his voice. "And you will go back to your homes. I promise."

Someone tugged at his leg. A tiny old woman, barely reaching up to his knee, proffered a small wooden cross with a trembling hand.

"May God protect you, lord," she rasped. "Take this. From all of us. With all our love and faith. You are our only hope."

He took the cross from her, kissed it and held it aloft. Soldiers and civilians cheered, in one mighty voice.

Many miles farther down, after the long line of the refugees had finally disappeared, the men came across a large crowd, who had gathered in a field. Right in the middle, standing on a small makeshift platform, an elderly Franciscan friar was preaching in Latin in a thundering voice. Sándor dispatched a rider to find out who those people were.

"Giovanni di Capistrano, the Pope's envoy," the man said when he returned. "They say he's God's answer to the Ottomans. He has united lower nobility, townsfolk and peasants with his fiery speeches and promise of absolution of sins. Hungarians, Croatians, Germans, Polish and Bohemians, they're all coming in their thousands to defend Nándorfehérvár."

Sándor swept his arm dismissively towards the crowd. "If this is the army that the Pope has promised, we are doomed. Look at them: full of faith and passion but light in weapons and armour.

Knives, slings, scythes, pitchforks and other... farming tools cannot win against cavalry and cannons."

On the twentieth day of June, they arrived in Nándorfehérvár – the frontier city which the Serbians called Belgrade. Sándor had been there before; the last time was thirteen years earlier. Not much had changed since then. Its fortifications were an impressive specimen of military engineering, with three lines of defence: the outer city walls, built around the lower town and the port on the Danube; the double walls and moat with two drawbridges, protecting the upper town, where the barracks of the garrison were also located; and finally, the inner castle walls, surrounding the citadel on the top of a hill. Tall watchtowers, some of them with flat tops and crenelations and others with pointed tiled roofs stood at regular intervals, all along the fortifications. In addition, a wide ditch, dug around the outer ring of the city, made approach even more difficult. Teams of builders and masons, in straw hats and only wearing knee-length linen braies and shirts with the sleeves rolled up, stood on high scaffolding at certain spots along the curtain wall, working hard to repair its weakest parts.

Sándor and his soldiers initially reached the eastern gate but ran into the back of a long line of carts and wagons filled with supplies, slowly trickling into the city. Armed guards examined each one lest Ottoman spies tried to enter Belgrade in disguise. Quarrels erupted several times because of the inevitable delay. The air was thick with all kinds of smells, from food and smoke to human sweat and animal droppings.

Sándor flapped his hand about, trying to scare the flies away. Waiting there would be a waste of time. He ordered the men to march to the southern gate. The tired soldiers grumbled about having to walk the additional distance in the searing heat, but at least they did not need to wait so long to enter this time.

He let his men unload their equipment and find their quarters in the upper town. After jostling his way through buzzing groups of soldiers, knights, workers, washerwomen, merchants and townsfolk, he climbed uphill to the centre of command in the citadel. As he walked along the corridor, looking for any of the high-ranking officers, he came face-to-face with a strapping long-haired young man. The stranger cast a glance at the coat of arms on Sándor's tabard and smiled. "The Szilágyi mountain goat. Good to see family is here to help."

"Sir, I do not have the honour of knowing you."

"I am László Hunyadi."

Sándor bowed his head. "Oh, forgive me, sir. I did not recognise you. I am Sándor Szilágyi of Szentimre in Hunyad County."

"Relative of my mother's, I assume?"

"Yes. I fought alongside your father and your uncle Mihály in many battles."

László beckoned to him. They entered the command room, where the other officers had gathered.

"Good to see you again. It's been a long time," said the familiar voice of the fortress commander, Mihály Szilágyi.

"Likewise, sir." Sándor glanced around. "Where is the

general?"

"Jankó has returned to Hungary to muster reinforcements. Let us pray that he will be here soon."

The military council was brief, and the news bad. Spies had just brought information that the Turkish army of sixty to seventy thousand was on the way, led by Sultan Mehmed himself. They were transporting large siege machines, cannons and a fleet of combat and support ships. On hearing this chilling news, everyone in the room fell silent. A dark and ominous cloud lingered over those brave men. The Ottomans would arrive much earlier than anticipated. It was now certain that Hunyadi and Capistrano's reinforcements would not be there in time. This meant that the defenders had to face a force twenty times their number.

21

Under Siege

July 1456

The scouts entered the city in such haste that they raised a thick cloud of dust after galloping on the dry ground. "They are here! The Turks are coming!"

The news was expected, but it still made the blood freeze in the defenders' veins. The gates of Belgrade were shut and sealed. With most of the inhabitants and merchants gone, the city was as quiet as an empty church.

By midday, the large army appeared on the horizon.

"Like a swarm of ants," Imre jested, observing from the walls of the citadel.

The Ottomans arrived, set up their tents and prepared their artillery machines. Right in the middle of it all, stood the magnificent pavilion of Sultan Mehmed, with the imperial banners flapping in the wind.

"Sixteen years ago, Murad tried to take the city but failed. This one believes that he will do better than his father," Sándor said. "Let us hope we shall stop him again."

"With God's help and with Lord Jankó's reinforcements, we

may have a chance."

***

They had barely sat down to have some broth – their first meal of the day even though the sun was already high up in the sky – when the building was hit. The blast hurled pieces of timber and masonry in all directions, sending the soldiers into a frantic search for cover.

Sándor caught sudden movement from the corner of his eye, jumped up and kicked Imre forward, making him fall flat on his face. His friend's bowl shattered into a hundred pieces, and the broth spilled all over him.

"Are you mad?" Imre screamed.

"Show some gratitude. I have saved your life," Sándor said.

He should not have opened his mouth. The dust, which now floated everywhere, choked him. The irritating tickle at the back of his throat turned into violent coughing.

Only then did Imre see the long shard of timber that had fallen on the exact spot where he had been sitting. "*Krisztus!* Where did that come from?"

Still coughing, Sándor pointed at a large hole in the ceiling.

"If this continues for long, I'll starve," Imre complained.

Sándor eventually caught his breath, but his voice was still hoarse. "If it is any consolation, I cannot eat my broth either. The rest of the missing ceiling is in it now."

"Those accursed cannons! They haven't stopped for two days. Where on earth is Lord Jankó?"

A squire stormed in, panting and with cheeks ablaze. "All officers in here, Commander Szilágyi wants to speak to you."

Sándor brushed as much dust as he could off himself. "I must go. Make sure you do not die before I return."

***

"Where are the reinforcements?" was the question on everybody's lips.

"I have news," the younger Hunyadi said. Conscious that all eyes were on him, he nervously tucked some stray strands of hair behind his ears. "An army is on the way, together with thousands of Capistrano's crusaders. But they can't approach the city because the Sultan has chained his ships together from one bank of the Danube to the other. That's why my father is assembling a fleet. They are still building the last few ships. But it will be at least a week before they arrive."

Sándor cleared his throat rather loudly.

"You want to say something, Szentimrei?" László Hunyadi asked. His face flushed at the interruption and the possibility of a challenge.

Sándor knew he had to be polite, but he was not going to keep silent. "With all due respect, gentlemen, we cannot sit and wait for a week. The walls have been breached in many places, the lower town is in ruins, flaming cannonballs are causing fires everywhere, the supplies are diminishing, the men's morale is low. My soldiers and I were nearly killed by the cannons. And this morning, I had to break up several scuffles among men fighting over food, wine, women, weapons, supplies and even over who will have his linen washed first."

Mihály nodded in agreement. "You are right. Thus far, we have not been as diligent as we should." He swept his arm around the room. "This is why all of you officers need to make sure all idle men are kept busy. Not only to protect the city, but also to protect themselves. We already have teams on the battlements, shooting with bows, crossbows and cannons. We need teams to patrol the walls for breaches and repair them; we need others to defend every tower and repel any enemy attempt to enter through the breaches; we need people tasked with quenching the fires, keeping the order and supervising the distribution of supplies. Now, go back out there and arrange all that. In the meantime, I'll send a message to Jankó to make haste."

***

Imre dashed up the tower stairs like a madman. "We won! Lord Jankó destroyed their ships!"

Sándor put the crossbow down. He blessed himself and embraced his friend. "Thank God! I regret I missed it. But I had orders to stay here with the archers to keep the Sultan's troops occupied and prevent them from aiding the fleet." He shook his fist in the air. "And we did a good job, boys!"

The soldiers cheered and patted each other on the back.

"Oh, you should've seen it, sir!" Imre's face lit up with the innocent enthusiasm of a little child while he flapped his arms about. "Our ships looked so menacing and powerful with those huge battering rams on their bows. They came down the river in the shape of an arrowhead. They broke the chains and crushed the Sultan's fleet. Jankó's army fired from the land too. And then, the Serbian boats came out of the city port, crept up on the Turks from behind and completed the victory."

"I saw the smoke. And the noise shook the walls. But I had no notion of what was happening out there."

"Oh, it was magnificent! The wrath of God fell on the heathen like a holy hammer. And now Jankó's here with thousands of men, munitions and food supplies. Now we have a chance."

With all its hopes pinned on the general, the exhausted garrison lined up to watch while Hunyadi made his entrance on a white horse, in full battle armour and escorted by his fierce Székely bodyguards carrying his banner.

His thundering voice echoed in every corner of the city. "My children! You are weary and disheartened. But do not despair. Trust in Christ and fight bravely in his name. Do not be afraid of your enemies. You know them; you know their tactics and their weapons. You have faced them many a time before. You have defeated them many a time before and sent them running home, scared. You know that they are the ones who are afraid of you. So, arm yourselves with courage. Be a bright example to future generations. And, with God's help, we shall defend this glorious city. Victory will be ours once again!"

22

A Dark Twist of Fate

As the Ottoman cannons battered the fortifications again the next day, one of Sándor's men came to him in great haste. "My lord, your son is here."

"What? Are you certain?"

"There is a band of lads with the banner of Szentimre among the newly arrived soldiers. Boys from the estate. Their leader is your son."

"Did you speak with him?"

"No, my lord. I came here to tell you."

"Very well. Thank you."

How did his son dare disobey? He had to deal with the matter forthwith.

He found István in the main square together with a dozen boys, all sons of knights and soldiers from his estate. They were often in his armoury, practising with their fathers.

"István Szilágyi!"

The boy turned around. Instead of being afraid or ashamed that he had been discovered, he smirked at his father.

Sándor stood with hands on his hips and legs astride. "What in God's name are you doing here?"

"I came to help," was the defiant answer. "The king and Lord Jankó sent a new call to arms, and so my friends and I decided to join."

"How did they let you leave the castle?"

"We left at night. We told the guards we were going to exercise in the forest."

"Does your mother know?"

"No, but she will have found out by now."

The blood rose to Sándor's head. He gave his son a slap across the face. "Are you out of your mind? I told you to stay at home. This is not for you. People die here. It's not a game or exercise."

István winced in pain and rubbed his cheek. His mates looked on in silence and with eyes wide open.

"And you, rascals! You will be in trouble when your fathers learn that you are here."

"What's the matter, gentlemen?" A voice of authority came from behind them. It was János Hunyadi. The youths all bowed their heads at his sight.

"These boys are from my estate," Sándor explained. "They disobeyed their fathers' orders, including mine, and came here to fight."

Hunyadi pointed at István. "And I guess this fine lad is your son?"

"Yes, sir. He is not even fifteen yet, although he is almost as tall as I am. But he must go home now. They must all go home. Szentimre is a small place. We cannot afford to lose two generations of men in a single campaign."

Hunyadi nodded. He took a good look at the youths once again. "Well, lads, I do not object to your presence here as I need every soldier I can get. However, a good soldier is the one who respects the orders of his superiors. If your fathers believe that you are not ready yet, you must obey them. The captain is right. This is not your fight. You are the next generation of warriors. You must wait until your time comes. I'm sure you will make Transylvania and Hungary proud, but you must be patient. Now, off you go, back to your mothers while the roads to the north are still open and clear of enemy forces."

The boys expressed their annoyance by mumbling and shaking their heads, but they packed their things and prepared to depart.

"I hope you have learned your lesson," Sándor said to István.

"I was trying to make you proud." The boy was in tears.

Sándor put his arms around his son and patted his back. "I am proud of you. That you came here despite what I told you was a brave decision. But you must wait until you are ready."

He watched them leave the city through the back gate. A huge weight lifted off his chest, and he could breathe freely again.

***

The bombardment continued during the next three days and nights. Although the loss of life inside the city was minimal, the defenders were exhausted as they had to be on the watch even at night. Every now and then, a few men napped in any sheltered place they could find, only to be woken up by their comrades or by the sound of cannon fire.

"Keep up the good work! It will be some time before their cannons cool and fire again," Sándor encouraged them. They were struggling to repair a broken section of the wall during a brief lull in the bombardment. It was an arduous and dangerous task to perform in the darkness, but the men laboured without complaint.

"Intruders!" someone shouted from the top of a nearby watchtower.

"Where?"

The guard pointed to a spot around the corner. "Five."

Sándor handed the torch to one of the men, put the helmet on and drew his sword. "Radu!" he called his Wallachian squire. "Come with me."

Those breaches in the wall were small but so dangerous. The Ottomans had been trying to squeeze through them all night.

They came upon five soldiers, who were moving stealthily in the shadows.

Sándor signalled to his squire to take the two on the left and so split the enemy group, drawing each part away from the other.

It would have been easier had he carried a shield. Without it, he had to use different tactics. He stood with his back to a wall for protection.

The Ottomans paused for a brief moment. Then, the one in the middle shouted an order, and all three attacked at the same time.

Sándor kicked hard at the hip joint of the axe-bearing short man on his right, sending him to the ground screaming in pain. As the one on the left flung himself at him, Sándor stooped and extended his elbow. Using the power of his whole body, he jumped upright and tossed the Ottoman over his shoulder. The enemy crashed violently against the wall behind, and by the sound the body made, Sándor knew the soldier's back was broken. In the meantime, he had parried the sword hits of the man in the middle.

He could not be beaten in a one-on-one sword fight. Only a short exchange of blows and the Ottoman was mortally wounded. But it was not over yet.

A heavy strike to his leg shook Sándor. He lost his bearings... The shorter soldier had recovered. He had crept on him from the right and was now swinging the axe at him.

Sándor was hit again in the same place: the spot of an old injury. Despite wearing armour, his thigh muscle burned like the fire of Hell. He screamed. A third blow. He was on his knees. The sword fell out of his hand. He frantically fumbled about but could not find it. No time. He raised his arm. At least, stop the axe from striking his head or neck...

A blade pierced the Ottoman's body from behind. He crashed to the ground, face-down.

"Look, Father! I've killed my first Turk."

Sándor peered at the dark figure, trying to discern his saviour's features. Was it true? Had the boy returned?

"István?"

His son helped him up. "Please, don't be angry, Father! My mates are all on the way home, but I had to come back."

"Why?"

"To be part of this. I feel it's my time to become a man. And I have just saved your life."

Sándor shook his head. No matter how hard he had tried to keep his son away, his efforts had failed. Perhaps it was István's destiny to be there. "Stay close to me at all times and don't try to be a hero."

"Yes, captain!" the boy replied in a firm voice.

***

The following day, Sándor was up on the battlements, commanding the artillery teams because their captain had fallen ill. None of the men in those units were his own soldiers. There were a few Hungarians, but the others came from different lands: Bohemia, Poland, Austria, the Holy Roman Empire. Even though they did not all speak the same language, it did not take him too long to get used to the task.

István was there with him, helping the soldiers load the cannons. The boy was eager to assist and prove his worth, but his youthful excitement made his father's heart rise to his mouth. Many a time, he knelt at the parapet wall and looked down through the embrasures, trying to see if any enemy soldiers were approaching or attempting to scale the walls.

"Come back here!" Sándor shouted at him. "This is not your duty, and it's also too dangerous."

"I wish you stopped treating me like a child!"

"I shall, when you start behaving wisely like a man and listen to my orders."

István grunted and finally moved away from the edge.

At the same time, a powerful bang shook the ground. It was

followed by the loud cheers from the Serbian cannon crew stationed on a flat-topped tower to the left. A section of the Ottoman artillery line had gone up in flames and with it, the viewing platform where a major enemy commander was standing.

For a few moments, all Sándor and his men could see was thick smoke. They stood still and waited. When the smoke settled, the effect of the blast became clear. Dead and mutilated bodies lay in the area, their cannons broken or overturned, while the wounded soldiers were screaming in pain and calling for help.

Scarcely able to contain his joy, Sándor cupped his hands around his mouth and shouted towards the Serbian team with all his might, "Well done, men! Next one hits Mehmed!"

But the Sultan sent the Janissaries to control the situation, and the Ottomans were back on the attack. It was not long before Sándor's men came under severe fire. Arrows flew at them, and cannonballs shook the earth below them and the walls around them.

They crouched or fell on all fours. Sándor shouted across the tumult to one of the soldiers, "Go and tell the general we need help. He must do something to distract them, or we shall all be dead soon." And turning to his son, "Go with him. It's too dangerous here now."

István, however, refused to leave his father's side.

Cursing his son's obstinance, Sándor pulled the boy to the cover of the parapet wall. He forced István to curl into a ball while he bent over him to protect his head with his own body.

The unrelenting pounding of cannonballs and whooshing of

arrows went on and on until a detachment in another part of the fortress began shooting at the Ottomans and drawing the enemy assault in that direction.

Some of the men got up, ready to resume firing duties. Still wary and crouching, Sándor pulled away from István, listening for the sound of incoming missiles. Before he could command his son not to move, the boy had already risen.

"Down!" Sándor shouted. As he launched forward to grab his son's arm, István fell backwards, the clang of his steel helmet reverberating against the stone floor.

Seized by an ominous dread, Sándor was rendered motionless for several moments. A cold sweat trickled down his back. His heart thumped with the weight of iron. "István!" he screamed. And crawling towards him, no sooner had he reached him than his anxiety was confirmed.

A crossbow bolt protruded from István's throat.

"No!" How could this happen? With trembling hands, Sándor checked his son's padded gorget. Warm liquid trickled out of a small opening. One of the straps had come undone. The bolt had pierced the boy's neck from one side right through to the other, severing the artery.

István's head tilted; blood spurted out of his mouth with each failing heartbeat, spattering over Sándor's face. And as Sándor stared into his son's eyes, they were filled with fear, growing dimmer with each dying breath.

Tears burned Sándor's eyes. He could not save the boy's life. All he could do was console him in his last moments. "I am proud of you." He drew his son nearer and spoke tenderly in his ear. "You are a hero."

Pulling back to gaze at István's contorted countenance once more, Sándor observed a semblance of a smile spread across it before the last breath of the boy's life was consumed by the blood which he choked on.

"No! No!" Sándor's heart crumbled. He turned his eyes to the smoke-filled sky. "How could you do this to me? How could you take him away from me?"

Having received no answer, he looked mournfully at his son and with a gentle movement, closed István's eyes.

"Sir!" A voice of desperation brought him back into the battle still raging around him. "Let us take you to the infirmary." His second in command tried to pull the dead boy away from him.

But Sándor would not let go. He did not wish to live anymore. He did not care if twenty cannonballs landed on him and tore him to pieces.

"Take cover!" someone shouted.

The enemy shot blew away the top of the parapet wall that protected them and sent debris and dust flying in all directions.

The blast threw Sándor to the ground. His hearing went. All around him, men with gaping wounds, missing limbs and broken bones screamed silently; others staggered about like drunkards coming out of a tavern. Blood obscured his vision. His face and chest hurt as if he had been trampled by a horse.

What happened afterwards went by like a dream: the soldiers who came and took his boy away; the ones who carried him to the infirmary; the surgeon who took care of his injuries... A single image kept flashing in front of him: his beloved son dying with the crossbow bolt through his neck – a sight that would be forever burned in his memory.

23
A Father's Plea

The bruise on Sándor's chest was as big as his hand. Every breath hurt. Once more, his trusted armour had saved him by absorbing the impact of the blow when fragments of the smashed wall hit him. No ribs or other bones were broken. But his face had not been protected. The wound under his eye was nasty. A deep cut on the skin and a bruised cheekbone had made the right side of his face swell badly. With shaking fingers, he felt the wetness of fresh blood still seeping through the dressing that the army surgeon had put on him after stitching the cut. His head throbbed. Yet the physical pain was nothing compared to the grief that tore him apart inside as he stared at his son's body, which lay on a blood-smeared pallet in the undercroft of the infirmary.

But for the dark red mark on his throat and the ghostly paleness of his skin, István looked at peace – just like the angelic little boy Sándor used to watch sleep so many times before. Only this time he was not going to wake up... ever again...

A massive lump rose to Sándor's throat. His eyesight blurred. He coughed up phlegm and spat it on the floor. It was not the putrid smell of death hanging in the air of the vault but his own guilt that choked him. What kind of a father was he? Useless...

unable to protect his child.

A flicker of the candlelight alerted him of someone approaching. Hunyadi emerged from the shadows, carrying a wooden stool. The general sat beside him and put a hand on his shoulder. "I'm sorry this happened to you. He was a fine lad. At least, he fell doing his duty as a soldier."

Sándor acknowledged the condolences with a nod. "I must take him home." With each word he uttered, a wave of deep, sharp pain shot from under his right eye down to his jaw. But he had to speak to the general.

Hunyadi's eyes narrowed. "What do you mean?"

"I cannot bury him here in a foreign place. He has to be laid to rest in his land."

"You are an experienced soldier and officer. Did you think I would let you leave? I need you here. This is the most important battle of our lives. The very existence of our country and our people hangs in the balance."

Sándor's heart was seized by pain as if an invisible hand had grabbed it and was squeezing all the blood out of it. Once again, he had chosen his duty over his family. But this time, he had done so at the most terrible cost.

"You must wait until this is over." The general's voice was cold and dry.

"The siege may last for weeks or months. I may die here and never take him home."

Sándor paused. How could the man he admired most in the world be so cruel to him? But no, it was not cruelty. Lord Jankó would have applied the same rule to himself if his own son had died in the middle of a situation like this. Those were tough and desperate times.

"At least, sir, let me send him home with some of my men."

"No, this is not possible either. Your soldiers are battle-hardened. I need them here too."

"Why? You have thousands of men inside and outside the walls."

"Have you seen Capistrano's army? They will be slaughtered if they enter the fray. I need every experienced soldier I can get."

A groan of immeasurable pain escaped Sándor's mouth. He fell to his knees in front of Hunyadi. "I beg of you, sir! I appeal to you as a father and not as my general. István was my only child. Please, do not let his final resting place be among strangers, so far away from his home and his family. Who is going to visit his grave and think of him?"

"Don't kneel in front of me, *barátom*," János said sympathetically. "I am not the Sultan." He rose and helped Sándor up. "I'll tell you what I can do for you. You can send your son home with one of your men. I shall also give him money to change horses on the way. Three of my servants will accompany him, on my expense. They will go all the way to your castle. And I shall provide them with a small military escort until they exit the conflict area. How is that?"

Sándor grasped Lord Jankó's arms and squeezed them. "Thank you, sir. I am grateful to you. I promise I shall not disappoint you out there."

With Hunyadi's help, he bought a lead-lined coffin, which would help preserve the body during the long journey back to Transylvania in the heat of the summer. He chose Imre as the man to bring István home.

His friend, however, was distressed with being given the task. "I can't do it, sir. How am I going to face your good lady? I gave her the news, years ago, that you were missing after the battle of Varna, and it broke my heart. How am I going to bring her dead son to her now?"

Sándor put a brotherly arm around his loyal knight's shoulders. "Listen, *kedves barátom*. Out of all my men, you are the one I trust most. I know you will do your duty, and you will protect my boy no matter what happens on the way. For the sake of all the years that we fought together, I beg of you to do this for me."

Imre could not say no to this plea. He accepted with a heavy heart.

They left before sunrise; men, horses, cart and coffin transported across the Danube on a barge. Unarmed, in his shirt and hose, Sándor lingered on the pier, his eyes brimming with tears. The dank smell of the river blended with that of gunpowder and fire, making him retch. He coughed to clear his throat and stood upright. Like his son's life, the barge floated away from him and slowly disappeared into the darkness.

24

Heroes

21 / 22 July 1456

The drawbridge leading into the upper town was down. Margit stood on it. She held István as a baby in one arm and a sword in her other hand. Her linen chemise was blood-stained; her long hair flowing in the wind. Around her, fire rained from the skies, and black clouds had descended upon the fortifications.

Sándor called her name. She replied with an otherworldly scream. Then, the cannons thundered, and the ground shook. The drawbridge broke in two and collapsed into the moat. Fire continued to fall from the sky, composing a near-apocalyptic picture.

"Margit!" he shouted again as he saw her fall into the moat, which had turned into a dark, bottomless abyss.

The ground moved under his feet. He began sliding towards the massive opening that was swallowing everything. He screamed in panic but could not resist. And the sound of the cannons continued...

"Wake up, sir!"

Sándor opened his eyes. His squire was standing over him.

"Radu! I was having a terrible dream. What's happening? What hour of the day is it?"

"It will soon be vespers, sir. The bombardment hasn't stopped since last night, and now the Sultan has ordered a full assault. The general has called for all men to gather in the main square."

"I must prepare. Help me put on my armour."

***

The first wave of the Ottoman attack reached what had remained of the outer city walls. Cannons and catapults supported the soldiers, battering the second line of the fortifications and bringing large sections to the ground.

Hunyadi sent the knights, the mercenaries and the most experienced members of Capistrano's civilian army to hold the enemy at the front line. Despite his advanced age, the good friar himself led the fight on the ramparts and urged them on in the name of Jesus Christ.

Alongside the general's own men-at-arms, Sándor defended the eastern entrance to the upper town. It was not too long before everything around him became eerily similar to what he had seen in his dream: the fight on the drawbridge, the screams, the sound of the cannons, the fireballs falling from the sky, the dead and wounded dropping into the moat. The end of that dream had been grim, but he did not care. If it were his destiny to die there, so be it. He was not going to yield an inch of ground to the enemy.

"Hold them, lads! Kill as many as you can!" Hunyadi kept encouraging his men. He was there with them, in the thick of it.

They fought wave upon wave of Ottoman attacks. The struggle continued well into the moonlit night while the machines of the enemy were still at work, spewing out their lethal load. The moat filled with bodies. Hunyadi's men were still holding, but they were too few. The rest of the Christian army had retreated, past their comrades on the drawbridge and into the upper town. They had done their part, which was to delay the Ottomans and reduce their numbers as much as they could.

The general had also returned to the citadel since sundown, but he sent out his son at the third watch of the night.

László Hunyadi pushed his way through to the front line. "Szentimrei!" he called Sándor over. The two of them found cover behind the entrance to the upper town. "I have orders from my father. When the horn gives the signal, you must bring all our men inside the gates and retreat towards the citadel."

"Retreat, sir?"

"Yes, this is the plan."

"And what if they pursue us?"

"Let them come in."

"Come in? After hours and hours of heavy battle, Lord Jankó is willing to let the enemy advance thus far? It will be the end of us."

László winked. "Do you trust me?"

"Of course, sir."

"Then do exactly as you are told."

"Yes."

"Good luck, cousin. Stay alive." László turned around and disappeared into the thronging mass of soldiers.

There was activity on top of the curtain wall, on both sides of the drawbridge. Moving quietly like shadows, archers were preparing their bows while other men were carrying something that looked like tree branches.

Sándor went back into the fight. He had to be much more careful now. Lord Jankó had trusted him with an important mission. He did not know what the outcome of that mission would be, but he had to complete it.

Within a few moments, the horn sounded.

"Everyone back!" he shouted, at the top of his lungs. "Now! Swiftly! General's orders."

Although surprised, the men obeyed him. He stood aside and let them hurry past him. He was the last one to retreat.

Sándor shifted the weight of his body from one foot to the other and back again countless times as he waited in line, together with his fellow fighters, below the citadel wall.

On the other side of the city gate, the Janissaries hesitated. But the doubt did not last too long. Like hounds smelling the blood, hundreds of them stormed into the upper town and headed towards the citadel.

At the same time, the movement on top of the walls intensified. Tree branches were thrown into the moat and around it. A strong, disgusting smell filled the air. Sándor covered his nose with the back of his hand. Sulphur and tar. Hunyadi was a genius.

The archers loosed a wave of flaming arrows, illuminating the night sky. Everything on the outside of the curtain wall went up in flames. All the defenders on the wall retreated. What was now raging in the moat was no ordinary fire. It took gigantic proportions and released poisonous gases, which were blown towards the enemy camp.

Sándor smiled. Lord Jankó had even used the wind to his advantage.

But the screams of the Ottoman soldiers made the blood freeze in his veins. Although far away from him, their faces, distorted by the pain of being burned alive or choking with noxious fumes, flashed before his eyes. And then, they all merged into the face of one person: a boy, dying in his arms.

He gasped and blinked to chase the image away.

Opposite him, the Janissaries stopped and looked around. They were trapped. The flames of Hell thundered behind them and Hunyadi's steel-clad warriors stood before them like a mighty fortress.

"Kill them all!" the general roared from the citadel.

Sándor screamed at them, the veins throbbing in his neck. Every doubt, every weakness had to be purged out of him. He clenched the sword in his right hand and the axe in his left. Let them come. Let death come if it may. It would be very welcome.

***

As the rays of the morning sun brightened up the city, the clamour of battle had ceased. All the Janissaries who had entered the upper town and tried to take the citadel had been either killed or captured. On the other side of the wall, the blaze had burned itself out. But it had served its purpose. The Ottomans had fully withdrawn to their camp.

Sándor's soldiers were still at their positions, manning the parts of the wall that were beyond repair. They had fought in the front line all night, and they could barely stand on their feet. After a unit of Bohemians came to replace them, their next duty was to guard the Ottoman prisoners in one of the city squares. This was an easier task, requiring a smaller number of men, so Sándor let them take a short nap in rotation. They needed it, and they were grateful.

As for himself, he could not sleep. He removed parts of his bloodied armour and sat on the ground. His whole body was in pain. The lack of food and sleep made him nauseous and dizzy. Fortunately, some of the city's inhabitants – mostly women – went around and gave ale, bread and a bit of meat to the defenders. It was not anything substantial, but it tasted like the best feast ever.

"Thank you," he said in Serbian to a young girl, who had brought the food to him and his men. "You are an angel."

She smiled and whispered something in her language. She then moved on to another unit of soldiers farther down. Sándor's knowledge of Serbian was limited, but the gist of what she had said was 'thank you for protecting us.'

These people could have left weeks earlier to save their lives. The sorry sight of the long columns of thousands of refugees fleeing towards southern Hungary came back to his mind. But some of Belgrade's inhabitants had chosen to remain in their homes and help the soldiers defend their city against the mighty

Ottoman army. Their support was invaluable even though they would not receive any of the glory of a potential victory or a heroic mention in the chronicles.

The girl was about István's age, and that brought tears to his eyes. He had not had the time to mourn his son. He would not be able to make it to the funeral either. He could just imagine Margit's grief and despair at seeing the coffin with their boy in it and her anger that her husband had not returned with it. She would not forgive him for this.

The rest of the morning went by without incident, and the dreaded second Ottoman attack never came to pass.

Sándor gave his weapons to Radu to sharpen and finally sat down to clean his armour and iron out the dents with a small hammer. Like everyone else in the city, he was on edge. But it was important to concentrate on the task. The quicker he repaired his equipment, the better. They could be called out to fight again at any moment. He prayed for the calm to last a little longer.

He put down the hammer, stretched and flexed his fingers. They were swollen and throbbing. The muscles in both his arms burned. He wiped the sweat from his face. The sun was high up in the sky now. He gritted his teeth and got on with the repair work.

The shouts of men and the clashing of weapons shattered the peace and quiet. It was all coming from the back of the city, outside the walls – the place where Capistrano's civilian army had camped. Sándor stood up, holding his breath for a few heartbeats. Yes, it was the clamour of battle. But why? The general had given strict orders to the troops to refrain from any offensive activity. What was happening? Were they under attack again?

The ear-splitting sound of war horns inside the city sent the men scrambling into their armour.

Hunyadi called the captains and commanders to him. He spoke to them while his two squires dressed him for battle. "Capistrano's peasants attacked the Turks who were camped on the opposite bank of the Sava. They disobeyed my orders. But something good may come out of this foolish act. They have disarrayed the Sultan's army. We must take advantage of this. We'll strike them with everything we have from the other side. This is our last chance. We must make it count."

The squires and pages brought in the horses and helped the knights and men-at-arms prepare for battle. The multi-coloured banners were up, the weapons in hand, the last pieces of armour in place and secured.

As they rode off, making their way through the destroyed lower town, the smell of death hit Sándor in the face. Burnt and maimed bodies lay everywhere. Small fires were still smouldering. Smoke wafted out of the ruins. Behind the earthen defences that the Hungarians had put up during the early days of the siege, the cannon and gun crews stood ready to support the main attack.

In normal circumstances, a battle in the open field was not wise, given the numerical superiority of the enemy. But Hunyadi gazed far into the distance and smiled. "It seems that the Sultan has committed a major error," he said to the officers, who had gathered around him. "He has attacked the peasant army with all his forces. Look, gentlemen! There is barely anyone guarding the artillery positions."

"Perhaps he's trying to create a distraction," Mihály commented.

"I think not. Capistrano's attack has surprised him as much as it has surprised us. He is reacting hastily. But he is a clever man and will realise his mistake soon. So, we must strike immediately."

Hunyadi turned to his son and his brother-in-law. "László and Mihály, take 200 men and return to the citadel. If things go wrong, you and the city militia will lead the remaining civilians to safety."

Then, he called the names of the other officers and ordered them to lead a head-on attack on the Sultan's forces to relieve the pressure on Capistrano's crusaders, who were now struggling.

There was only one name that he had not called yet. "Szentimrei," he said, at last. "I saw the way you fought yesterday. As if you didn't care about your life. Your death will not bring back your son, you know."

"Sir!" Sándor protested, but the general cut him short with an abrupt wave of his hand.

"The last thing I need now is an officer with a death wish. That's why I'm going to give you a mission of utmost importance. You will take your men-at-arms and a hundred from my *banderium* and attack the artillery positions. You have worked with cannons before. You know how to use them. Secure the batteries, destroy the heavy guns and turn the lighter ones against the Ottoman camp. Our gunners have orders to get there after you."

"Yes, sir."

"We shall all ride together. When I give the word, you will turn left and head towards the batteries. The enemy will throw everything at you as you approach and when you arrive. Our artillery will do its best to provide covering fire. I'm giving you my own men for this mission, Sándor. The best of the best. Lead them bravely but also wisely."

"Of course, sir."

Hunyadi signalled to his chosen hundred to stand in formation behind Sándor and his soldiers. "He is your commander now."

The Ottomans had just succeeded in gaining some ground against Capistrano's army when the heavy cavalry of the Hungarians and their allies hit them with incredible force from the other flank.

At the same time, Sándor's unit veered to the left, towards the enemy artillery positions. They were about two to three hundred paces away, but the area was too rough and unsuitable for cavalry. There were ditches, trenches, a wooden palisade and earthen defences to negotiate. More than half of his men were on horseback, and they were riding at a suicidal pace.

"Slow down!"

For some of them it was too late. A few horses stumbled over the earthen mounds and crashed to the ground or fell into the ditches and broke their legs. Cries of pain and despair filled the air. Those men who were not seriously wounded by the fall stood up and continued on foot.

Straight ahead, the few Ottomans who were still guarding the cannons scrambled to repel the sudden attack. But it would take too long to prepare and load the larger cannons. The enemy would only be in a position to fire the smaller guns and only once until he and his men reached the batteries.

Several loud, successive bangs cracked from behind. Their own artillery had fired first. The projectiles flew over the Hungarians and made the Ottoman soldiers duck for cover. An explosive cloud of dirt and dust spread everywhere, blinding and choking enemies and friendlies alike. A few moments later, the Turkish guns roared. Three iron balls the size of a man's fist blasted through the air. Sándor ducked instinctively. The missiles whizzed over him. The screams of the men, the neighing of the horses and the disturbing sound of bone and metal being crushed made him curse. He did not turn back to see how many soldiers he had lost. He had to lead the rest of them to the batteries before the Ottomans fired for a second time.

It was not long before they were on top of them. His horse jumped over a ditch and landed on an enemy soldier, trampling him to death. The Ottomans were too few and not properly armed. They did not have time to run away. Most of them were cut down by the heavy swords and maces of the Hungarians. Those who escaped with their lives huddled together in one of the trenches.

Sándor ordered his men to destroy the heavier machines and turn the smaller ones around towards the Ottoman camp.

"Load!" he shouted, but the men-at-arms looked at him as if he had two heads. "Damn! They don't know how to prepare and fire a cannon," he thought. It would take him too long to show each team.

A cloud of arrows flew towards them from the direction of the Ottoman camp. The setting sun reflected on the drawn swords of the approaching Janissaries, blinding Sándor momentarily. The enemy had realised what happened and was coming to take the cannons back.

He had to act swiftly. "Hey, you!" he called at the enemy gunners, who were hiding in the ditch. They were Christian mercenaries or slaves. Italians mostly but also Germans, Serbians and Greeks. "If you want to live, help us!" he said to them in Latin and then in Serbian. They nodded, climbed out of the ditch and took their positions behind the cannons.

"Protect them!" he ordered his men.

Most of the Hungarians prepared to face the Janissaries, who were now trying to climb the embankment. The rest of them raised their shields to cover the gunners from the arrows that rained from the sky. The latter, skilfully and speedily, loaded the cannons and fired. Within a short time, the Bohemian and German gunners had also arrived from the Belgrade side to take over the remaining cannons.

Sándor drew a deep breath and, with axe in hand, moved to help his men fight the enemy.

25
Head-to-Head

Sándor bit hard on his belt while the surgeon reset his dislocated shoulder and then stitched all the cuts. A few cracked ribs, concussion and several bruises made the suffering even worse. The wound on his face was already healing. The swelling had subsided, but it was still sore, and it had left a scar.

"A magnificent victory," the surgeon said.

It certainly was. And Sándor had been part of it. Seeing Mehmed's army abandon all hope and take flight was worth the pain.

But he could not celebrate. He had to go home. Transporting István's body, Imre would be about three days ahead of him by now. There was no way he could catch up; only a slim possibility that he would be there in time for the funeral if he left forthwith.

If he left now...

A sudden wave of nausea washed over him. He turned to the side and threw up... Again. How many times today? He had lost count.

The surgeon helped him up. "You must rest, sir."

Sándor staggered out of the infirmary, stumbling at every step. He barely made it to the barracks. He slumped on the first empty pallet he could find. The world went dark around him.

When he opened his eyes, in the afternoon of the following day, he felt much better but was still weak. He called for his knights to hear their reports about the state of his men. Out of the hundred soldiers that left Szentimre two months earlier, eleven had died. Twenty-three were seriously wounded and unable to travel yet. The remaining men had either light injuries or were unharmed and were ready to be on the way home soon.

"I must leave tomorrow," Sándor said to the most senior of his knights. "I shall take Radu and three of the men with me. The rest can follow us in a few days, together with the baggage train. I need you to stay here with the wounded and lead them back home when they have recovered."

They departed at first light. As they needed to ride fast, they left most of their armour behind and carried just the necessary weapons.

On the seventh night of travelling, they made camp for the last time, hoping to arrive at Szentimre the following morning. But as soon as they fed and watered the horses and were about to sit down around the fire, they heard galloping in the distance. A lone rider approached in haste. The men stood up and drew their swords.

"It's me, Imre Gerendi!" he shouted. He jumped off his horse and hurried towards Sándor, almost tripping over his own feet. "Sir!" he gasped. "I'm so glad I found you here. I feared that I'd have to ride for days to reach Nándorfehérvár, or that I'd miss you and you'd fall into the trap."

"What trap?"

Imre took him aside, out of earshot from the rest of the men. "We had István's funeral yesterday, and your brother came to pay his last respects."

"My brother? I haven't heard from him in years. He said he did not want to know me."

"Yes, sir. He came with his soldiers. We didn't think ill of that, and we let them all in. But he had the most evil plan in his head. After the funeral, he asked if he could stay for a day or two. Your lady said yes. All was well until the last watch of the night when his men attacked our garrison and took over the castle. Balog and the guards are in the dungeon cells."

The blood rushed to Sándor's head. "Are you telling me the truth?"

"Why, sir, of course. You've known me for years. I wouldn't lie to you."

Sándor's legs gave way, and he fell to his knees. He remained quiet until a worrying thought crossed his mind. "And Margit? Is she safe?"

"Yes. I went to her chamber to warn her. She said she knew of a secret passage. She, her maid and I took that and escaped just in time. She's in the mine now. The workers are protecting her. But they won't be able to last long if your brother's soldiers attack them. She sent me out to find you for fear that you'll be murdered the moment you set foot in Sasfészek."

Leaning on Imre's strong arm, Sándor stood up, walked back to where his men were sitting and said in a decisive voice, "We have a situation at home. I shall ride to Sasfészek with Imre now. We should be there before dawn. In the darkness, they will not see us approach if we are careful. You must follow at a safe distance and go straight to the mine to protect my wife. I shall call for you after we take over the castle."

"Take over? Just the two of us?" Imre asked.

"Yes. You said the garrison is held in the dungeon. If we disable their guards and free my men, we shall take the castle in no time. We shall catch them by surprise."

"I hope you've thought this through well."

"Trust me, Imre, we can do it."

They left their horses at the foot of the castle hill and climbed up. There was no path, but the bright moonlight illuminated their way until Sándor found the spot where the secret passage opened onto the hillside. It was just below the base of the walls, at a place well hidden from sight by thorny bushes and rocks.

"I hope no one else knows about this."

"No one knows, and no one will," Imre assured him. "Your lady had both me and her maid swear on the Holy Book that we'll never reveal it."

They squeezed through the small opening, which could only fit one person at a time. Then, it was a long climb of a hundred steps inside the hill, in complete darkness and with nothing to hold on to but the rough cave walls. The underground passage ended at the basement of the keep, behind the dungeon. From there, a steep spiral stairwell led up to the third floor and into Sándor's quarters through the secret door in the wall panelling.

"Thank God your brother isn't using your bedchamber," Imre said.

"He would never dare to."

Sándor opened the door carefully and waited. Not a sound. He signalled to Imre to follow him. They crept along the dimly lit corridors with their weapons drawn and then down the stairs to the dungeon. Some of Miklós's soldiers were sitting around a table, talking and drinking. One of them had a bunch of keys hanging from his belt.

"We shall fight them," Sándor said. "Two against five is fair, don't you think?"

"No, we needn't fight. I've another plan."

Imre ran into the room with such speed that, before anyone realised what was going on, he had grabbed one of the men and held a dagger against his throat. "Stay where you are, or I'll kill him!"

The other soldiers did not even have the chance to reach for their weapons. They remained seated while Sándor entered, holding a dagger and a sword. "Come with me!" he ordered the man who had the keys.

The soldier stood up and followed him to the cells, where he unlocked all the doors to free Pál Balog and the garrison.

"Thank God, you came, sir!"

"Good to see you all. Now, let us take back the castle."

Sándor ordered some of his men to tie Miklós's soldiers. Then, they took any weapons they could find. They stepped out to the courtyard through a side door, silent as shadows. They knocked out the two men who were guarding the armoury and armed themselves properly. Sándor sent some of them to the gatehouse and some up the towers and battlements to surprise any of his brother's soldiers who were keeping guard there. "Try not to kill anyone if you can. We have all seen enough bloodshed already."

He signalled to Imre to follow him to the barracks building. "Let us find their captain now."

The leader of Miklós's men was sleeping alone in the garrison commander's room. Imre woke him up and held a dagger to his throat while Sándor whispered in his ear, "I have come to take my castle back from my brother. I have no quarrel with you or your men. So, go and lock them all in their sleeping quarters. I promise I shall let you leave unharmed."

Dawn was breaking when Sándor and Imre returned to the courtyard. In the dim early-morning light, Balog waved to them from the top of the walls that everything had gone according to plan.

Sándor heaved a sigh of relief. He sent Imre to fetch Margit and Erzsi.

Moments later, shouting came from the family residence. Miklós appeared at the doorway and ran out towards him, calling for help.

"No one will come," Sándor said.

They stood face-to-face in the courtyard. Miklós looked around and then upwards. The soldiers of the garrison aimed their arrows at him.

"You are on your own." Sándor signalled to his men to stand down.

Miklós trembled with anger. "What happened? How did they let you in? What did you do to them? Did you kill them all?"

"No! What did you do? On the day of my son's funeral, you took over my castle. Have you no respect at all? I have no heir anymore. All this would have been yours on my death. Why did you do this? Did she make you?"

"No, she didn't. This time it was all me. You don't know how it feels to be rejected and shunned all your life. You took everything from me: Father's love and respect, my rightful share of the estate, my pride, my dignity, my wife, my whole life. I was nothing to you. And now, you ask why I did this? Does the word 'revenge' mean anything to you?"

He fell to his knees, sobbing. "I tried to prove to her that I am a man, but I failed again. Kill me now. Put me out of my misery."

Sándor winced. He approached Miklós and helped him stand up. "I regret you feel that way, brother. You are my blood, and I have always loved you. I know I did not treat you as well as I should, and I apologise for that. But you did not try much either."

"Yes, certainly, I am to blame too," Miklós admitted. "Will you forgive me, brother?"

"Of course."

"Embrace me then. Let's forget the past and start anew."

Sándor finally smiled. It was about time they put their differences aside and became a family again. He took his brother in his arms and held him tight. Before he even knew it, sharp pain ripped through his left side and then once more, a little higher.

"You should have killed me when you had the chance," Miklós whispered in his ear. "Now it's time you paid for that mistake."

Sándor pushed him away and looked down. A knife was stuck into him, just under his heart. There was another wound, a bit lower, on the left side of his belly. He pressed his hand against it. Blood streamed through his fingers. His body felt heavy as lead. His knees buckled. Everything dimmed around him. Suddenly, he was on his back.

At the same time, six arrows hit Miklós. He sank to the ground.

Tears flooded Sándor's eyes. In the space of a few moments, his whole world had come crashing down. Gritting his teeth in pain, he crawled towards Miklós. He stretched out his trembling arm. It was time for the last farewell. "Brother... Brother... I am sorry."

Miklós convulsed as life was leaving his body. Blood trickled out of his mouth, and within moments, he lay still with his eyes wide open.

Sándor continued to stare at his brother until darkness descended upon him and covered everything.

26
The Biggest Fight of His Life

The sun was well on its ascent in the summer sky. Margit shaded her eyes with her hand. They still stung from the tears she had shed mourning István's death and then fearing for her life after the attack. But it was all over now. The castle had been liberated, and her husband had come home safe. She could not wait to hold him in her arms again.

She, Imre and Erzsi ran into the long convoy of Miklós's soldiers, who were marching through the town gate, unarmed and gloomy-faced. She halted them with a raised hand. "What happened? Who is the dead man on the cart?"

No response. Imre dismounted and walked towards the cart. She held her breath. The knight slowly lifted the cloth that covered the man's upper body and head.

"*Krisztus!*" he exclaimed.

Margit gasped. "Miklós!" She crossed herself. A dreaded thought ran through her mind. Had Sándor slain his brother?

Imre waved the convoy on, and it continued its slow and sombre march.

Margit turned to Erzsi. She opened her mouth, but no words came forth.

"We must hasten to the castle, my lady," the maid said decisively. "We must find out what happened."

Silence and emptiness greeted Margit when she entered the keep. "Where is he?"

Imre rushed in behind her. "Dear lady!" His face had turned pale. "He's wounded. His brother tried to kill him."

Her legs were shaking as she entered her husband's bedchamber. He lay there motionless, stripped from the groin up, his skin the colour of ash. Erszi helped her sit down by his side.

"How is he?" the maid asked the physician, who was looking after him.

"Thanks be to God, the knife struck his ribs and missed his heart. But he has a second wound in his belly. I have stanched the bleeding, cleaned and stitched both wounds... The one in his belly is deep. I don't know... I think we should all pray."

"No, no," Margit whispered. "I can't lose him too. Please God, help us!"

"Do you want to go to the chapel, my lady?" Erzsi asked.

"No, I shall stay here with him. Please, leave. All of you."

She stroked and kissed her husband's face, begging God not to take him from her. Many years earlier, when Imre had brought her the news that Sándor was missing after the battle of Varna, she was grief-stricken, but everything had happened far away from her. She did not have a body to mourn. Now that he lay there, right in front of her, her heart ached with helplessness and despair for there was nothing she could do to save him.

She stayed awake all night, praying and talking to him. From time to time, he twitched and mumbled or called his son's name. But he did not come round. As the hours passed by, he developed a fever. His face became hotter and hotter despite the cold compresses that she put on his forehead. The physician returned during the night and bled him, but that did not help. By the morning, Margit could not keep her eyes open any longer and fell asleep in a chair.

People's whispers woke her up. The priest was in the room, together with Erzsi. Margit sprang to her feet. "Father, why are you here?"

"Unlike you, my lady, your husband rarely attended mass or had a confession. He has killed people, committed adultery and allowed the operation of a house of ill repute in his estate, as well as of a number of pagan 'healers'."

Margit's back stiffened. The priest's words were harsh. He had no right to speak of Sándor like that. "Forgive me, Father, but you are being unfair. My husband is a soldier. He only killed people on the battlefield while protecting his homeland, his family and the Christian faith. As for the adultery, it happened a long time ago, and he has done his penance. And trust me, he believes in God even though he doesn't go to church as frequently as he should. He shows this in his actions every day; in the way he cares for his family and his people. So, please judge him a little more kindly."

"I am still concerned about his soul. I was told that he is at death's threshold, and I have come to give the last rites."

Margit gasped. Did the priest know something that the

physician had not told her? Or perhaps, he was only being overzealous. "No, no. He is not dying. He will get better. I know he will."

"Well then, at least, let me pray for him."

"Of course."

As soon the priest opened his prayer book, Sándor stirred. He mumbled and cursed in the beginning, but then he gasped for breath. His entire body shook violently as if possessed by an evil force. Some of the stitches tightened and ripped his flesh. Blood seeped out of his wounds.

"Get help, now!" Margit shouted to Erzsi.

The priest stopped reading and took a few steps back. He crossed himself. "The Devil is in him!"

Sándor's eyes opened wide. He sprang upright and stared ahead, his face a mask of terror and rage combined. "Stay away from my boy! I'll kill you!" He jumped out of the bed, grabbed the earthen pitcher of water from the bedside table and hurled it against the wall, smashing it into a hundred pieces.

The door burst open. The physician, his assistant and Imre rushed to him. Sándor flapped about like a madman, screaming at an invisible enemy.

Margit covered her mouth with both hands. The world swirled around her. People were moving and talking, but their voices were distant, like coming from the other end of a tunnel.

The physician and his assistant seized Sándor's arms. He screamed again and pushed the two men to the floor as if they were made of straw. Dazed, they scrambled to their feet.

"Stay behind him!" Imre ordered them. He stood in front of his friend and shouted, "There's no enemy here. You're home. You're safe."

Sándor growled and swung at him wildly. Imre ducked. He clenched his fist and punched Sándor in the face. The hit shook him, but he did not fall. Imre punched again and again, with all his might. A red mist of blood rose in the air. Sándor's legs gave way, and he staggered backwards. The physician and his assistant caught him before he crashed to the floor. Together with Imre, they carried him to the bed.

He lay with his eyes closed and breathing normally. His nose and mouth were still bleeding, but the assistant cleaned them with a cloth.

The physician nodded to Margit reassuringly and then went on to stitch the wounds on Sándor's body again.

She let out a deep sigh. The world became loud again. Tears of relief poured down her cheeks.

Imre approached her. "I apologise, dear lady, but I had to do this. The fever must have troubled his mind. He's calm now."

"Thank you, my dearest knight. God bless you," she whispered, desperately trying to brush the tears away.

"I care for him very much, my lady. He's my best friend. We've been through so much together since we were young squires in the king's court." He held her by the arm and supported her as she went to sit near her husband.

"He is not out of danger yet," the physician said. "The wound in his belly has started to fester, and this keeps him hot. If the fever does not subside soon, he may not survive."

He bled Sándor again while the priest read another prayer. Then, they all bowed to Margit respectfully and left, except for Erzsi. "Is there anything else you need, my lady?"

"Yes. Bring me that wise woman, Marina. She saved my life when I also had a fever."

"Of course, my lady. I'll fetch her now."

An hour later, the door opened, and Erzsi entered with Marina. The two women were followed by the priest, who was fuming. "My lady! The witch has no place in your noble house. She is the Devil's instrument. She must –"

"Father, I beg of you! I am trying to help my husband. This woman is my only hope."

"This is a terrible sin. You are selling his soul to the Devil."

"I shall gladly take the sin upon me, Father. I would sacrifice my life and my soul to save him."

The priest became red in the face. He huffed and puffed awhile, but Margit would have none of it. Unable to persuade her, he left but not before throwing threats at her for condemning herself to the flames of Hell.

"I also do God's work," Marina commented. "I help people. But priest hates me. He thinks I'm a witch."

"Well, can you help us?"

Marina examined the inside of Sándor's forearm and shook her head. "The physician bleeds him?" she shouted. "Not good. He lost much blood from injury. The man fights with death. The hardest fight ever. Bleeding makes him weak."

She rummaged through her sack and took out some strange-looking leaves. She stuck those on his wound. While waiting for them to work, she got Erzsi to fetch her a cup of water, into which she stirred a bluish powder until it turned into paste. She spread this paste on his forehead. In the meantime, the leaves had caused some sort of green, frothy liquid to seep out. It looked disgusting, but Marina explained that it was the 'poison' coming out of his body. When this stopped, the old woman placed a handful of maggots on the wound.

Margit recoiled, but Marina held her arm to reassure her. "Fear not, lady. They clean wound. They help heal."

Before the wise woman left, she told Margit that it was still too early to say if Sándor would survive or not. She would be back the following day in any case.

Margit kept vigil all night at her husband's side. There was no visible improvement in his condition, but his forehead was not so hot now. Marina continued the treatment for the next five days, and little by little the infection subsided. But Sándor remained in deep sleep most of the time. During the brief periods that he was awake, he was still incoherent and confused, groaning in pain and mumbling incomprehensible words. He was unable to take anything except water.

27

Facing Reality

On the morning of the seventh day after her husband's injury, Margit was summoned to the town. The soldiers had returned from Belgrade. Even though some of the men had serious injuries, they had been forced to flee the city to escape the plague that had broken out. The wounded had been carried home on carts. Two had died on the way. The families of the survivors rejoiced to see their loved ones return alive, but heart-breaking scenes took place when the names of the dead were announced. Margit thanked them all for their service and returned to the castle.

At the entrance to the keep, the priest was arguing with Marina. Margit stepped between them. "I beg of you, Father! This woman is a great help. I believe she can heal my husband. And she is not a witch. She uses no magic or alchemy, only herbs, plants and God's other creatures. Please, let her continue, and I pledge to make a large donation to the Church if he survives."

At the mention of money, the priest backed down immediately, which surprised Margit. But she did not make any comment, only thanked him and hurried into the house.

When the women entered Sándor's bedchamber, he was awake. Margit's heart leapt. She threw herself into his arms.

"*Szerelmem*, I'm so glad!"

Sándor screamed in pain.

"Oh, forgive me!" Margit said, pulling away from him. How silly of her to forget about his injured ribs! She sat on the bed and lovingly stroked his face.

At length, he smiled at her. "I have missed you. So good to see you again." He looked around. "Where is István? Where is our son?"

Margit waved Erzsi and Marina out of the room. She took a deep breath. "I am sorry, *kedvesem*. He is with God now."

"No!" he shouted in despair. "It can't be! I was talking to him, only a few moments ago."

"It must have been in your dreams."

He squeezed his eyes shut. "You are lying to me."

"I wish I were, *szerelmem*. We had his funeral many days ago. He is in the family crypt."

"I want to see him." He tried to get up, but the pain did not let him move much. He winced and sank back onto the bed.

"You are too weak to go anywhere. I shall take you there as soon as you feel a little better."

He lay down again, exhausted even by that small effort. "It's my fault," he whimpered. "I failed to protect him... And Miklós... Oh, God! He is dead too. I have failed him too. They are both dead because of me."

What could she say to him? On one hand, his desire to go fighting again was the cause of everything that followed. Had he stayed home, both István and Miklós would still be alive. On the other hand, he was heartbroken. And she had nearly lost him. Her life would have no meaning without him. "It's not your fault. You told István to stay here, but he did not listen. And Miklós caused his own death by attacking you. It was God's will for all this to happen. There is nothing you could have done to prevent it."

Sándor gasped. "You speak of God? I fought for Him all my life. And yet, where was He when my son lay dying in my arms?"

"Dear husband, I beg of you! Those are blasphemous words."

"Hush, Margit! You were not there. I had his blood on my hands, on my face..."

She stood up and glared at him. "Do you think that I did not love my child? I was the one who carried him, brought him into the world, fed him when he was little, sang to him before he went to sleep, wiped his brow and comforted him when he was ill, taught him prayer and good manners. He was a part of me too. Do you think that I did not suffer? When they brought him back, I wished for my life to end. I wept for days, I –"

He silenced her with an abrupt wave of his arm.

She pressed her hand against her chest, trying to calm herself. Arguing with him would not achieve anything. It would not bring their boy back.

***

Sándor wept day and night and refused to take any food. Margit became worried, not only about the state of his body, but also about the state of his mind. It looked as if he did not want to live anymore. Afraid to leave his side, she took care of him with the greatest devotion. She changed the dressings on his wounds, helped him wash and put clean clothes on, talked to him about things that were happening in the estate to keep his mind occupied. She lay beside him at night to make sure he would not do any harm to himself.

He finally started to accept reality. He eventually had some food, and with Imre's support, he went to the great hall to meet his counsellors and inform himself of the affairs of the estate. And within a few days, he asked to see István.

Margit accompanied him to the family burial vault underneath the castle chapel. Sándor sat beside his son's stone coffin and asked her to leave.

Three hours later, she went back to the crypt and found him sitting in the dark, like a weary ghost refusing to leave its haunting place. He was whispering to his boy but became quiet as soon as she approached.

She set her candle in an iron wall sconce, then sat beside him and took his hand in hers. "Come, *szerelmem*. Let us return to the house."

"Return?" he snapped. The flickering light accentuated the angles of his hardened face. "I wish to stay here. My only child is here. I do not have another one. I cannot have another one."

Margit sighed. "No, it is I who can't have another child. You can. I'm sure there are many women who would be willing to help you."

He inclined his head towards her. "What do you mean?"

"Your family has had this estate for generations. It's important that you have an heir to bequeath it to. I promise I shall love your child and treat it like it's mine, no matter who the mother is."

Sándor gaped at her. "You ask me to commit adultery?"

"You must preserve your bloodline. I shall have to accept it."

His face opened into a smile. "You are a woman of remarkable loyalty, Margit Bátori. But no, I shall not do what you ask. When you were ill after giving birth, I made a pact with God. I promised never to lie with another woman if He kept you safe. I intend to keep that promise for as long as I am on this earth. For it hurt me so much when I betrayed you that I'd rather let the king take my estate when I die."

Relief washed over Margit. She embraced him with the utmost tenderness and held him for a long time.

"I have lost most of the people I loved so dearly," he said. "You are the only person in this world that makes me want to stay alive. Land, gold, glory... they don't matter to me anymore."

28
A Surprising Turn of Events

September 1456

The woman, dressed in black and her face covered with a transparent veil, held a little boy by the hand as she stood in the great hall of Sasfészek.

"Who are you?" Sándor asked.

She lifted the veil.

His heart jumped. "Anna! What in God's name are you doing here?"

"What happened to your face?"

Instinctively, he touched the scar but then grimaced at her. "I'm sure you did not come here to talk about my face."

"Can we speak somewhere more private?"

He led her to his study upstairs.

"Where is Margit? I wish to speak with both of you."

"She has gone to the town. But even if she were here, she would not like to see you."

Anna raised her eyebrows. "I know she hates me, and I don't blame her."

"What is it that you need? I don't have all day."

She looked at the boy, who was clinging to the skirt of her gown. She gently nudged him in front of her. "This is my son, Márton. Your nephew. He is seven years old."

Sándor opened his mouth to say something disparaging about the paternity of the child. But the boy looked so much like Miklós when he was small that he could not dispute the fact that this little one had his family's blood running through his veins. "Pleased to meet you, Márton." He patted him on the head. "I am your uncle, Sándor."

The boy smiled but kept his eyes fixed on the floor. Anna asked him to go and wait outside.

"I really need your help," she said.

"And why do you think that I would help you?"

"I am going to live the rest of my life in a convent, and I wish you and Margit to look after Márton."

Sándor looked at her askance. "You? In a convent?"

Anna fiddled with the knot of her girdle. "I have done horrible things in my life, and I have such a burden on my conscience. I let my father arrange the murders of my two husbands, and then I conspired with him to marry Miklós. The plan was to do away with you eventually and take your estate. A short time after that, it would be your brother's turn to disappear. But I thank the Lord that none of this came to pass. When we met for the last time, eleven years ago, you told me to go and live my life. But in order to do that, I had to cut all ties with my past. I had to start again. I am sure you know that my father died later that year."

"Yes."

"The truth is I convinced Miklós to kill him. He suffocated him with a pillow while he slept."

Sándor's jaw dropped. He had never liked Holman, and he did not care about his death. But at the same time, he shuddered at the thought that Anna had turned his brother into a cold-blooded murderer.

"My father was the cause of my misery. He had mistreated me for so many years. As soon as he was gone, I felt liberated. Everything changed. Miklós and I had a good life together. We had a child, and for the first time, we were happy... or so I thought. But the truth is that he was still carrying all that hate, which kept eating him from the inside."

Wincing, Anna leaned on the writing desk for support; but then, she straightened up and swallowed hard. "He wanted to destroy you. I begged him to stop thinking about it, but he would not listen. He believed that I went against him because I was secretly in love with you. Well, I did desire you a long time ago, but I loved my husband too. And so, he bided his time. When your son died, I could not imagine what was to follow. He left with the soldiers, pretending he was going to attend the funeral. The next time I saw him, he was dead."

She stopped talking again and pressed her hand against her mouth, trying to keep herself from bursting into tears. "And now I feel responsible for all the terrible things that befell me and my family," she whimpered. It took her a few moments to regain her composure and continue, "I cannot live with this burden anymore. That is why I am going to lock myself away from the world and finally search for peace. And I beg of you to look after my child until he comes of age and is able to take care of his estates."

Sándor remained silent awhile. He did not know if he felt pity or anger towards her. But what had brought about this big change in her?

"All this time you and Miklós have been trying to take what is mine, and now you wish me to look after all that is yours. Why?"

Anna gripped both his arms and looked him straight in the eye. "I only wish to protect my boy. Márton needs a father to guide him until he becomes a man. You have lost your son. I know that he will never replace your boy, but he may bring some joy into your life."

Perhaps her plea was sincere after all. She would not entrust her child to him or enter a convent unless she had regretted her past life.

He stepped away from her. "I don't know. I must talk to Margit."

"Of course. Take your time. As soon as you have decided, I shall send you my people with papers to sign, and Márton can move here."

Footsteps and whispers echoed from above as Margit ascended the stairs. She had just arrived home after consoling a grieving family in the town. She was not in the mood for visitors... And it was not just any visitor. Her mouth opened wide when she saw Anna and the boy. They did not exchange a word, but the smirk on the Saxon woman's face made the blood rush to Margit's head.

She quickened her pace and burst into Sándor's study.

"I hope you are not actually considering this!" she shouted when she found out what Anna had asked them to do.

"Why not? The boy is my blood. He is my closest male relative, and he will inherit my estate when I die. He has lost his father because of me. The least I can do is take care of him."

"He has her blood too. That vile strumpet will finally have her way."

"How can you talk like this? The woman has regretted what she did to us and is trying to make it right."

"And you believe her?"

"Yes. You must calm yourself and think more clearly. It's obvious that your jealousy is clouding your judgement."

Margit gasped. "Are you out of your mind? What would I be jealous of? Her evil soul or her scheming mind?"

"Perhaps because you think she may still be after me?"

How presumptuous! She clenched her fists, struggling to hold herself from slapping him. "Don't flatter yourself! She did not come here because she loves you, but because she wants to take advantage of you – of both of us. You may be clever and strong and generous, but sometimes you let yourself be deceived. You believed Miklós was seeking forgiveness, and he tried to murder you instead. And now you believe that Anna has changed and has become a good person. Well, I must warn you: people do not change so easily."

"Why do you always dispute my decisions?"

"Not always, husband. Only when they are wrong."

He shook his head.

"Do as you wish," she said. "But you should know one thing: this boy will never become our son."

Erzsi had just finished helping Margit prepare for bed and was plaiting her lady's hair when someone knocked on the door. The maid answered. As soon as she saw who was there, she bowed and left.

Sándor entered. He had a sombre look on his face.

Margit did not even acknowledge his presence.

He approached and put his hand on her shoulder. "I am sorry about the way I spoke to you earlier. I have been heartbroken after losing István. So, I thought that instead of disrespecting you by having a child with another woman, I could adopt Márton. What Miklós and Anna did to us is not the boy's fault. He has now lost his father, and he has a mother of questionable morality. He needs parents like us to lead him through life."

She sucked her lower lip. At least, he had apologised. "I have no problem with the child. My issue is with Anna. I may be wrong, but I cannot trust her. She is not the kind of woman who would live the rest of her life in a convent."

Holding her by the arm, Sándor made her stand up opposite him. She looked away, but he gently turned her face towards him with his hand. "I have all those counsellors and officers, but in the end, you are the only one who gives me the most honest and fair advice. I don't know what I would do without you."

His words made her anger melt away. "*Kedvesem*, I shall always be by your side," she whispered in the most tender manner. "As for this case, I would say yes, look after the child until he comes of age, but do not adopt him. At least, not until Anna's intentions become clearer."

"Yes, you are right. You are always right..." A broad smile softened his stern countenance. "I am so fortunate to have you. Not only are you my best counsellor, you are my anchor too. Every time I falter, you bring me back in line. Pity you were born a woman. You would have made such a great leader for our homeland otherwise."

"Really?" Margit struggled to keep a straight face. "Would I have given you the same amount of pleasure had I not been born a woman? Would you enjoy taking me to bed as much if I were a man?"

He burst out laughing. "*Úristen*! Of course not!"

"Then, stop pitying me for being a woman and count your blessings. Our homeland's loss is your gain."

***

A few days later, Anna arrived at Sasfészek with her legal advisers. Sándor and his steward examined the accounts of her two estates in detail. They did not see any serious issues, but it was not good news either. After the payment of the various taxes, there was very little profit left. A lot of work needed to be done, plus the estate near Szeben was too far away. Anna said she had competent people looking after it, but Sándor would have liked to see this for himself. He would have to pay a visit there when he felt a little better.

They finally signed the papers, which named him as Márton's guardian and trustee of his two estates. This meant that he would administer the youngster's fortune to the best of his ability until the boy became of full age.

After the signing, Erzsi took the child and showed him around his new home. The servants unloaded his belongings and brought them into Miklós's old bedchamber.

Anna talked to Sándor and Margit about what education she wished her son to receive, and what were the things that he liked to do in his free time.

"Do not fret," Sándor said. "He will be looked after very well."

"Thank you. I knew I could count on you."

She smiled at him, but it was nothing genuine. It seemed more like a conceited smirk, even a sneer. It was as if she were saying, "I can make you do whatever I please. I can make you dance to my tune."

"So, which convent will you enter?" Sándor asked.

"I have not decided yet. There is one near Hermannstadt – or 'Szeben' as you Hungarians call it. It is close to the place where I was born."

"Are you sure? Would it not be better for you to remarry instead?"

She fluttered her eyelashes at him. "You know that the only man I would marry is... you."

Affronted by Anna's impudence, Margit left the room in a huff.

Anna threw her hands up in the air. "What's wrong with her? I was only jesting."

"You know very well that she will never like you after what you did to us."

"Really? And what about you? Do you hate me too?"

Sándor looked away. "I do not hate you. But you are not my favourite person either."

"That makes two of us."

"What do you mean?"

"I used to like you, Sándor. But now, I am not sure anymore. You murdered my husband. How am I to feel after this?"

His pulse quickened. He had tolerated her up to that point, but now he was losing his patience. "I did not kill him. He attacked me, and my soldiers shot him with their arrows. They were protecting me."

"Exactly. They killed him for you. You are still responsible."

"I do not understand. How am I responsible if he stabbed me in such a cowardly manner?"

He folded his arms. Of course. He could now understand why Margit was so suspicious of Anna. It was strange that she would relinquish her fortune and, more importantly, her own son to a man whom she held accountable for her husband's death. Was she really abandoning her previous way of life, or was she plotting something else? So hard to know the truth.

"You could have been mine," Anna said. "And none of this would have happened. But you married that self-righteous bitch instead, who thinks she is above everyone else."

How dare she? He raised his hand to slap her but stopped halfway. Despite her insults, he still could not bring himself to hit a woman. He wagged his forefinger in front of her face instead. "Don't you ever talk about Margit like that!"

"I apologise." She sniffled. "I simply cannot bear the thought of you getting inside her every night while it could have been me in her place."

"*Úristen!*" he gasped. "You are disturbed. To tell you the truth, I am glad that your son will be here with us for the future, as far away from you as possible."

She pushed him out of the way and stormed out.

Sándor slumped in a chair. His heated encounter with Anna had brought on a sudden, sharp pain in his heart. She had lied to him. Margit was right. Anna had not changed. She was as evil as ever, and through her false tears, she had misled him. What was her plan? He did not know. But now he started to have doubts about the contract he had signed with her.

29

Serious Problems
and Desperate Solutions

Sándor's hands trembled as he read the letter. The silence and emptiness of the room around him only amplified the effect of the unexpected news. János Hunyadi had died in Belgrade, a short time after contracting the plague that had ravaged through the camp, following the end of the siege. His body had been transported to Gyulafehérvár and had been buried in the Cathedral of Szent Mihály.

Sándor felt sick in the stomach. It was like losing a family member. Lord Jankó was his hero and, perhaps, a second father to him. Through an irony of fate, the man who had fought and survived so many military and political battles in his life had been taken away by disease. Sándor wanted to go and pay his last respects at the grave, but he was still too weak to travel.

Hunyadi's death could not have come at a worse moment. With the exception of the castle garrison and whatever was left of the local troops after all the battles they had been in, the majority of Sándor's soldiers were mercenaries paid by János. Those men had not received their wages since the start of the siege of Belgrade.

It was a serious situation. He could not afford to lose the

military protection of his estate at a time when the Ottoman danger had not disappeared completely, the king was hostile towards any supporters of the Hunyadi family, and the new Prince of Wallachia had launched a series of raids on Tranyslvanian soil.

He sat down with his steward and the leader of the mercenaries, and they managed to put together some money to pay the soldiers' wages up to that point in time. However, this was not the answer to the problem. He would not be able to afford his small army in the long term and needed to find a more permanent solution.

By the middle of October, his health had improved significantly, and he was able to travel on horseback again. His financial troubles had not disappeared though. Not only did he have to make sure that he administered his own estate properly, but he also had to look after little Márton's affairs. He had not visited his nephew's estates yet. It was about time he did so.

The fact that Miklós had taken over Sasfészek with the help of mercenaries was encouraging. If there were soldiers paid with his brother's money, Sándor could use those to protect his own land, instead of employing Hunyadi's troops.

The nearby estate was called Grossenwald, which means 'Big Forest' in German. It bordered his land, and its main village was about three hours' travel from Sasfészek. Sándor rode there at a leisurely pace, without an escort. The lack of human interaction let him savour the beauty of nature in the most intense way. After his injury, he had to do things at a slower pace, instead of rushing to attend to every matter at once. He stopped several times on the way to let both himself and his palfrey rest. He refreshed himself, drinking from clear springs and small waterfalls.

Grossenwald was mostly covered with a dense forest, at the edge of which stood a handful of farmhouses and a church. The road led him past an abandoned military camp. Sándor had been there once before, following his return after the battle of Varna, when he escorted his brother home. The camp was in use back then, but now it lay empty and open to the elements. What had become of the mercenaries?

Upon entering the estate's main village, his heart sank. Overgrown weeds, roaming animals, neglected houses – some of them abandoned and boarded up – muddy narrow streets that stank of waste, peasants in dirty clothes, watching him with sad eyes. He gave a few copper coins to the barefoot children, who followed him all the way through the village.

It was not the Grossenwald he remembered from eleven years earlier. Anna had not said a word about all that. What on earth had happened?

He rode to the fortified manor house, which stood on the top of a small hill.

A Saxon man greeted him. "Welcome, my lord. I am Hermann Stolz, the steward of the estate."

Stolz spoke fluent Hungarian, with an accent similar to Anna's. He was well-dressed, in complete contrast to the people who lived only a few hundred paces downhill. He led Sándor into the main room of the manor and ordered a female servant to bring in some refreshments.

Sándor expressed his disappointment at the state of the place and asked about the soldiers.

"They all left after your brother died. The mistress let them go."

"Why?"

"She was not interested in continuing this business venture."

That was unexpected. Sándor's face heated. What else had she hidden from him? "And what about the other activities of the estate? The accounts show revenue from agriculture, timber and animal trade. I did not see any of that today."

"All trades have ceased. Many people have left to seek their fortune elsewhere."

"I thought the estate was making a small profit."

"Yes, it was. But everything has stopped since the master died. We have no money to pay the taxes now."

"I am sure Holman and Miklós had revenue from the mercenaries. There must be some money."

Stolz shook his head. "No, my lord. When the mistress left, she took all the money, jewellery and anything valuable with her. We have been left here with nothing."

Sándor surveyed the room around him. It looked as bare and empty as the entrance hall of the manor. No ornaments, tapestries, paintings or heirlooms; not even candlesticks anywhere. The curtains had disappeared too, leaving the house at the mercy of draughts. The few dying embers in the fireplace could do nothing to dispel the smell of damp that pervaded the air.

"This is strange. No one takes their earthly possessions with them when they enter a convent... Or perhaps she has not actually entered a convent." He paused. That evil woman had tricked him. "She lied to me. What am I going to do with this place now?"

Stolz turned his gaze to the floor. "I'm sorry, my lord. I didn't know this was going to happen."

"No, it is not your fault. She probably tricked you as well. But I am responsible for this estate now on behalf of my nephew. I cannot let it go to ruin."

"We could start again," the steward said hesitantly, "but that would require a great expense."

"Money which I do not have."

Sándor returned to Sasfészek the next day and told Margit the news.

"I had always been suspicious of Anna's behaviour," she said, "but I had never imagined anything like this. You are right. If she has taken all her money and valuables with her, she has not entered a convent. God only knows what she might be plotting now."

"I must visit the other estate in Szeben. I need to see what the situation is there as well."

How on earth had he been deceived so easily? He could not back out of the contract now and was afraid of what was to come.

Thankfully, things with Anna's other estate were not so bad. There was a large fortified house and extensive pastureland, on which sheep were bred for their wool. This was, in turn, sold to the merchants of the town. The steward was another Saxon man. He was the last person to have seen Anna. He told Sándor that she had arrived about a week earlier. She had taken all the money and valuables and then left without saying where she was going. The estate's sheep business was still operating. This was a good sign even though there was no money left to pay the farmers' wages due in the next couple of weeks.

Sándor could not keep both estates because he could not afford them. He had to sell one in order to save the other. There was no specific clause in the contract to say that he could not sell; only that he would administer his nephew's fortune in the best way possible. Between the two estates, the one near Szeben was the most attractive; the only one that could be sold. It was near the town and the merchant guilds. Still in business, it was worth much more than Grossenwald. The latter lay in a remote, mountainous area; but it abutted Szentimre, and it would be easier for him to keep an eye on it. He could use the money from the sale to invest there. And so, he put the Szeben estate up for sale.

***

"What are we going to do about Márton?" Erzsi wondered. "I can't understand how the shy and quiet boy turns into a demon every time your husband is away. It's a blessing that we don't speak his language. At least, we're spared all the vile words he's probably using about us."

Margit covered her ears with her hands. If only the screaming and noise would stop! The front of her kirtle was full of stains from the food that the boy had thrown at her during supper. And now the servants were having a hard time trying to put him to bed.

"He hates me. I am sure his mother has put some evil notions into his head."

"You must talk to your husband."

"He will not believe me. He will think that I only complain because of my feelings about Anna. He has grown fond of Márton. And now that we have no child of our own, the boy will inherit the estate because he is Sándor's closest male relative."

Erszi helped her prepare for bed. "I'll have your clothes cleaned, my lady."

"Yes, thank you. You can leave now."

Margit sat on the bed and took a deep breath. The screaming had finally stopped, but the pressure on her chest had not subsided. Her head was in a spin. Anna's suspicious disappearance from the face of the earth and Márton's change of behaviour every time Sándor was away, were signs that something sinister was at play. Her husband had worked hard all those years and had put his life in peril, fighting to protect their home and make sure she was always safe and lived a comfortable life. She would not forgive herself if she let anything bad happen to him as a result of that woman's plotting. And what would become of her if Sándor died before her? She would be at Anna and Márton's mercy. If they did not lock her in a convent, they would certainly make her life hell. She would rather be dead.

With a trembling hand, she opened her wooden medicine casket. She took out the two jars of Marina's herbs. She stood in front of the fireplace, holding them against her chest for a long time. It was a difficult decision; one that could cost her life.

"Help me, God," she whispered and crossed herself.

She removed the lid of the first jar and emptied the contents into the fire. Then, she did the same with the other.

***

Sándor lay on the bed and let Margit take the initiative. After his rather strenuous journey to Szeben and back, his wound pained him some. But this did not prevent him from enjoying the pleasure of his wife's naked body as she straddled him like a skilful amazon on her stallion. He slid his hands from her hips up to her breasts. She had broken into a sweat, and her skin felt pleasantly warm.

It was not long before they lay beside each other, out of breath and with flushed faces.

Leaning over her, he ran his fingers through her hair and kissed her on the forehead. "You are still as beautiful as you were on our first night."

"I am not," she replied, with a coy smile. "I am sixteen years older. My body and face are not like they used to be."

"Your body and face are not like they used to be? Well, have you seen my scars? I meant what I said. To me, you are the most beautiful woman in the world. I swear to God, even after all these years, I still feel like a lovestruck adolescent when I am with you. I wish I could last a little longer to please you more, but I really can't. I am so tired. I am getting old and weak."

She playfully jabbed her finger at his chest. "No, you aren't. You only need a little more time to recover fully from your injuries, and you will be yourself again soon."

That delightful smile was still on her face.

"You were particularly... eager tonight," he teased her.

She covered her mouth with her hand and giggled. "You went away for a few days, and I have missed you."

"Should I be absent more often?"

She blushed and buried her face in the pillow.

He gave her a light kiss on the shoulder and then lay his head back on the pillow and fell asleep.

Margit pulled the bed covers over both of them. She squeezed herself against his body, put her arm around him and rested her head on his shoulder. She closed her eyes, praying that her plan would work.

30
The Price of Loyalty

There was a lot of interest in Anna's estate in Szeben. That it included pastureland and flocks of sheep sounded like a great opportunity to the textile and weavers' guilds of the town. They were not willing to buy the land because the price was too high, but they offered to lease it. This solution was ideal. Sándor would receive a steady income, which he could invest in the other estate. At the same time, he would not lose the land for good.

With one issue resolved favourably, he had to look at the problem of paying his soldiers' wages. He had been able to cover them only for a few months; and now, well into November, he was already a month behind and needed to find a solution soon.

It was best to meet with Hunyadi's eldest son, László, who had inherited his father's title and vast fortune. The young man had recognised Sándor as family when they met in Belgrade. There was a good chance that he would agree to continue paying the mercenaries' wages.

Sándor arrived at Hunyadvár in mid-November. He stopped at the castle to spend the night and on the off-chance that the family might have returned. But the Hunyadis were in their other estate in Temesvár, further west. On arriving there, he found the town teeming with soldiers and guards. He had to submit to a full interrogation as to what business he had there. The reason was the presence of King László in Temesvár at the time.

"Have you not heard, sir?" one of the soldiers said. "Count Ulrik Cillei was killed in Nándorfehérvár while he and the king were guests of Lord László and Mihály Szilágyi."

Sándor gasped. "Cillei? The king's relative? The arch-enemy of the Hunyadis?"

"That very man, sir."

"*Úristen*! And why is the king here?"

"To meet with Countess Erzsébet."

Sándor had to wait until the king had left before being allowed into the castle. By that time, László Hunyadi had already departed for Buda as well. The only person who could help him was Erzsébet, and so he requested an audience with her. He had met her before, when he and Margit visited Hunyadvár castle, but many years had passed since then. What mood would he find her in after the recent death of her husband and the trouble her son and her brother had got themselves into? Would she even be willing to help him amidst all that?

He arrived at her residence at the agreed time. A female servant brought him into the audience hall. After counting – over and over again – how many times each of the four different decorative patterns appeared on the glazed tiles of the massive stove, he paced around the room, admiring the opulence and superior craftsmanship displayed by the various items of furniture, ironwork and tapestry. Then, he sat down and waited.

An hour must have passed, but still no sign of Erzsébet. Perhaps she had forgotten about him, or did not wish to see him at all.

When Lord Jankó's widow finally entered the audience hall, solemnly dressed and looking imperious, she was flanked by two of her personal guards. Both soldiers approached Sándor. One asked him to hand over his sword, and the other told him to kneel and introduce himself.

He bent down on one knee. "Sándor Szilágyi, lord of Szentimre. We are third cousins."

At last, Erzsébet cracked a smile. She signalled to him to stand up. "Give the man his sword back and leave us," she ordered the soldiers.

His voice quavered as he explained the reason for his visit. Surprisingly, the countess agreed to help without hesitation. But she wanted something in return: his absolute and unconditional loyalty.

"I have proven this already, my lady, by offering my own services and those of my men to your heroic husband."

"Yes, I know that, and you have my sincere gratitude. But times are dangerous. Cillei had been poisoning the young king's mind against our family even before my husband's death. He was afraid of all the land and power that we hold. He convinced the king to take most of our castles back from my sons by making false accusations of treason against my László."

"How dare he? Cillei never sent a single soldier to fight the Ottomans. And then he accused the hero of Nándorfehérvár of treason?"

The countess grimaced in disgust. "The king made him commander-in-chief of the kingdom. They both went to Belgrade to take over the fortress from my son and my brother. They brought thousands of mercenaries with them, but Mihály had the gates closed before the soldiers could enter the city. The next day after mass, László confronted Cillei about his traitorous behaviour. They both lost their temper. They drew swords and fought. My son's friends came to his aid, and they killed that accursed man."

"I have heard that the king has promised not to hold your family responsible. Do you believe that he will keep his word?"

Erzsébet pursed her lips. "Not at all. He is a frightened little puppy now, but as soon as he returns to the palace, he might change." She took a step towards him and clasped his forearm. Her voice was as firm as her grip. "That's why I want to count on my family and friends if things go wrong and my two sons need help. If you swear you will be under my command whenever required, I shall gladly pay the wages of your soldiers."

Unnerved, Sándor turned away to avoid her penetrating gaze as he contemplated his response. The countess was a tough woman and in a tough situation. Swearing loyalty to her meant that he would have to go to war again, possibly very soon, given the circumstances. Despite his kinship with the Hunyadi family, he knew that Cillei's death was nothing short of a political assassination. The king would not let that go unpunished. It was only a matter of time before the Hunyadis found themselves in the eye of a storm of unpredictable proportions. By supporting them, he was running the risk of being branded a 'rebel' against the

Crown. He had hoped that after the disaster in Varna, the loss of his son in Belgrade and his narrow escape from death following the attempt on his life, he was done with fighting. But he had no choice. He needed the protection of his powerful relatives.

He bent down on one knee, drew his sword and held it up before the countess. "I swear on my honour as a knight and nobleman of Hungary to serve you and your family whenever needed. My sword and those of my men are at your disposal."

"Thank you, cousin," she said, with a broad smile on her face. "Two of my servants will escort you with half a year's wages for your soldiers."

***

"I'm sorry for what befell you, my lady," the physician said. "You have not suffered damage, thanks be to God. But you must rest for a few days."

A female servant took the bloodied sheets and clothes away.

Margit burst into tears. It was not the pain that really hurt her but the heavy burden of her failure. Would she ever be able to bear the child that she wanted so much?

"Thank you, sir. Please don't say anything to the lord," Erzsi told the physician while escorting him out of the bedchamber.

She turned to Margit, shook her head and folded her arms. "My lady, I knew that you were with child even though you never said a word. I kept quiet and prayed that all would go well for you. But after what happened today, I cannot be silent any longer. I know why you wish to have a baby, but you must promise me that you won't try again. There are other ways to prove your loyalty to your husband than putting your own life in danger. If you don't listen to reason, I swear I'll tell him."

Margit raised her hands. "Hush, Erzsi! And don't you dare threaten me! You don't understand my suffering."

"I'm sorry, my lady, but this is foolish. You can't plot behind your husband's back either. He has enough troubles and certainly doesn't need you to add to them."

"Very well, I shall not do it again," Margit lied. She just wished her maid to stop and leave her in peace.

When Sándor returned, she managed to hide her pain and pretended all was well. But she was not going to give up. She was going to try again and again for as long as there was life in her.

31
Surprise

A few days after Christmas, the soft, downy snow flurrying down from the grey sky did nothing to diminish the gloom that hung over the land. From the window of her chamber, Margit watched as the bitter wind swirled the flakes into a frenzied dance until they came to rest upon the frozen ground.

Sándor was out on estate business in that wild weather, and she did not envy him in the least. Confined in the house, she expected it to be another dull and uneventful winter day when the servants informed her that there was a visitor at the castle, looking for her husband.

Downstairs, at the entrance hall, stood a woman. She had honey-blonde hair in plaits coiled at the back of her head, hazel eyes and lightly tanned skin. She did not look a day over twenty years of age. Although her clothes were of good quality wool, they were creased, dirty and untidy. Her long, hooded cape was soaked through; from the hem of her gown melting snow dripped onto the floor. In her gloved hands, she clutched a small bundle of her personal things, and she shivered from the cold.

Margit led her to the great hall and told her to sit by the fire. When the girl took her cape off, Margit was surprised to see that she was with child.

"Who are you?"

The stranger replied in a foreign language. Slavic. Somewhat familiar but also different from the Polish that Margit had learned from her mother. "Do you speak Hungarian? Wallachian? Or Polish?"

The girl shook her head.

"Does anyone know her language?" Margit asked the servants.

A kitchen hand came forward and told her that the stranger was Serbian. He tried to find out what she needed but to no avail. The girl insisted on speaking only with Sándor.

"What does she want from my husband?" Margit wondered, with a dose of suspicion.

"She won't tell me. She said it's a personal matter."

"Well, he will not be back before sundown. Take her to the kitchen, give her something to eat and drink and tell her to wait there until he returns."

Who was this woman that had appeared so suddenly? It had been about five months since Sándor's return from Nándorfehérvár – a city with mostly Serbian population – and the stranger looked five months pregnant. Margit trusted her husband was faithful to her. Yet, the thought that perhaps he was hiding something lingered on her mind for the rest of the day. She had told him that she would not object to him having a child with another woman. But now, as she was faced with such a possibility, the pangs of jealousy tormented her heart; and even more so because the stranger was so young and pretty.

When Sándor entered the house, she gave him no time to take

off his hat and gloves, not even to brush the snow from his cloak. Threading her arm through his, she ushered him to the great hall.

"What's the matter?" he said, alarmed by her behaviour.

The servants brought in the girl.

Margit scrutinised her husband's countenance. "Do you know her?"

With narrowed eyes, Sándor surveyed the stranger's face. "She looks familiar. But no, I don't think I know her."

Margit waved the servants out of the room. "You speak Serbian. Talk to her."

The young woman knelt in front of him and grabbed his hand. She spoke fast, letting out little gasps after each sentence. It took him some time to understand what was going on. "The damn fool!" he shouted.

But he was not angry. On the contrary, he was smiling, which confounded Margit even further. He removed his hat and gloves, called the servants and asked them to bring Imre to him.

"*Krisztus!*" his friend exclaimed as soon as he saw the stranger. The astounded look on his face revealed it all. It also put Margit's fears to rest.

"You, rascal! What were you doing with this young lady?" Sándor teased him.

"Umm... I... was... lonely," Imre stammered.

"And careless too. You are forty years old. At your age and with your experience, I thought that you had mastered the art of 'withdrawal'."

"Sándor! Don't be so rude!" Margit rebuked him, but she could not keep a straight face anymore.

The Serbian woman rose and regarded them with a worried expression on her face.

"The poor girl thinks that we are laughing at her expense," Margit observed.

Imre's face turned scarlet.

Sándor waved to him to come closer. "Where are your manners, *barátom*? Will you not introduce us?"

"Umm... yes. This is Dragoslava Lazarević, the daughter of one of the town officials in Nándorfehérvár. She kindly offered me company during the long nights of the siege."

"Sadly, her father banished her because of that. But she is comely, from a noble family and carrying your child. She will make a good wife for you."

Imre almost choked. "W... wife?"

Sándor's eyes twinkled like those of a mischievous child. "Jesting aside, you must make this right. You must wed her."

"Is this an order?"

"Yes. An order from your superior officer and your lord."

Margit burst out laughing. "Imre, don't you think it's time you took a wife and had a family?"

"Umm... yes, my lady."

"That's settled then," Sándor concluded and then turned to the girl, "You... him... wedding," he said in Serbian.

She knelt again and kissed his hand in gratitude. He helped her up, took her by the arm and led her to Imre. "For the sake of all these years that we have fought together and for the loyalty you have shown me, I shall make you my castellan. After Balog let Sasfészek fall into my brother's hands without a fight, I have lost faith in him. He is nothing like his father. I even have a suspicion that he was bribed by Miklós. So, he will be demoted, and you will take his place as garrison commander too. And I shall give you the guest quarters in the castle so that you can live here with your future family."

***

"So, you thought I was the father of her child?" Sándor asked Margit when they were in bed that night.

"She insisted on talking to you only. She is Serbian, and you were in Nándorfehérvár for over a month. Even the timing of her pregnancy was correct. I don't know, the thought just crossed my mind."

"Is this what you think of me?"

She blushed. "No, of course not. I am sorry."

"My dear wife, this is such disrespectful behaviour."

"I said I am sorry."

He chuckled. "That's not good enough. You need to be 'punished'."

Margit covered her mouth with her hand but failed to suppress a giggle. "And how do you intend to punish me? Lock me in the dungeon with no food until I repent?"

"Oh, no. That would be too severe."

"March me through the town naked on a horse?"

Sándor scratched his chin. "Hmm... It is tempting. But I do not wish to share your beauty with every man in the estate."

"What then?" she continued to tease him. "You must do something to restore your honour."

"If you insist." He gave her a playful slap on the backside. "There, naughty girl! My honour has been restored."

32

Civil War

April 1457

The news hit Sándor like a thunderbolt. "László Hunyadi? Executed?" He stared at the messenger, doubting he had heard right.

"Aye, sir. Accused, tried and condemned to death for high treason. Beheaded in Buda a month ago. And young Mátyás a prisoner of the king. The most important allies of the Hunyadi family have been arrested too."

"One son dead and the other held captive. The countess must be heartbroken."

The messenger shook his head vigorously. "Erzsébet Szilágyi is unlike any other woman. She won't lie down and cry. She's vowed to avenge the death with blood. The revolt has begun, and she's asking all family, friends and allies to take up arms."

Sándor quickly read the letter that the man had handed him. The countess was calling on him to support the cause against King László and join the rebellion. She reminded him that he was indebted to her for the favour she had done him.

His young relative's brutal treatment and subsequent

execution made Sándor seethe. But go to war against his own people? Even though the king had little Hungarian blood in him and had spent most of his short life outside Hungary, he commanded the loyalty of a large number of native barons, noblemen and ordinary folk. It was a grim dilemma.

Sándor did not return to the great hall where his wife and his friends were celebrating the birth of Imre's son, completely unaware of the news. During all his life, he had avoided getting involved in internal political conflicts. But this time he had to choose a side. He read the letter again and again, but its message remained the same: either join the rebellion or face the wrath of his powerful relatives.

It was all happening at a time when he had just sorted Grossenwald and had put it back into good order. A war would prevent him from making any further progress. And what about the other estate near Szeben? The Hunyadi and Szilágyi influence in Transylvania was so strong that most of the province would certainly side with the rebellion. The only exception would be the Saxon towns. Traditionally, they had always been loyal to the king. As Anna's land had been leased to the Saxon guilds, the rebels could see it as 'enemy territory'. Sándor could not afford to let the estate be attacked and ravaged because it was in Saxon hands.

A knock on the door jolted him out of his deep thoughts. Margit entered his bedchamber, with a concerned look on her face. "What happened? Why did you leave our company so suddenly?"

He showed the letter to her.

She turned pale as soon as she started reading it. "What will you do?"

"I have no choice." His voice quavered. "I must go."

"No. Only send your soldiers. In this way, you will do your duty without putting your own life in danger. You have only recently recovered from serious injury. You must not expose yourself to further peril."

Sándor shook his head. Her suggestion was not feasible. "Erzsébet has requested my personal involvement in the rebellion. I must lead my men and add myself to the list of noblemen who are publicly supporting the Hunyadi-Szilágyi league. All this is part of a game of intimidation, whereby the larger the number of nobles opposing the king the more frightened he will become."

Margit drew a deep breath but did not give up. "And what if you find yourself in a situation where you have to kill people? What if you are ordered to slaughter women and children because they are on the other side of the conflict? This is not a war against the Ottomans. It's something monstrous."

"I know. Perhaps this is the reason I should be there. I must make sure that my men are properly led and do not commit any violent acts."

"True, but have you thought what would happen to you... what would happen to us if the king won? We could lose everything; you could be arrested and imprisoned; you could even be... executed."

"Then, I must make sure that my side wins."

Margit slumped on the bed, pressed her hand against her forehead and closed her eyes.

He sat beside her and put his arm around her waist. "Do not

fret, *angyalom*. I shall not let anything bad happen to us."

But would he be able to keep his promise?

***

Sándor had the flag of the Hunyadi-Szilágyi league raised on the towers of his castle and in his nephew's neighbouring estate. As he was going away for an unknown length of time, he had to ensure that the land under his care would not be attacked by the rebel forces, which were sweeping across the province.

Many Transylvanian towns and villages welcomed the armies of the Hunyadi family, cheering the hero's widow and her brother as they rode through in triumph. The Saxon towns, however, were hostile to the idea of rebellion and remained loyal to the king.

Sándor and his men were initially ordered to march to Guylafehérvár, where they would link up with the rebel army. From there, they would have to move north to the Saxon town of Beszterce, the inhabitants of which had decided to put up resistance against Mihály Szilágyi. However, Sándor wished to secure his nephew's estate first and foremost. He instructed his men to march ahead while he rode towards Szeben, planning to catch up with them later.

He tried to convince the guilds to raise the rebel flag to keep themselves out of harm's way. The estate did not have any significant fortifications and would have been destroyed during an attack. The guild members resided in the town, so it was left to the peasants to look after themselves, the land and the animals. Despite his good arguments, the Saxons would not comply. They considered it an insult even to pretend that they were against the king. After hours of negotiating, a solution was found. They agreed to raise Sándor's family banner, which would be recognisable by the insurgents as friendly and, at the same time, it would not offend the Saxons.

The town of Beszterce was under siege when he arrived. Columns of dark smoke billowed from behind the walls while the cannons were mercilessly pounding the fortifications. Szilágyi's men were close to breaking in.

Sándor gathered his soldiers as they waited for the command to enter the town. "I know you are eager to join the fray. I ask you to restrain yourselves. You are not facing the Ottoman army or the king's mercenaries but defenceless townsfolk."

"They are Saxons. Greedy merchants," one of the soldiers grumbled. "All they care about is money."

Sándor would not allow such behaviour. "Saxon, Hungarian, Székely, Wallachian or Slav, we are all one people," he said sternly. "We were all born in this Transylvanian land that we call home. So, I ask you to treat them with mercy. Yes, we must take the town, but we need not kill and destroy. Do you understand me?"

Within half an hour, the main gate opened as the town had surrendered. The army pushed its way in, burning, plundering and assaulting the inhabitants. Mihály Szilágyi wanted his revenge on the people who dared to stand against him.

"Sir!" Sándor shouted, trying to make himself heard over the hubbub. "We have taken the town. Isn't this what we wanted? Isn't this enough?"

"We must make an example of them. So that the other towns take notice."

Sándor swallowed hard to smother his indignation. His relative was a tough military man, loyal to his family and his homeland. But he was not a good politician. He was sometimes impetuous and rash, even violently tempered. While Lord Jankó was alive, he had Mihály under control and had succeeded in bringing out the best in him. But now, Szilágyi had too much power, and he did not know how to use it wisely.

"I shall not be part of this," Sándor muttered under his breath. He turned his horse around to leave.

"Are you disputing my orders, cousin?" Mihály shouted after him. He had deliberately stressed the word 'cousin' to warn Sándor that any disobedience would be considered betrayal and even more so because of their family connection.

"No, sir!" Sándor turned back again to face Szilágyi. "I only think it's better to win these people over to our cause by showing mercy rather than –"

"I shall let it go this time. You are fortunate to have my sister's favour. But if you do that again..."

Sándor had to yield. He would not participate in any acts of violence, but it was imprudent to disobey his relative's command. A more subtle circumvention was required. "I apologise, sir. My men and I will march on towards the next town and clear the way for you to follow," he told Szilágyi, who did not argue with that.

33
Suffering and Salvation

Margit bit hard on the pillow to muffle her agony. The pain was tearing her insides apart. If only she could scream for help. Yet, she had chosen not to. Death would be a just punishment and, perhaps, even a welcome relief. "Dear God, please take me. I cannot suffer anymore. I have failed my husband again. Please take me so that he can have his freedom." But the pain continued to come in waves, a stark reminder that she was still alive.

She drifted in and out of consciousness several times until the suffering finally ended. She stared at the wall for a long time. Her mind was blank, empty of thoughts and feelings; her body so light as if drained of its blood and devoid of its organs. She just existed like a shadow...

The crackling of the fire brought her back to reality. Groaning, she made a gigantic effort to get out of bed. She staggered about the room with her hand on her forehead. What was she going to do? Warm blood trickled down her thigh. She frantically mopped it with the end of her chemise. Guilt grasped her body and mind. "Clean everything. Make all traces disappear. No one must know."

She stood, shivering in her nakedness, and waited until the fire consumed the bloodied bedsheet, and then she threw in her chemise and underclothes.

A knock on the door made her jump.

"My lady! Are you well? I thought I heard a stir."

Margit gulped. She had deceived Erzsi this time. Although she had continued buying the usual herbs from Marina, she kept replacing them with similar-looking, harmless ones at night. And she had sent her maid on various errands outside the castle to give herself time to procure animal blood, which she then used to feign her monthly bleeding.

For once, she could do without Erzsi's lecturing.

"All is well. I only had a bad dream. Go back to bed." She put her ear against the door, holding her breath until the sound of the maid's footsteps faded and the door of her bedchamber was shut.

A little later, Margit stole down to the family crypt and knelt on the cold stone floor. She silently wept as she placed the small wooden box with the remains of her miscarried child in a dark corner, out of sight. She had lost babies before, but they had been taken from her before she had even seen them. This one, though, she had held in her hands. It was smaller than her little finger. But it was still her child. Trembling, she mumbled a prayer and begged God to admit its innocent soul into Heaven.

Although the storm had passed, Margit kept sinking deeper and deeper into an abyss of despair. Perhaps God was punishing her. Perhaps all those herbs and pessaries that she had used for years had caused so much damage to her insides that her body could not keep a baby anymore. Perhaps she would never be able to have a child again.

Márton's disrespectful behaviour in Sándor's absence made matters worse. The more Margit pleaded with him to stop, the more aggressive he became. It was like a game to him. He enjoyed seeing her distressed and desperate, and that was why he was working hard to drive her over the edge.

But one day she had enough of it. As usual, Márton threw his food at her at the dinner table and shouted obscenities in the Saxon language. Margit remained still while the pieces of meat and vegetables hit her face, and the cursing echoed in her ears. Then, she stood up, gripped his arm and dragged him kicking and screaming all the way up the stairs and into his bedchamber. She sat him on the bed and gave him a loud smack in the face. The boy pressed his hand against the red mark on his cheek but did not make a sound.

"Listen to me," she said in a calm but menacing voice. "You are a guest here and you must show respect."

Márton spat at her. But before he savoured his 'victory', another slap landed on his face. "Your mother asked us to look after you. But be sure that if you don't behave, she will learn all about it."

"You are a filthy bitch!" he shouted, at the top of his lungs.

"So, you can speak Hungarian when you wish to?"

He sprang to his feet. His eyes searched around the room for a way to escape, but Margit sat him down forcefully again. "I'll tell my uncle that you smote me," he whined.

"And I'll tell him that you have been insolent and bold. Let us see whom he is going to believe."

"Me. He loves me because I am his only heir."

"You will never inherit from him if he finds out how much mischief you make every time he goes away."

"He will leave everything to me because you can't have children."

Margit tugged at the skirt of her kirtle, barely holding herself from slapping him again. "Not necessarily. He can decide to leave the estate to the king instead. There is no law against that."

Márton's brow furrowed defiantly.

"If you think that you can be a pig without suffering the consequences because you are the only heir to the estate, think again," Margit continued. "I shall lock you in your bedchamber with no food until you reflect on your behaviour towards me and the servants and apologise."

The boy snorted.

Exasperated, Margit folded her arms. "You don't believe me?"

A mocking smile played on his lips.

As insolent as his mother! He needed to be put in his place.

Margit searched through the bunch of keys that hung from her girdle, picking out the one to his chamber. She headed to the door, listening for his reaction behind her; but there was only silence. With her hand on the handle, she lingered for a few heartbeats. Nothing. She exited the room, slowly, still hoping for some response, which did not happen.

As soon as she closed the door, however, and turned the key in the hole, there came the ouburst. "No, don't do that!"

Several moments later, a bang on the door. "Please! I'll be good."

She paused.

Another bang; this one stronger, perhaps a kick. "Please, open!"

Margit smiled to herself. She believed she had won this battle. But a troubling thought crossed her mind.

Unlocking the door, she opened it with caution and slid in through the narrow opening lest he had hidden behind it, waiting to pounce on her or to escape. To her relief, Márton stood with his head hung low. As he raised his eyes, she saw pleading and desperation, and his face flushed with dejection while he muttered, "Ummm."

With hands on her hips, Margit scrutinised his expression. "So, what is it that you wish to say to me?"

His gaze dropped to the floor again. "I am... sorry."

"What?" She leaned towards him. "I can't hear anything. You are mumbling."

"I am sorry!" His voice was loud and clear this time.

"Very well. You can go and finish your meal. But make sure it ends up in your belly and not on my face."

After that conversation, Márton changed his behaviour. He became quiet and withdrew into himself. He did not bother anyone and only spoke when he was spoken to.

But that incident was Margit's salvation too – as if someone had thrown her a lifeline and had pulled her out of a nightmarish quagmire. She had not felt so alive for a long time. All she wished now was for her husband to come home safe so that they could continue their life together. And perhaps, finally, to be able to have the child she wanted so much.

34

A Short Break

Summer 1457

Margit paced to and fro in the entrance hall of the keep, wringing her hands, until Imre returned.

She grasped his arm. "What's happening? Are the miners still causing a disturbance?"

"Yes, my lady. They've gathered in the town square now, shouting and threatening to plunder the shops and warehouses. Master Kendi and I tried to talk to them, but they don't listen to us. The townsfolk are terrified. Shall I send my men down there?"

Margit shook her head. "No. They are not to blame. This accursed rebellion is the reason. The king's men abandoned the mine and ran away. No metals have been transported to the royal mint for months. We have received no rent this year. There is no work for these people. And now they demand to be paid even though they are sitting idle."

"Is there news from your husband yet?"

"No. I don't believe he has received my message. If he had, he would be here now... I cannot tarry any longer. I must deal with it myself."

She rode to the town with Imre by her side and an escort of ten foot-soldiers. But for this crowd of twenty to thirty miners, the square was empty and the shops closed, with their doors and windows securely locked.

"When's your husband coming back?" one of the men shouted.

"I don't know, but I am here to talk to you on his behalf." The angry stares of the crowd were unnerving. She took slow, deep breaths, clenching the reins in her hands.

"He's out there killing his fellow Transylvanians, instead of looking after his people. We want our wages!"

A small group of men rushed forward in a threatening manner. The soldiers formed a shield wall in front of Margit and Imre. But so much sudden movement made her palfrey jerk under her so violently that she lost her grip on the reins. She desperately clutched at the pommel of the saddle. Her heart raced. She was going to hit the ground any moment now.

But no... she did not. Imre grabbed the bridle with his steady hand. Bending over, he whispered in the horse's ear and stroked the animal between the eyes until it calmed down.

"Stand back or you'll be arrested!" he shouted at the miners.

The men settled at last, but their piercing stares did not relent.

"Send your representatives to the castle tomorrow at Nones. I shall do my best to help you." Margit had regained her composure in a surprisingly short space of time. "Drive them home if they don't leave voluntarily," she ordered Imre. "But don't hurt anyone. We are not barbarians." She turned her horse around and rode away under the derogatory shouts and whistling of the crowd.

"You heard the lady," Imre shouted. "Now, go back to your village until tomorrow!"

Margit used some of the tax money, which she had not sent to the king because of the rebellion, to pay the miners and prevent them from creating further trouble. But this could not continue for long.

***

In early July, Sándor returned. Accompanied by his squire and two more men, he rode through the castle gate, his helmet and steel pauldrons glinting in the afternoon sunshine. He rushed into the house and called for Margit. The servants told him that she was not there, but they were not sure where she had gone.

This gave him some time to take off his armour and clean himself. The cold, refreshing bath was more than welcome after such a long journey. After he washed and shaved, he looked at his face in a well-polished hand mirror. The memories of the day when he had come home to his dying father, seventeen years earlier, appeared in his mind's eye.

He still remembered his younger self from all that time ago: fitter, stronger, healthier and full of life. And now, forty years old and after fighting countless battles and narrowly escaping death twice, he was but a shadow of what he used to be. Although he had no grey hair yet, his face was drawn and hollow-cheeked, and the scar under his right eye appeared much nastier than it really was.

He glanced down at his scarred and bruised body. How much more pain could he take? He needed to stay home and recover, instead of taking part in rebellions and more fights. But war was in his blood. It was something he could not live without. When he was on the battlefield, his strength, skill and resolve miraculously kept coming back, making him feel young and powerful again.

As he touched the two deep scars on his left side, the ones caused by his brother's murderous attempt, he closed his eyes and winced. Fate had not been kind to him. He had lost his mother when he was but a little boy; he was not home in time to prevent his father's death; he had seen his only child die right in front of him; and finally, his brother had betrayed him and had to be killed by his soldiers. Perhaps this was a way of God telling him to stop running away and look after the people he loved instead. Every single death was a warning and yet, he had not listened. He kept ignoring the signs. Margit was the only one he had left now. Would he end up losing her too if he continued his stubborn obsession with war?

He threw some more cold water on his face, trying to banish those dark thoughts from his mind. Then, he dressed and went downstairs to the great hall to wait for his wife.

Margit and Erzsi returned at sundown. While the maid went upstairs to light the fire in her lady's chamber and prepare her bed for the night, Margit was stopped by a female servant, who told her that she had a visitor.

"Who is it at this hour? I'm tired."

"I don't know, m' lady. He didn't give his name. But he said to tell you that he's tall and pleasing to the eye."

"I don't have time for games!" Margit snapped at the woman, who was trying hard to keep a straight face.

"Please go to the great hall, m' lady. You shouldn't keep this man waiting."

"What on earth is all this about?"

She had just taken off her veil but did not bother putting it back on and walked into the great hall with her head uncovered.

Her husband was standing there with a broad smile on his face.

She let out a shriek and ran into his arms. "Thank God, you have returned!"

"The messenger had trouble finding me," Sándor said apologetically. "The army kept moving from place to place. The moment I received your message, I dropped everything and rode here in full armour, almost killing my poor horse. The fighting has stopped for now, but I may need to leave soon if I receive new orders. Is there trouble?"

"Yes. Production in the mine has stalled; the king has not paid; the workers are restless. I was able to sort it out for now, but it will not last."

"Do not fret, *angyalom*. I shall deal with it tomorrow." He smiled and stroked her face. His voice deepened; his breathing became short and fast. "My beautiful lady, you cannot believe how much I have missed you." He took her by the hand and hurriedly led her up the stairs.

"Why are you in such a rush?" Margit asked. They were running along the upstairs corridor.

When they reached the staircase that led to the next floor and their quarters, Sándor stopped and gently pushed her against the wall. He kissed her on the face, lips and neck. At the same time, he lifted her skirts and slid his hand between her legs.

She giggled. He was going to take her right there, in plain sight. Recklessly impulsive and highly inappropriate. But she could not resist him. His touch sent a warm wave of desire surging through her veins. She closed her eyes and surrendered to him. The two of them were equal in all matters except one: when it came to lovemaking, he held all the power.

A muffled laugh came from the shadows.

Margit opened her eyes. "Stop!" She pushed her husband away.

"What's the matter?"

"I heard something."

They both turned around. Márton appeared at the turn of the corridor. The light of the torch above him illuminated his face, distorted by a strange and rather disturbing smile.

"Leave!" Sándor shouted. "Begone! Disappear!"

Márton did not move but kept staring at them. "Now!" Sándor shouted again. Finally, the boy spun on his heel and ran out of sight.

Sándor shook his head. "Come!" He gripped her hand abruptly and climbed the stairs, towing her along behind him.

"So, what's happening out there?" Margit asked later that night as she snuggled up to him and rested her head on his shoulder. "We have little news. Only whatever passing travellers and merchants can tell us."

"It is not good. The king has fled to Vienna, taking young Mátyás Hunyadi with him as a hostage. The realm is in disarray. We are fortunate that the Turks have not attacked us yet."

"Did you do a lot of fighting?"

"In the beginning I did as little as possible. Mihály soon noticed that and wanted to know why. I had enough and told him that I'd rather face the king's mercenaries than defenceless peasants and townsfolk. And so, my wish was granted. We were ordered to march towards Buda, with the royal army blocking our way. I really had to fight then."

"And when must you go back?"

"As soon as I can. My cousins are negotiating Mátyás's release presently. If they fail, the fighting may start again. But do not fret. I shall resolve our problems here first."

Margit sighed and averted her eyes.

Sándor brushed her cheek with the back of his hand. "I know you are distressed, *angyalom*. Sadly, I'm indebted to my relatives. If there were a way for us to support ourselves and our land without their help, I would not need to fight. So, until this war is over, I cannot do otherwise."

She turned to him with a bittersweet smile. "I understand. Perhaps we should take back control of the mine. The king has not paid. Until the current situation is resolved, we should look for other buyers, who may be willing to offer a good price."

He pondered for a moment. "You are right. I shall discuss it with my counsellors tomorrow, and we shall see... Now, let us sleep. I am spent."

***

Sándor studied the faces of his counsellors as they sat at the long table in the great hall. Lowered eyes, pursed lips, raised eyebrows, head-shaking, mumbling. He could understand why. The rebellion had cost the whole area a lot. The miners had no work; the business of tradesmen and merchants was slow; the farmers' products could not reach the markets in towns due to insecurity on the roads... The list was long. And if his own large estate suffered, their smaller ones would feel the pinch even more.

His new steward rose and approached him. Kálmán Havasi was old Péter's second son. A timid man of about Sándor's age, with a ruddy beardless face and narrow dark eyes. He had inherited the position after his father's death just before the rebellion broke out.

"The accounts of the last three months, my lord," he said in a whisper.

Sándor skimmed through the papers. Kálmán's neat handwriting distracted him, momentarily. It looked similar to his own. And his well-organised recording method was a welcome surprise. But the numbers did not lie. The situation was dire.

"Gentlemen, we are not the only ones facing such problems," he tried to appease his counsellors. "We are at war. I have seen the devastation with my own eyes from Szeben to the plains of the Tisza river. Until we have a strong king on the throne, the realm will suffer. This is why we have rebelled. King László has run away, letting the barons do whatever they please. They do not care about Hungary. Most of them have not even bothered to defend her against the Ottomans. I do not say that the Hunyadi and Szilágyi families are saints either, but at least they have fought and shed their blood for Hungary. They are our people, and we must support them."

"What are our chances of winning the war?" Kendi asked. "Will it be soon?"

"I don't know. Neither side is any closer to winning. I fear that if the negotiations fail, Transylvania and eastern Hungary might separate from the rest of the kingdom."

"That would be a disaster!" Josef Roth exclaimed, and all the others agreed, bobbing their heads.

Sándor nervously ran his hand through his hair. Everyone was waiting for his response. "Regardless of what is happening out there, we must find a way to survive."

"How, my lord?" Kendi said. "We're totally isolated, travelling is unsafe, and no one wishes to come here to buy our produce."

"Correct. This is why we need to take our products to them."

"This won't be possible. We don't have enough soldiers to escort us anywhere."

"We can use our people," Imre proposed. "If we give armour, weapons and horses to some of them, they'll look like soldiers. No one will know the difference."

"And what if they have to fight? They'll be slaughtered," Kendi countered.

"Who will be foolish enough to attack a small army? Plus some of the men are already trained in fighting."

"Imre may be right," Sándor said. "I cannot pull my soldiers out of the war; at least not while I depend upon my relatives for support. But if we can stand on our own feet, I shall be able to bring them home. The biggest reason for our troubles is that the mine is at the king's disposal. My family had royal permission to sell one third of the metals to whomever paid the highest price until I made an agreement with Lord Jankó and King Władysław. But now they are both dead. King László has left, and he has not paid us this year's rent. He has broken the contract. We should take back the mine and look for buyers."

After some thinking and discussion, everyone agreed that this was the best course of action. Sándor would bring samples of smelted gold and silver to the goldsmiths and craftsmen of Szeben and other towns and would attempt to negotiate a contract with them. The plan was not guaranteed to work, but they had to try.

***

Sándor set off the next day. He needed to secure a successful trade agreement so that he could return to his soldiers. Margit and Márton travelled with him. His wife was to continue taking care of business during his absence; for this reason, she insisted on accompanying him. As for his nephew, Sándor wanted to show him his land near Szeben and let the boy have a glimpse of the opportunities and difficulties that he would have to face in the future as a landowner.

On the way to Szeben, they stopped in Gyulafehérvár to visit the grave of János Hunyadi. In the cold and dimly lit crypt of Szent Mihály's Cathedral, Sándor crossed himself, knelt and said a prayer for the soul of his hero. The good, old memories came back to his mind. Despite his faults, Lord Jankó was one of the great men of Hungary. The void he had left behind was not easy to fill. Barely a year after his death, the kingdom had been divided again by bitter civil war. No one knew what the future would bring.

During the days that followed, the discussions and meetings went on and on in Szeben, but no positive outcome was reached. The guilds were not willing to enter into any type of contract with Sándor for fear that either the current king or any future one would wish to bring the mine back under royal control. But there was also another reason why they did not wish to trade with him: a political one. As a member of the Szilágyi family and known to have sided with the insurgents, he was viewed with suspicion by the Saxons, who had remained loyal to King László.

Under pressure for time and with his confidence waning, Sándor was losing his patience. "It's not working. I cannot convince them to trade with me."

"Don't give up," Margit tried to encourage him. "There are other places you can go and look for business. This town seems to have suffered because of the rebellion. They are a close-knit community. If one of the guilds has a problem with you, they will all shun you. Why don't you try Segesvár? They were your biggest clients before. They know you and may wish to trade again."

"Too far away. Don't forget we need to transport the products there ourselves. It's too dangerous, especially when the escorts are not proper soldiers but disguised peasants."

But the failure and disappointment they experienced in Szeben was a blessing in disguise. Returning home, they followed a different route and stopped in another Saxon town called Sebes. It was a smaller place, severely damaged by a number of Turkish and Wallachian attacks some years earlier. The town was struggling to get back on its feet. This was exactly what gave Sándor the idea that he could find trade partners there.

Their jewellers and weapon-makers were eager to buy the precious metals of his mine, at least for the short term and on condition that the products would be transported to them. They were in direct competition with nearby Szeben, and due to their past misfortunes, they had not been able to secure any good contracts with suppliers. An agreement was signed. The price they were to pay was not as high as Sándor had hoped for, but at least it would provide an income for him in the near future.

When they returned to Szentimre, new orders from Mihály had arrived. The negotiations had failed, and Sándor needed to re-join his men.

On his last day at home, he spent as much time as he could with his wife. He did not know when he would be back again, and so the two of them expressed their love in an intense and emotional manner.

"Dear husband, I beg of you, stay one more day," Margit pleaded, her eyes overflowing with tears.

He could not do that. But it broke his heart to see her cry.

Unable to utter a word, he nodded in agreement, just to make her feel a little better. He cradled her in his arms until she fell asleep.

He did not keep his promise. To avoid any more distressing moments, he left quietly before the sun was up and while she was still sleeping.

As he rode out of the town gate in the faint early-morning light, he turned his head back to cast one last glance at Sasfészek. His wife's presence still lingered about him. The raw scratches of her passionate embrace still stung his back and shoulders; her scent pervaded his skin and hair; the taste of her kisses clung to his lips; and her warm breath and whispers still caressed his ears.

With the passing of time, it was becoming harder and harder for him to leave his home and his beloved behind and put his life in great peril for the sake of his country – a country which, during the last twelve months, had changed so much that he feared it was only a matter of time before it would come apart at the seams and disappear from the face of the earth.

35
Surprising News

Winter 1457/58

Winter had set in for good. The heavy December snow blanketed the entire land. Trudging ankle-deep and with their breaths visible like puffs of steam coming out of their mouths and nostrils, men and horses entered the courtyard at Sasfészek.

It was good to be home again. Imre was the first one to welcome Sándor with a hearty embrace and an important question: "Have we won the war?"

"You could say so. The king is dead."

"*Krisztus*! He was only seventeen. He wasn't murdered, was he?"

"No. Some illness, they said."

"So, Hungary is again without a king."

They climbed the steps and entered the keep. Sándor unstrapped his fur-trimmed cape and gave it to a servant while a page knelt at his feet and removed the spurs. He was still wearing his armour and could not wait to get out of it. But Imre was so anxious to hear more news that he followed Sándor all the way up the stairs. "What will happen now?"

"Erzsébet and Mihály are working to promote Mátyás as the new candidate for the throne," Sándor explained. "The boy is held in Prague. They are trying to gather enough support and money to ransom him out of the Bohemian governor's hands."

"*Szerelmem*, you are home!" Margit ran to him from the other side of the corridor. Even the jingling of keys and other metal objects that hung from her girdle sounded cheerful and welcoming. She gave him a tight hug and would not let go for a good while.

Sándor winked at Imre. "I shall talk to you later."

He followed her into the bedchamber. He always enjoyed having her help him take off his armour, instead of a servant or his squire. There was something sweet in the way she stood on the tips of her toes to reach the straps on the top of his pauldrons. He pushed her veil back, bent his head towards hers and breathed in the familiar smell of her hair.

She put on a brave face as she removed his brigandine, teetering under its weight. Amused by the sight, Sándor helped her carry it to a corner, where all the other pieces were also laid.

Margit brought him a change of clean clothes. "It was about time you came home," she said as soon as he took off his shirt. "You need to eat some good food. I can count all your ribs."

Sándor bobbed his head. "Yes. I have been away for too long. I have missed our cook's delicious dishes. I could only dream of them while I was out there." He stopped and touched her face with his fingertips. Her smile was the most beautiful sight in the world. "I have also missed the warmth of my wife's embrace."

He drew her into his arms and kissed her while he ran his hand up her body. Her figure felt curvier than usual; her breasts larger and harder than he remembered. But that was just a fleeting thought. There was only one thing he wanted now. He led her to the bed, where she lay on her back, and he knelt astride her. His mouth found hers in a long, hungry kiss. Fumbling under her skirts, his hand sought the soft skin of her thigh and then slowly glided upwards.

Margit grasped his hand and pushed it away.

"I'm sorry," he said, surprised, as his face heated in embarrassment. "Whatever I have done to you, I'm sorry."

She looked equally perplexed by his reaction. "Why are you apologising?"

"You do not wish to lie with me. I must have done something to distress you. Or..." He sniffed his body under the shirt. "Is it because I stink? I have not washed for weeks."

She giggled. "No, no, you don't stink so much. And you have not done anything wrong." She took a deep breath. "I did not write to you about it. I did not wish to trouble you while you were away... I... I am with child."

Sándor nearly fell off the bed. "What?"

"Since your last visit, five months ago."

Only then did he notice the swell of her belly.

A shadow flitted across Margit's face. "Are you not pleased with the news, *kedvesem*?"

He sat at the edge of the bed. For a few moments, everything around him became a blur and then slowly cleared up again. He struggled to get his voice back as he turned to face her. "Of course I am pleased. But I am also worried. You are putting your life in danger. The physician clearly said that you should not have any more children."

Margit fiddled with one of her plaits, her hands shaking slightly. "That was a long time ago. It may be different this time. Apart from feeling a little tired at times, I have had no trouble thus far."

He gripped her wrists and squeezed them. "I don't want to lose you, Margit. You are the only person I love that I have left in the whole world. Are you not afraid either?"

"Listen," she said in a soft and calm voice. "I thought about this, and I made my decision. You went to war so many times to protect your homeland and your family. Neither you nor I ever knew if you would return alive; and yet you went. This is now my battle to save my family. I shall not let Anna's son or any king take our land."

"This is foolish! What if both you and the child die in the end?"

"At least, I would have tried. And you would be free to marry again."

He let go of her hands and stood up. "You make me regret being loyal to you," he said bitterly. "Had I accepted to have a child with another woman, this would not have happened. Is this how you repay me for respecting you?"

Margit burst into tears.

Sándor instinctively bit his tongue as though to punish himself for his harsh words. He sat on the bed and put his arm around her shoulders. "Forgive me, *angyalom*, for what I said. I did not mean to distress you. I must admit, I'm so afraid. I could not bear to lose you. Please, calm yourself. I shall do whatever I can to make sure nothing happens to you. I shall be by your side all the time. I promise."

Margit stopped crying and wiped her tears with the end of her sleeve. She rested her head on his chest. "I am afraid. But I have made my choice. There is no way back."

"You are so brave, *szerelmem*. You put me to shame."

***

Margit waited until the messenger had left. "What's the news?"

Sándor silently read the letter and smiled. "Good news this time. My cousins have succeeded in gaining the support of most of the opposing barons in their plan to make young Mátyás the new king. The assembly of the higher nobility and Church leadership will meet in Buda in three weeks to decide. To make sure the barons and bishops will do their duty, Mihály has called his army to follow him to the capital. He has asked me to join."

She frowned. "Is he expecting a fight?"

"He says we shall be there to ensure that any decision will be made for the good of Hungary."

"Oh! I hope there will not be bloodshed if the decision goes against his wishes."

Sándor tossed the letter on the desk. There was a fight inside him. He wanted to go to Buda, but he would not forgive himself if anything bad happened to her while he was away.

"You should go."

Her words made him look askance at her.

"You fought for our homeland and our faith all your life. I know you are eager to join your old comrades and march again in glory. This is your chance to be part of such a historic moment. I would go with you, but sadly I cannot travel now. But I shall pray that the boy is elected king and that your service to his father and to him is deservedly recognised."

Sándor stood in silence. She had always tried to keep him home; yet, right at that moment, she was urging him to do the opposite.

Margit inclined her head towards him. "You are wavering. Why?"

"Umm... I do not wish to leave you on your own."

Her face opened into a loving smile. She approached him, raised her hand and caressed his face. "Do not fret, *szerelmem*. All will be well. I am not due for another four months. God willing, you will be back by then."

And so, once again, Sándor put on the battle armour and mounted his horse. He took ten of his men with him. They had fought alongside him the longest and deserved to be part of those important moments. Imre was one of them. He wore the armour and his old friend's family coat of arms with pride.

It warmed Sándor's heart to see all the Transylvanian veterans – noblemen, knights and ordinary soldiers – march together with the new generation of warriors under the Hunyadi and Szilágyi banners. Men who had taken part in and survived all those legendary battles, riding or walking alongside the younger ones, some of them their sons or even grandsons. They all had one thing in common: their love for their homeland and their hero, János Hunyadi, whose boy was now a favourite candidate for the throne. Thousands of them joined the lesser nobility and ordinary citizens from all over the kingdom, who had gathered in the streets of Pest as the barons and prelates prepared to vote in the castle of Buda across the river.

Inside the castle, Mihály Szilágyi and his supporters negotiated with the delegates. Outside, standing on the frozen Danube, the crowd chanted Mátyás's name. The breaths of thousands rose in the air, creating a cloud of steam. Despite the cold, Sándor felt intoxicated by the enthusiasm and cheerfulness that surrounded him. His heart was beating fast in anticipation of a better, united future.

"This is unbelievable!" he shouted.

"I hope our blood wasn't shed for nothing," Imre said. "I hope the 'boys' up there will listen to the voice of the people."

"Oh, they will, *barátom*. Or else they will not come out of the city alive."

It was not too long before Mihály appeared on the castle walls. Everybody fell silent as they waited with bated breath to hear what he was about to announce.

"*Vivat Matthias Rex!*" he shouted at the top of his lungs.

Still, he was too high up and too far away to be heard by everyone. He signalled to the four soldiers who were standing by him. They unfurled a massive flag of the Hunyadi family crest and hung it from the wall. At the sight of the raven and golden ring, the crowd erupted in cheers so loud that they could shatter the ice on the Danube.

Celebrations in Buda and Pest continued all day and all night – people embracing each other, singing and dancing in the streets.

"The people see this as their victory," Sándor said. "But the truth is that the boy's election today was nothing but the result of intense negotiations, complemented by bribery and intimidation. That was the reason we came here all the way from Transylvania. It was a show of strength that no baron could ignore."

Imre shrugged. "I'm not one for politics, but I know that we're all tired of fighting. Hungary suffers. The only person who can unite all sides is young Mátyás. So, let the people have their victory. And let's join in and celebrate with a few drinks."

"I must return to Margit. I am worried about her. You can stay as long as you like, but I must leave."

36
Love and Pain

March 1458

The door of the chapel had been left ajar. Sándor crept in, silently like a mouse. Margit was there alone, praying on her knees. With a flowing white veil covering her hair, she was the image of the statue of the Virgin Mary, which watched over her from the left side. For so many years, his dear wife had tolerated his sins and vices, his mistakes and misjudgements, his long absences, his selfishness and outbursts of bad temper. If he had become a better man, it was all thanks to her. She had the kindness and patience of a saint.

He knelt and bowed his head. He did not wish to intrude on her private moments. Even Erzsi had left her alone. But he could not bear to be away from her, not even for an hour. He had spent so long fighting in all those wars and battles. And now the time they had left together could come to an end at any moment. His heart ached. "Dear Lord, please protect her. Keep her safe."

Margit finished praying and crossed herself. She tried to stand up but did not make it.

Sándor was by her side in a heartbeat. "Wait! Let me help you."

She turned around, surprised. "I did not hear you enter."

He extended his arm. "Here. Lean on me."

Grunting, she propped herself up. "I have become so heavy."

"Come. I shall take you to your bedchamber."

She folded her arms and inclined her head towards him. "Are you my shadow? You follow me everywhere... Dear husband, do not fret. I feel tired at times, but I am not ill."

She walked away with proud and resolute steps as if she wanted to prove her words even more emphatically.

***

Margit let out a sigh. "The pain is growing stronger every time. It seems this little one is eager to come into the world before it's time."

Erzsi handed her a steaming wooden cup. "Here, my lady. Drink your herbs. They'll help with the pain."

Margit took a few, careful sips and winced. "It tastes terrible. I don't want it." She thrust the cup back at her maid. "You can go now." Pressing her hand against her belly, she drew a deep breath.

"Sit down and rest," Sándor entreated.

Her head was about to burst. "I cannot bear being locked in any longer. I wish to go outside."

"It's freezing cold. You will get ill."

"I shall put the fur blanket on me. Do not fear." She made a move towards the double door that led to the small terrace, but he stepped in front of her, blocking her way. "You cannot keep me inside all the time," she complained. "I need to breathe some air. I spend most of the day in this chamber. I am not a prisoner!"

"Very well. I shall bring a chair for you to sit on."

Margit stood by and waited as he opened the door. He carried a wooden chair for her and a folding stool for him and placed them close to the wall, where it was a little more sheltered from the wind. They were three stories up, and the breeze whipped his hair across his face. He stopped for a moment to catch his breath.

Wrapped in the blanket, Margit walked out onto the terrace and sat down.

After an extremely harsh winter, the mountain tops were still white with snow, its brilliance contrasting with the verdure of the trees on the slopes. The sun played hide-and-seek among the grey clouds, which rolled eastwards. The escaping rays caused the landscape to vibrate in this game of light and shadow.

Sándor leaned on the parapet wall. He gazed into the distance awhile and then turned around to her. "I have been to many places, but there is nowhere more beautiful than here. Nothing compares to my homeland. I have her in my heart wherever I go."

"Is this the poet-warrior talking now?"

They both laughed heartily.

He sat down beside her. He took her hand and held it in his, stroking it gently.

"I'm so happy," Margit said. "I wish this moment lasted forever."

"Are you not afraid of what is to come?"

Her chest tightened. "Of course I am. But I have made my peace with God, and I am prepared for my fate, whatever it may be. The only regret I have is that I wasted more than three years keeping you away because of a foolish grudge."

"That was a long time ago, and you were right to be angry with me."

He leaned towards her and kissed her. She responded by putting her hand on the side of his face and holding him close to her.

"*Angyalom*," Sándor said, "not one day of my life does pass without me thanking my father for choosing you as my bride. I swear to God, you are the only woman that I have ever loved and that I ever shall." His voice quavered. "You have always been by my side, no matter what. I am so sorry for all the heartbreak I caused you over the years." He turned away from her and looked to the other side.

Something moved inside her. "Dear husband, are you... crying?"

He did not respond.

"Sándor! Look at me!" she said in a firm voice.

He slowly turned around. His wet eyes glistened deep green like the forests that surrounded them.

Margit thought her heart was going to melt. Despite his faults, he was a good man, a loving and loyal husband. He deserved every sacrifice on her part. "I shall speak to you in a language that you will understand. You stood against thousands of enemy soldiers and did not falter. You saw death all around you on the battlefield and did not break. You were ready to give your life for the ones you love. And so am I now. Do not feel sorry for me. This is my war, and I shall fight it with bravery and dignity, in the same way that you would. And if I die in the end, you should be proud of me as I would be proud of you if you had fallen in battle like a hero... Now, dry your tears, and let us go back inside. It's too cold out here."

***

Margit's screams woke Sándor up. He opened his eyes and fumbled about in the dark to find his bearings. He had fallen asleep in his study, still dressed.

He rushed to her bedchamber and found her kneeling on the floor, in a small pool of liquid. "What happened? Are you bleeding?"

"No. It's only water. Call for help. The baby is coming."

He and Erzsi lifted her up and helped her lie on the bed. Dragoslava went to fetch the midwife, who arrived a little later with one more female servant.

"Summon the physician, just in case," Sándor asked Imre, who had followed the women.

The midwife instructed the other women to bring various things that would be needed: clean towels, hot water, pots and vessels, herbs, oils and other items that Sándor had never heard of. She rolled up her sleeves and moved her hands on Margit's belly, pressing in different spots. "The baby is coming the wrong way."

"Again?" Erzsi exclaimed. "She's going to suffer like the first time."

The midwife smeared some oil on her hands and rubbed them

together until it was spread evenly. "I'll try to make it move around."

Sándor stood back a bit, his body numb and his brain frozen.

Erzsi turned to him. "Please, my lord, you must leave. It's improper for any man to be present at a birth unless he's a physician."

Utter nonsense! "No! I wish to be with her. I don't care if it's appropriate or not. Tell me what to do to help."

"You can't do anything, really. Perhaps sit and talk to her. Try to keep her mind occupied so that she doesn't feel the pain so much."

He sat on a chair by the bed. He held her hand and spoke comforting words to her.

Three whole hours passed without any result. The women had tried everything: bathing, rubbing, warm towels on her belly, herbal drinks, oils, prayers, charms... They had even made her walk around her chamber awhile. But nothing seemed to work. Margit was dripping wet with sweat and tears, vomiting and still screaming in pain.

The veins in Sándor's temples were throbbing. He could do nothing to alleviate her suffering. Every time blood-tinged fluids came out of her, a powerful wave of nausea overcame him. He could not bear it anymore. He ran out of the room in a panic, slamming the door behind him.

The physician arrived just at that moment, together with Imre. They were both out of breath. "I'm sorry, my lord. I was at the mine, treating a man who had a terrible accident."

Sándor acknowledged him with a nod and stepped aside to let him pass by and enter the bedchamber.

Imre looked at him anxiously. "What's going on?"

Sándor raised his hand, signalling to his friend to stay away. He went to a corner and threw up. He leaned against the wall, his chest and throat burning as if he had swallowed molten iron. "Dear God, help us."

Margit screamed much louder than before. Then, there was silence until the physician emerged from her chamber in an agitated state. "My lord, I'm sorry to say this, but I must cut the child out of your wife."

Sándor could hear the words, but he could not speak no matter how hard he tried. His brain had gone completely blank. Even his breathing stopped for a brief moment.

"Is there any way we can avoid this?" Imre intervened.

"No, sir. The poor woman is... is dying. Her womb has ruptured, she has fallen in a swoon, and the baby is in terrible distress. I'm sorry, I can do nothing to save her... Nothing... I can only try to save the child, but I must act at once, and I need his permission."

"Sándor!" Imre grabbed him by the shoulders and shook him forcefully. "Please answer!"

He came back to reality. "Do whatever you have to do," he whispered.

The physician answered him only with a nod and rushed back inside.

"I'll fetch the priest," Imre said.

Sándor closed his eyes. He needed courage, like never before, to support her in her last moments. With a quiet prayer on his lips and inhaling deeply, he entered the bedchamber.

Erzsi was crying loudly in Dragoslava's arms. The physician was in the process of making an incision on Margit's abdomen with his surgical knife. The midwife and the servant were holding towels to absorb the blood.

Margit woke up and screamed.

Seeing her in such pain, Sándor felt paralysed by a deathly chill. But he soon came to his senses, flew to her bedside and took her hand in his. "I'm here, *angyalom*."

She grasped his sleeve with her other hand, holding on to it as if to her very life that was slipping away.

"You are so brave, *szerelmem*," he said softly, striving to hide the fear in his voice.

Her grip weakened with each breath she drew. Twisted in agony, her face paled into a transparent whiteness. Her wailing cut through Sándor's soul like the sharpest blade. His heart beat at a frantic rate. Everything around him faded into obscurity. It was just the two of them, alone in the world. Nothing else mattered...

And then, the baby cried.

"It's a girl. Thanks be to God." The midwife's relieved voice lit a faint spark of joy amidst the gloom.

Momentarily, Sándor's heart filled with hope. "Did you hear that, *angyalom*?" he said, gazing into her clouded eyes. "We have a child."

A trace of happiness flitted across Margit's face. Pulling him nearer to her, and with heavy, gasping sighs, she uttered, "Please... look after her... Make sure she... takes a... good husband... just like... I did."

Sándor embraced her shivering body. His face touched hers; his burning tears mingled with her own into rivulets of sorrow and loss. He kissed her on the forehead. "I shall see you again, *szerelmem*... In another life, where there is no pain... where there is no death."

Margit smiled at him before her eyes closed, their lids drooping as she lapsed into unconsciousness. Her chest rose and fell slowly, then rose no more.

The chamber suddenly turned cold, empty, hostile.

Laying her down gently, Sándor stared at her, numbed by grief and guilt. Every fibre of his soul cursed at God for not sparing her, for not taking him in her place. He was the sinner. It was all his doing. If only he had not allowed himself to be seduced by that wicked Anna; if only he had remained longer by his wife's side instead of going off to wars. And, above all, if only he had protected their son, she would not have sacrificed her life to preserve his bloodline.

The priest arrived too late. All he could do was read a prayer for Margit's soul and ask God to accept her in Heaven.

Then, they all departed in gloomy silence, taking the baby with them.

Sándor, however, could not leave her side. Holding her in his arms, he stroked her face, her hair, her shoulders. He kissed her a hundred times. He talked to her about the past, about the future, about their love, about their child... He was going to protect her. No one was going to hurt her anymore...

When the servants returned in the morning to clean her and prepare her for the funeral, he still would not let go. "Get lost, all of you! Demons and vultures! You will not lay your hands on her!"

Then, Imre walked in. "You can't keep her here, *barátom*. She must have a proper Christian funeral so that her soul can rest in peace."

Why wouldn't they leave him alone? All he wanted was to be with her. He would not let anyone take her away from him.

"Do you hear me?" Imre shouted.

At length, Sándor turned towards him. "What?"

"If you truly love her, you'll let her go. You don't wish her soul to roam around tormented. She must rest in peace."

"Yes, yes, of course." His friend was right. Margit's place was in Heaven. He had no right to prevent that.

The last thing he heard was Imre calling the servants in. He closed his eyes and lost himself in the dark forest of oblivion.

37
Into the Darkness

The voice came from far away. "Wake up! Wake up!"

Sándor ignored it. Whoever was calling him had to wait.

He was in a beautiful place, lying on fresh-smelling grass, under an apple tree; his head resting in Margit's lap. A few transparent clouds dotted the bright, blue sky. The summer breeze brushed like silk across his face. His wife's soft fingers ran through his hair. She was singing an old song about a soldier coming home...

"Sándor! Please, wake up!" The voice was louder now, more demanding of his attention. "Wake up!" It sounded familiar.

The dream faded. He slowly opened his eyes. The face in front of him was blurred. He blinked. "Imre. What is it?"

"You must prepare for the funeral."

"Whose funeral?"

"Your lady's, *kedves barátom*. She's in the chapel. The service starts in two hours. You must get dressed. You must look your best for her as you say your last farewell."

"Margit." Sándor sat up on the bed and covered his face with his hands. It was still so hard to believe that she was gone.

A short time later, he immersed himself in a tub filled with cold water. He stayed there until he felt the iciness burning his skin. The pain was welcome. It was his punishment for being alive while she was not.

The servants brought his best clothes. He let them dress him, numbly obeying their instructions to raise his arms, move his legs or stand still. Lastly, they put on him his favourite: a tight-fitting, knee-length dark-red coat with golden embroidery on the front, the edge of the sleeves and the stand-up collar.

"One moment," Imre said, looking at him gloomily. He picked a red felt hat with black fur trim and placed it on Sándor's head. "Were she here now to see you..." He choked up, but recollected himself. "She would say you look perfect."

Sándor entered the chapel. The sheer number of people both inside and outside the building overwhelmed him. Everyone stepped aside to let him pass. Imre held him by the arm and ushered him to the front row of the benches.

During the service, Sándor stared at the floor, not paying attention to the priest's words. It was all merely noise. It was all a bad dream. He would wake up from it any moment now... any moment now... But why was he not waking up? He turned and looked at Imre. Why were his friend's eyes wet with tears?... No, no, it was not a dream. Margit was dead. She lay there in the coffin, in front of him. A massive lump blocked his throat and made him gasp.

"I have lost a wife, a lover, a friend, a mother, a sister, an adviser. She was the whole world to me."

Neither the support of his people nor the sincerity of their sorrow did comfort his grief-stricken soul. No kind words, no praise for Margit would bring her back. After officials, knights, soldiers, servants and locals came to him to express their condolences, he followed the coffin-bearers to the family burial vault in the crypt underneath the chapel. There, they placed her into a stone coffin, next to that of her son.

Sándor asked them to leave.

Tears of despair filled his eyes. "How am I going to live without you?"

He sat on the cold stone floor and closed his eyes. If only he would die this instant and be reunited with her... If only...

The chilly and damp air of the crypt went through him. He shivered. But he still would not move. He would not leave her side.

When he came out of the vault, it was the next morning. He silently walked past the servants and climbed the stairs to Margit's bedchamber. Everything had been tidied there. All her things still lay about, and yet the room felt so empty. He took them in his hands, one by one: the finely carved comb, the ivory-backed hand mirror, the perfume bottle, her elegant decorative hairpins, her jewellery box... Her image flashed in the mirror. He recoiled in disbelief; he turned on his heel, but she was not there.

He would never see her again. The thought made him shake and gasp for air. After flinging the terrace door open, he ran towards the edge and leaned over the parapet. The ground seemed as if it were coming towards him; as if it were only an arm's length away. Some strange power was pulling him downwards. All he had to do was let go, and then he would be free...

His heart stopped for a brief moment. His body jerked backwards as if pushed by an invisible hand. He stepped away from the edge and touched his forehead while the world spun around him. Breathing heavily, he staggered back inside and lay on the bed. He cried awhile and then drifted in and out of sleep.

A knock on the door woke him up.

Erzsi and Imre entered the room. "My lord," the woman said, "would you like to see your daughter?"

"My daughter?"

He had forgotten about the baby. His child... He should ask that they bring her to him. He should hold her in his arms, like a loving father... But an all-consuming darkness chased away the endearing image. The little girl was the symbol of a new life, and he hated life at this moment. Seeing her would only augment the war that raged within his soul. "No! Begone! Leave me in peace!"

"Give him time," Imre whispered to Erzsi, and they both left.

Sándor walked out of Margit's bedchamber in the evening. Lightheaded, he teetered and leaned on the wall for support. When was the last time he had eaten? He ordered the servants to set the table in the great hall, and he sat down with Imre. Unable to attend to his duties for some time now, he asked his friend to inform him of any developments.

Wishing to block out the pain, he soon saw the advantage of keeping busy with matters pertaining to his estate. He did not talk about his wife and tried not to think about her either. It worked during the day when other people were around. The nights, however, were the reverse. Lying in bed, in the dark, he floated in the abysmal void that she had left behind. He would never get over the loss. His life had no meaning without her. He was completely alone in the world.

A month later, he still refused to see his daughter. Despite the pleas from Erzsi and Imre, he did not even want to decide on a name for her, and the little girl remained unbaptised. The priest came to his house numerous times, threatening him with eternal damnation, but Sándor did not care. He was enraged with God too for taking away his only companion in life.

But as time passed, he finally relented and, albeit apprehensively, he visited the baby's chamber.

Erzsi jumped to her feet as soon as he entered. "My lord! It's so good that you're here. Look at her... So beautiful, so precious."

He did not say a word, only signalled to the woman to leave with an abrupt movement of his hand.

He stood over the cradle. The child was sleeping peacefully. He lifted her into his arms. But her face, instantly reminding him of Margit, drove the already crushing agony deeper into his heart. "I hate you. Your poor mother died so that you could live. You do not deserve this. You are not even a boy." Rage perfused his mind. He placed his hand around the baby's throat. It would be so easy to snap her little neck...

"Sándor!"

He recoiled in fear and gasped. Was that Margit's voice calling him, or was it all in his head? Whatever it was, it had stopped him from committing the most heinous crime of all.

The baby started crying and within a few moments, Erzsi burst in with a worried expression on her face. "Is she well, my lord?"

"Yes, yes," he mumbled and handed the child to her.

Erzsi gently rocked her from side to side, speaking tenderly in her ear. The little girl quietened. "She probably had a fright when you held her. She doesn't know you yet."

Sándor nodded. His hands were shaking so badly that he had to clasp them behind his back to make them stop.

"So, have you decided on the name?"

He answered without even thinking. "Margit."

"My lord, I'm so glad that you chose this name. She's the image of your wife. But she has your strength too. She's a little fighter, surviving against all odds and without her mother. And she has your red hair. May I suggest that she takes your name as well? She can be Margit Alexandra?"

"Of course."

"Thank you, my lord. I'll arrange the baptism forthwith. Who do you wish to be the godparents?"

He did not take long to decide. The best choice stood right in front of him. "You are a loyal and loving woman, Erzsi. You say your prayers and never miss church. You served my wife faithfully for many years. And the way you care for this child now makes me certain that you are the most suitable person to be my daughter's spiritual mother. So, I release you from service. I shall look after you like a member of my family."

Erzsi's mouth opened wide, and her face lit up. "Oh, my lord, this is the greatest honour! I thank you from the bottom of my heart." But suddenly, her mood changed. "My lord, I don't have enough money to buy her presents."

"Do not fret. Your love and guidance will be your best gift to her."

Sándor stared at the sleeping baby's face. Despite himself, he smiled. For the first time, he saw his daughter as an angel; a messenger of hope and love, sent from Heaven by his dear wife. The child was part of Margit; a blessed piece of her, which shone through the darkness of his miserable life like the Northern Star, destined to light his way back to happiness and joy. The thick veil of loss before his eyes had finally been lifted, and he could gaze at the beauty of the world again.

38

An Old, Familiar Face
Appears Again

Summer 1459

Sitting on a cushioned marble bench outside the king's audience room, Sándor held his hat in his hands and tapped his fingers on it. King Mátyás had summoned him to the palace in Buda, but he had no notion of why. It had been just over a year since the youngster took the throne, and he had already pushed the powerful barons aside and had given high-ranking government and military positions to lesser nobles and ordinary citizens. He had even gone as far as throwing his uncle, Mihály Szilágyi, in prison for plotting against him.

Sándor tried to think of his daughter to calm his nerves. He missed his Margitka very much. Day by day, he had grown to love her more and more. It was as if his beloved wife had come back to life. He could see her in the little girl's face. Her smile and laughter gave peace to his heart. And now, being away from her – even for a few weeks – was like torture to him.

It was not too long before a servant in the king's livery led him to the audience room. Mátyás was sitting on his ornate throne, wearing a serious expression, which made him look much older than his sixteen years.

Sándor bowed respectfully. "Lord King."

"Who can I trust?" Mátyás said. "My royal enemies from abroad have been conspiring against me since the moment I set foot in this palace. Even worse, some of my closest advisers have turned against me. My own uncle has betrayed me, blinded by greed and ambition. It seems the only reason he put me on the throne was so that he could govern in my place because I am too young. My father's struggles and my brother's murder have taught me two things: not to trust anyone and to rule on my own terms."

Sándor clasped his hands behind his back to hide the fact that they were shaking. Was the king about to accuse him of something?

Mátyás stood up and folded his arms. "Tell me, cousin, did my uncle ask you to join him in his traitorous plot to overthrow me?"

Sándor gulped. His whole body went numb. Did the king know about that and was trying to catch him out, or was he just speculating? "Yes, he did. At first, he tried to entice me. Then, he resorted to threats."

"And what was your answer?"

"Your father was my mentor and my hero, Lord King. I endangered my life fighting in the civil war to put you on the throne. No threats would make me turn against you." Sándor was surprised that such confident words had come out of his mouth. But it was the truth and he had nothing to fear.

Mátyás unfolded his arms. The stern expression on his face softened. "I appreciate your integrity and honesty. I also know that you are an experienced soldier and officer. That is why I summoned you. Enemies surround Hungary from every side. I cannot rely on the noble levies every time my kingdom is in peril. I have decided to establish a professional army. In this way, I shall have a well-trained force, ready to fight at a moment's notice and also one that would suffer minimum casualties thanks to its skills and advanced weapons. I ask you to be the commander-in-chief of this army."

Sándor almost choked. He wanted to shout 'yes' with every fibre of his being. But as he opened his mouth to answer, the image of Margitka's face appeared in his mind's eye. He had left his wife behind many times to go to war. She was a strong woman and well capable of surviving without him. But he could not abandon his little girl. She was so small and innocent.

"Well?" the king said. "I don't have all day."

"I am honoured by the generous offer," Sándor answered, hesitantly. "But I cannot accept."

Mátyás regarded him with narrowed eyes and flushed face. "Why not? I recognise your abilities, and I give you this great opportunity to advance yourself. You can join the ranks of the barons instead of remaining a mere provincial nobleman. I do not understand why you have refused."

Sándor's heart thudded. The last thing he wanted was to insult the king. He bent down on one knee and bowed his head to Mátyás. "Please, Lord King, do not be offended by my answer. I would seize the opportunity if I were ten years younger. But my fighting days are behind me, and war as an occupation does not appeal to me anymore. I have lost my son and my wife. My one-year-old daughter is all I have. And I am all she has. I must look after her and protect her."

He paused, raising his eyes to meet the king's cold and penetrating gaze. "I swear to you that I shall fulfil my obligation as a nobleman and take up arms to defend the realm whenever you call a general levy. And I shall continue to represent your interests in the assembly of Hunyad County and uphold the law and pass judgement in your name in the county court."

"And so, I have lost to a baby!" Mátyás threw his arms in the air, looking like a child who had his favourite toy taken away. But any signs of indignation quickly turned into a curled smile. He motioned Sándor to stand up. "Very well, cousin. I respect your decision. But if you ever change your mind, let me know at once."

***

A week after Sándor's return to Sasfészek, the servants informed him that he had a visitor.

He entered the study to find the woman sitting comfortably in his chair, behind the writing desk. She did not bother standing up to greet him but regarded him with a broad smile.

His face heated up. "Anna! I thought you had entered a convent. But you are not dressed as a nun."

"I didn't. I changed my mind," she responded, flippantly.

He exhaled loudly. "Of course. So, why are you here?"

She rose and approached him.

"I wished to see my son and give my condolences to you. I was only informed recently that Margit passed last year. I know how painful it is to lose your partner in life. I also want to thank you for looking after Márton's estates so successfully."

"Yes, it has been a struggle for me after you disappeared with all the money and valuables."

"Well, a woman on her own in this world needs the means to survive."

"Right. And where do you live now?"

"That is none of your concern."

Her answer was deeply offensive. She had saddled him with the responsibility of her child and her land, and now she was being secretive concerning her whereabouts. But he did not insist on interrogating her any further. He wanted her to leave. "I trust that you have already seen Márton and that you are on your way now?"

Anna did not reply immediately but stared at him for a few moments instead. "Yes... but there is something else."

"Oh, you need another favour," he said, rolling his eyes. "What is it?"

She thought awhile before answering, "This may sound unexpected to you, but I am here with a marriage proposal."

Sándor staggered backwards. "What?"

"I know it's not allowed because I was wed to your brother. But I also know someone in a high position in the Church, who will provide us with a dispensation."

"Someone you bedded?"

"That's impertinent," she dismissed the accusation. "So, what do you think? We are both widowed and growing older. You are the guardian of my son and my land already. And your daughter needs a mother."

Her insolence certainly knew no bounds. "You gave up on motherhood when you brought Márton here. Why do you now think that you can be a mother to my child? Or is it perhaps because you have spent all your money, and you are looking for a fool to take care of you for the rest of your life? I shall not be that fool. I shall never marry you."

Anna shook her head. "Wrong answer." She stepped right in front of him and glided her hand down his arm and then, slowly, up the inside of his thigh. "You must feel lonely in your bed at night. Do you pay someone to give you pleasure? I can offer that to you for nothing. And you can do to me whatever you desire."

Even though they were both much older now, her intoxicatingly sweet lavender scent and her seductive touch still made the blood rush through Sándor's body like a raging stream. But at the same time, Margit appeared to his perturbed mind, rising from her grave in anger. He could not betray her again.

He grunted and moved away from Anna. "You are disgusting!"

"Disgusting? You used to like all that a long time ago. But Margit changed you. She made you self-righteous and... dull."

"How dare you?" He pointed at the door. "Leave now! If you ever come near my nephew or his land again, I shall have you locked in the dungeon."

"You will regret this," she muttered under her breath and

stormed out.

Sándor sat down, still shaken by what had happened. But he did not dwell on those thoughts for too long. He was glad to see the back of her and hoped that she would not dare come visit him again.

Anna hurried towards the door, fuming.

"Mother! Are you leaving already?"

She stopped and turned around. Her son ran to her and they embraced. She knelt down and held him by the arms. She spoke to him in the Saxon language so that no one would understand them. "I must go. Your uncle has banished me from this place."

"When am I going to see you again?"

"In time, my boy. That accursed woman has made everything too difficult for us by having a child. Do not fret though. The little girl will not be a problem. She cannot inherit the estate. She is only entitled to a dowry when she weds. And who knows, she may not even survive until then. I promise you that I shall find a way to bring Sándor down. He must pay for what he did to us. In the meantime, stay quiet and let me know of everything that happens here. Do you understand?"

Márton bobbed his head eagerly. "Yes, Mother. How shall I communicate with you?"

"We have a friend in the castle. He will take your messages and bring them to me. And when the right time comes, we shall strike."

"A friend? Who is he?"

She pulled him close to her and whispered in his ear. Márton nodded, smiling.

"Be good and respectful to your uncle and try to learn to fight and use as many weapons as you can. Now that his wife is not here to poison his mind against us, you must make him trust you." She stroked his hair. "Your dear father loved you so much. After suffering endless humiliation in his youth, he wished to give you a better life than his. I have now come to understand what he tried to do that fateful day. He sacrificed himself so that you can become the next Lord of the Eyrie. It was the bravest thing he ever did even though he did not succeed in dispatching his haughty brother. You must do your part now."

"Of course, Mother. I promise I'll make you and Father proud."

She gave him a tight hug again and kissed him farewell.

39
The Contract

Spring 1462

After that visit, Anna disappeared again. But every now and then, Márton would receive a note from her, pushed under his door at night by their 'friend'. He did not have much to report back to her as life in Sasfészek went on as usual, and nothing out of the ordinary happened for a long time.

Márton was growing up quickly. Sándor did take great interest in his training and education to the point that from his twelfth birthday onwards, the boy was allowed to sit at the meetings his uncle had with his council to observe and learn. He also received combat training, not by Sándor himself but by a professional instructor.

But when it came to friends, Márton had none. Since he was small, his only true companion had been his father. They had been inseparable. And now, the only thing he could hold on to were the memories. How he used to cling to his daddy's leg and follow him everywhere. How he sat on his shoulders to pick the sweet apples from the trees. How he fell asleep to the sound of his voice telling stories about heroes, wizards, kings and fair princesses... And then, the soldiers came into the house, carrying his beloved father's corpse. The worst day of his life. The world had suddenly become a dark and hostile place; and even more so, since he was sent to live with his uncle – the man who had caused his father's death.

His only comfort in those times of loneliness were his mother's messages. Her encouraging and determined words warmed his heart and gave him strength. He was destined to be the next lord of Szentimre. The castle of Sasfészek, the land around it and the mine were his inheritance by right. His uncle looked after his upbringing so closely. What else would this mean but that he was preparing him for taking over in the future? And his mother had promised him that the time would come sooner rather than later.

Still, there was the matter of his little cousin. If he inherited his uncle's estate, what would become of her? His mother would certainly devise of some sinister plan to get rid of her before she reached marriage age to avoid paying her dowry. But Márton was not going to let that happen. He had the solution to everything: he would marry Margitka. The girl was so adorable with her copper-coloured hair, her bright green eyes and her sweet freckled face. He could not wait to take her as his wife when she was a little older. All he had to do was show his uncle that he loved her. It was as simple as that.

***

Sándor came home before vespers. A refreshing bath would be welcome after being out on business all day. He ordered the servants to bring water to his bedchamber. As he ascended the stairs, screams came out of the playroom. Margitka and Imre's son, Endre, usually played there together under Erzsi's supervision. The two children got on very well. There was no reason for the little girl to be screeching like that.

When he opened the door, he gasped in horror. Margitka was lying on the floor, on her back. Márton had one hand on her chest, trying to keep her still, and the other under her skirt. The little girl was crying and so was Endre, who was sitting on the floor, holding his bleeding nose. Erzsi was nowhere to be seen.

"Take your hands off my daughter!" Sándor grabbed Márton by the scruff of the neck, lifted him off the ground and threw him on the floor with force. The boy fell with a thud and screamed in pain.

"I'm here, *kincsem*." He lifted Margitka up in his arms, gently stroked her hair and kissed her on the forehead. "You are safe. I'm here. I'm here."

She clung to him, her arms around his neck; tears and drivel staining his tunic.

Sándor turned to Imre's son. "Has this happened before?"

The boy shook his head vigorously. "No, sir. I tried to stop him, but he smote me. My nose is so sore."

"You are very brave to defend her. Go to your mother now. She will look after you."

Obediently, Endre ran out of the room.

At the same time, Erzsi entered in a state of panic. "What happened?"

"Damn you, woman! Where have you been?" Sándor's voice

shook the windows like a clap of thunder.

She shrank in fear. "I'm sorry, my lord. I had to leave for a moment. The two of them were alone, playing." She took the girl in her arms and tried to calm her.

"If you let her out of your sight again, I shall break your neck!"

"I'm so sorry, so sorry! It'll never happen again." Erzsi burst into tears. She left in haste, taking Margitka with her.

Sándor stood over Márton, who was still lying on the floor. "What the devil were you doing?"

"I'm sorry... I... I was trying to show that I... love her."

"What? Are you out of your mind?"

"I saw you do this to your wife, and she liked it. I thought it's a good thing to do to a girl that you wish to marry."

Sándor's breath caught in his throat. "What made you think that you will marry her?"

"I... I thought this is what you... wished too? Keep the estate within the family?"

"You, foolish boy! You cannot marry her. She is your first cousin."

"I'm sorry, Uncle."

Sándor clenched his fists, fighting the urge to kill him in cold blood. He lifted him off the floor, grabbed him by the throat and shoved him against the wall.

Márton screamed when his back hit the hard surface.

Sándor grasped the boy's left hand.

"Uncle, please! Don't hurt me!"

But he received neither forgiveness nor mercy. Sándor got a

tight grip on the boy's little finger and pushed it backwards with such force that the bone snapped. Márton let out a bloodcurdling wail and fell on his knees.

"If you ever touch her again, it will not be a finger. I shall smash your head and throw your body off the castle walls for the wolves to eat. Do you understand me?"

"Yes, Uncle," Márton whimpered.

"Get out of my sight!"

The boy dashed out of the room, terrified.

Sándor slumped in a chair. His heart was beating fast as if it wanted to jump out of his chest. What had happened was the most disturbing thing; something so evil that he would not forget it for the rest of his life. Yes, he had treated his nephew with extreme violence. But his daughter was the apple of his eye. He would not hesitate to kill anyone who dared to do her any harm.

***

Erzsi was horrified when Sándor explained to her what had happened in the playroom during her absence. She wept and begged him to forgive her.

"Don't let her out of your sight again! She is very young, and I pray she will forget this as she grows up." Holding Margitka in his arms, he spoke to her softly and reassuringly. "Don't be afraid, *kincsem*. I shall not let anybody hurt you."

The little girl sucked her lower lip. Exactly like her mother... Sándor looked away, fighting back tears.

"Daddy," Margitka said sweetly as she twisted a few strands of his long hair around her tiny fingers. "Márton is a bad boy. I'm scared."

He gave her a light kiss on the forehead. "He will not touch you again. I promise."

A knock on the door. Sándor nodded to Erzsi to answer. Endre walked in, followed by his mother. One of the boy's nostrils was stuffed with a piece of cloth to absorb the blood.

"Wants to see if friend well," Dragoslava said. She was able to speak Hungarian now, although with a heavy Slavic accent.

"You are a brave boy," Sándor praised Imre's son. "Do you promise me that you will always protect her?"

"Yes, sir!" Endre's voice was full of confidence and pride.

Sándor set his daughter back on the floor. The little girl ran to hug her friend.

"Oh, so sweet," Erzsi remarked, and all the adults smiled at the sight.

"Where is your husband?" Sándor asked Dragoslava.

"In garrison house."

"Ask him to come and see me when he returns. I must speak with him."

***

Later that evening, Sándor was writing a document in his study when Imre entered.

"I'm sorry to hear what happened. I hope she's well."

"I hope so too, *barátom*. I pray that she will forget it all eventually."

Imre nodded.

"Your boy was brave, trying to defend her. I am sorry he was hurt," Sándor said.

Imre smiled, beaming with pride. "Oh, it's nothing. He'll have to get used to that if he's to become a tough warrior like me."

Sándor invited his friend to sit down with a movement of his hand. "After what happened today, I am worried about my daughter's future. I must make sure she will be safe and looked after in case I die while she is still little. I want her to inherit my estate. Even though Márton is my closest male relative, I don't wish him to be my heir after what he did today."

"Why don't you marry again and have more children?"

Sándor shook his head. "I shall never love another woman after Margit."

"I'm not talking about loving another woman. Just marry a young one that can bear you a son. You don't have to love her."

"I hear you, but I still do not wish to do that. My daughter is all my life now. I shall not impose a stranger on her as her mother."

Imre shrugged. "So, what do you need to discuss?"

Sándor leaned forward on his writing desk. "I have looked through the legislation, and there is a way for Margitka to have my estate. Have you heard of the term *praefectio in filium* or 'prefection'? The Hungarian king has the prerogative to 'promote' a nobleman's daughter to a son, giving her the right to inherit land as if she were a man. This is how my Székely grandmother, who was an only child, kept this estate when she married my Szilágyi grandfather. Normally, this cannot be granted when there are close male relatives. But I believe that if the king hears about my brother's treachery, Anna's immorality and what Márton tried to do to my daughter, he will grant me the request."

Imre stared at him in admiration. "You're so learned, *barátom*. I've never heard of such a... thing."

"It means that if my daughter has a husband, he can inherit my estate through her. In this way, Márton can be completely excluded from it."

"Great! But how are you planning to do this? She's only four years old."

Sándor pointed at the document in front of him. "I have drafted a contract for you and me to sign, agreeing that our children are betrothed until they are old enough to wed. I shall also write to the king, requesting his approval of my daughter's right according to this custom of prefection. If I die before that time, your son will inherit my estate on the condition that he will fulfil his obligation to marry my daughter when she is fourteen years old."

Imre jumped in his chair. "You want Margitka to marry Endre?"

"Yes. If you agree, of course. My dear wife's last wish was that I find a good husband for our daughter. You are my best friend – my 'blood brother' if I may say. You have proven your loyalty to me so many times, both in war and in peace. And the children are fond of each other. Unless you are opposed to that?"

"No. On the contrary, I'm honoured. But he's below her standing. You're a member of the nobility, you have your own castle, town, villages and mine. I'm only a knight with no estates. My family lost its land and privileges years ago because of debts. That's why I became a professional soldier. Are you sure about this?"

"Your ancestors were noble once. With this union, your family will be elevated again. And I'd rather my daughter took a lower-ranking husband, who would love and respect her, than the son of some rich landowner, who would only wed her to increase his fortune and use her to bear his children. So, are we in agreement?"

"Yes, of course."

They stood up and shook hands.

"Excellent," Sándor said. "The notary will be here tomorrow to witness our signing and seal our agreement. And then, we can celebrate."

40
Endgame

On hearing the news of Margitka's betrothal to Endre, Márton wished the earth would open to swallow him. His actions alone had brought about his own downfall. Now there was no chance whatsoever that he would inherit Sándor's estate. He wrote to his mother, describing the situation. He left the letter at a specific place in the castle courtyard from where his 'friend' took it and forwarded it to Anna.

His finger was giving him terrible pain. Sándor had forbidden the physician from treating him. The broken bone was not healing properly. It appeared distorted. Gradually, the affliction spread to the rest of his hand. A curse on his uncle for being so cruel to him because he tried to show his love for Margitka! And damned be the Church for having that absurd law, which prevented him from marrying her because they were related! She was not his sister; she was only a cousin.

Following the incident, he was instructed to stay away from her. The little girl cried every time she saw him, so he had to make himself disappear. He spent most of the day in his bedchamber. He had his lessons and took his meals there as if he were not a member of the family any longer; or even worse, as if he were a prisoner. Sándor watched his every move, and that made the hairs stand on the back of his neck. He wished his mother would come and take him away from there.

He received an angry letter from her. She rebuked him for what he had done. He was useless. He had destroyed his chances to inherit. And now, she had to find a way to sort things out once and for all.

***

During the summer, Sándor received correspondence from the king. Mátyás had decided to take over the mine of Szentimre. The production of gold and silver was vital to the realm's survival. Sándor held a privilege which put him at an advantage over the other members of the nobility in Transylvania. The mine could not stay in private hands any longer. It would become the property of the king, who would have the full rights to the income from it. And as a punishment for taking this privilege without royal permission during a time of conflict and confusion, Sándor would also lose the land where the mine was located and the rent that would come from that.

Sándor understood that Mátyás was trying to pay for his wars in order to protect and even expand his kingdom. Maintaining a professional army and equipping it with the latest weaponry did not come cheap. The king had increased taxation several times. He had also imposed a monetary levy on all noblemen to relieve them from the obligation to provide men from their estates for the army. Even though these additional financial burdens made the upkeep of Szentimre harder, Sándor had accepted their necessity. But now, without the mine, he would struggle to maintain his land and his people and would have to look for other sources of revenue.

It was not the first time he had faced such difficulties since Mátyás ascended the throne. A year earlier, he had to let the mercenaries go and only kept the local castle garrison to protect his estate. Eventually pardoned by the king, Mihály had died fighting the Ottomans, while Erzsébet had left Transylvania and moved to her other estates in Hungary to be closer to her son. She did not need Sándor's help any longer, and so she stopped paying the wages of his soldiers.

After offering loyal service to the various kings for almost one and a half centuries, Sándor felt his family was being treated unfairly now. He met with his counsellors, who believed that there was nothing he could do. Mátyás was too powerful. Any resistance or dissent could be crushed with considerable force. But Sándor always thought that even though the king ruled the realm with an iron fist, he was a man of justice, and he would listen to his plea.

Despite the objections from his officials, he wrote a letter to Mátyás. He reminded him of the long service of his family and of the importance of the mine to the survival of Szentimre. He pleaded with the king not to take away his people's livelihood as the estate would be ruined without the mine, and the population would suffer. He was willing to negotiate an alternative solution, which would be beneficial to both sides. His letter was respectful, and he made sure it did not show any signs of disobedience or disloyalty.

A few months passed without a response, and life went on as usual. But in early October, a company of the royal army arrived in Szentimre.

Following the normal procedure, which applied whenever an uninvited military force approached, the portcullis at the castle entrance was winched down immediately.

The king's army entered the town and marched in formation towards the fortress. The inhabitants watched in disbelief. The soldiers looked so serious that no one dared question their unexpected arrival. They stopped outside the castle gate, and their captain asked to speak to the person in charge.

Sándor hurried down the stairs to the entrance hall just as Imre and two guards entered the keep.

"Why is the king's army outside?" he asked, his mind laden with an uneasy sense of foreboding.

Imre approached and spoke in a low voice. "They've come to arrest you."

Sándor felt the ground move under his feet. "*Úristen!* ... Why?"

"They didn't say. But they promised that they aren't here to cause trouble. They only want to take you on the king's orders."

"Why would the king arrest me? I didn't do anything wrong."

"What shall we do?"

"Let them in, Kovács," Sándor ordered one of the soldiers. "And tell the guards to stay calm and not to attack under any circumstances. I am sure it's only a misunderstanding."

As soon as the soldiers left, he gripped his friend's arm. "I need you to do something for me."

"Of course."

"Take my daughter, Erzsi and your family and leave the castle through the secret passage. I fear trouble is brewing, and I don't want my child to be in danger."

"I think you should escape as well."

"No! This is my land. I shall not run away. I have done nothing wrong. Fleeing would indicate guilt. The king sees conspiracies everywhere since his uncle and some of his officials betrayed him. I hope the issue will be resolved soon. I shall call for you to return then."

"Yes, I'll let them out, but I'll come back to help you. My place is by your side."

"You will stay with them. That's an order. You must make sure they are safe. You are the only one I can trust to protect my daughter."

"Very well," Imre conceded and turned around to walk away.

Sándor held him by the arm again. "Go to my study. Take all the documents that relate to Margitka's birth and title, my will and the marriage contract. If I do not come out of this alive, look that she weds Endre as we agreed."

"Of course, *barátom*."

"And make sure she does not forget her legacy."

As Imre ran up the stairs, Sándor buckled his sword belt and stood in the great hall, waiting for his 'visitors'. His heart pounded. He closed his eyes and prayed.

Four people emerged from the doorway: an army officer, Pál

Balog, Márton and Anna. The officer whispered something to Balog. The latter pointed at his lord. "It's him."

They all approached and stood around Sándor.

With his hand on the hilt of his sword, Sándor looked at each one of them. Balog averted his eyes, Anna remained stone-faced, and an evil smile played in Márton's eyes.

"Sándor Szilágyi of Szentimre, I am arresting you for treason," the officer declared. "I am Balázs Kardos, captain of his Majesty's royal army. Put your sword on the ground and your hands behind your back."

Sándor's stomach was in knots. He had to obey. Any resistance would certainly work against him. He took off the sword belt and placed it on the floor.

The captain stood behind him and tied his hands. He then made him fall down on his knees.

"You accuse me of treason. What proof do you have?"

"You wrote this letter to the king." The officer put the document in front of his face. "It is the most disrespectful and defiant piece of correspondence I have ever seen. You are presenting yourself as a rebel and enemy of the Holy Crown."

Sándor took a quick look at the letter and shook his head. What nonsense was that? "I did write to the king, but this is not my letter."

"Is this not your signature and your seal?"

"Yes, but it's a forgery. I am loyal to Mátyás. I would never rebel against him... Balog, help me. You took the letter and offered to deliver it to the messenger –" He paused. All was clear as day now. "You are the traitor! How much did this bitch pay you to be her spy? Or did she open her legs for you, the whore that she is?"

The former castellan remained silent.

"And who wrote the letter?" Sándor continued. "You couldn't have. It requires skill, and you are thick as a log... Was it Havasi? He is the only one who could imitate my writing and signature and use my seal. Did you force him, or did he do it willingly?"

No response again.

Sándor turned to the captain. "This is a conspiracy. Both this woman and her accomplice have personal grudges against me. They would not hesitate to lie to Mátyás and forge my letter in order to bring me down."

"If that's the case, you will have your chance to defend yourself in front of the king when I deliver you to him."

"I trust his Majesty's judgement. He is a fair man, and the truth will come out. Take me to him forthwith."

As the captain put his hand on Sándor's arm, Márton took a step forward and stood in front of them. The officer stopped and looked at him, surprised. "What is it?"

"This man mistreated my mother and is responsible for my father's death," Márton replied in a disturbingly cold manner. "He deserves to die."

The boy's hand covered Sándor's face, obscuring his vision. His head was violently pushed backwards. The light sound of a dagger being drawn was magnified in the silence. And then, Anna screeched.

The sharpest pain sliced through Sándor's throat like a stroke of lightning. Unable to hold the weight of his body any longer, he fell to his side. The sound of his skull cracking as it smashed against the stone floor sent waves of terror coursing through his soul. He screamed, but nothing came from his mouth. The world slowly moved away from him until he was left alone, floating in the darkness.

Then, Margit appeared against a beam of pale-yellow light, young and radiant like the first day he saw her upon returning home to his dying father. She beckoned to him. He wanted to follow her, but a dreaded thought paralysed his limbs. No matter how much he longed to be reunited with his dear wife, the moment had arrived much sooner than he expected. "What about our daughter?" he whispered. "I can't leave her."

A peaceful, loving smile spread across Margit's face. With a graceful sweep of her arm, a gentle breeze stirred about Sándor, carrying her words, "You need not fret, *kedvesem*. You have saved her. She is in good hands now."

He still wavered; for apprehension still claimed his heart. But then her image flickered. "Stay!" he implored. "I cannot lose you again."

Margit re-appeared, this time by his side. Her hand had already taken hold of his. Her touch was airy, like that of an angel's feather. "Soldier," she said, her voice riding on the crest of the once again swelling breeze. "Your wars are over. It's time to rest."

The pale-yellow light turned brilliant white, enveloping him in a comforting, reassuring warmth. Trusting to fate the life of their beloved daughter, he finally yielded and, closing his eyes, he let her guide him away.

***

"Stop screaming, Mother!" Márton burst out. "Did you not wish me to finish what Father started?"

Anna covered her mouth with both hands. Her eyes fixed on Sándor as he lay dying in an ever-expanding pool of his own blood. What had she done? That was not the plan. How could her beloved son betray her? That evil look on his face! She did not recognise him anymore... She had raised a monster.

"Outrageous!" The captain's thundering voice made her ears ring. "I'll arrest you all. You cannot play judge and executioner and kill a nobleman in cold blood when he is on his knees. He was entitled to be heard by the king."

Anna gasped. She was going to rot in prison; or, even worse, she could be hanged. Her knees shook. The world dimmed around her. She barely caught a glimpse of Balog nodding to the boy and drawing Sándor's sword. She only blinked, and the captain was lying on the floor with a dagger stuck in his stomach and the sword through his heart. She screamed again.

Balog raised his bloodied forefinger in front of her face. "Quiet!"

There was banging on the door of the keep. "The soldiers," she whispered.

Balog looked around desperately for a few moments, but then his face lit up. "Yes, we can cover this up. Yes, yes... The captain tried to arrest the lord. The lord attacked him and killed him. Then he assaulted us, and I had to take him down. There are no witnesses. As long as we stick to this story, we are safe."

He pulled Márton's dagger out of the officer's body, gritted his teeth and made a cut on the outside of his own arm.

More blood. Anna's stomach rose to her throat. Were Balog and the boy really shifting bodies and weapons, or was it a dream? She had no notion of what was going on anymore.

The door of the keep burst open. The heavy footsteps of a dozen soldiers rushed in like thunder towards the great hall.

Balog pressed his hand against his bleeding wound. "He killed the captain! Treason against the king!" he shouted with all his might.

Anna took a deep breath. Her vision slowly cleared. A glimmer of hope fluttered in her chest. Perhaps her old friend Fortune would smile upon her once again.

41
Out of Darkness Came Forth Light

Erzsi sat on the cold and dirty ground of the cave, trying to catch her breath. Her body was still shaking. Their descent down the escape passage had been frightening on those steep and slippery stairs. She had gone ahead of the others to light the way with a torch. Dragoslava went behind her, holding Endre by the hand. At the back, Imre followed with Margitka in his arms. The little girl had been quiet during the whole time, but as soon as Imre set her back on the ground, she cried and called for her father.

Erzsi hugged her and kissed her on the forehead. "Calm yourself now, *édesem*. All will be well. Your daddy will be here soon."

They hid in the bushes and waited awhile. Soldiers were shouting from the castle, and there was commotion in the town. As night fell, it would be difficult for them to be discovered, but they could not stay there for too long. They moved slowly and carefully until they saw some of the king's men running along the path below them with torches in their hands.

Imre led them back inside the entrance of the cave. "This doesn't look good. I'll run to the miners' village to find out what's happening. Stay here and don't move."

It felt like an eternity until he returned. He was out of breath. "We must leave. Run for our lives."

"What happened?" Erzsi asked, her heartbeat throbbing in her ears. "Where's the lord?"

"The estate is under attack. We must go, now!"

Imre went ahead to make sure the way was clear, and the others followed him. They moved, crouching and taking cover every now and then. The two children were scared. Margitka cried a few times, but Erzsi put her hand over her mouth to make her stop. All this time, they heard shouts and screams and the sound of weapons clashing. After wading through the shallow waters of a small stream, they crossed to the other side of the valley, where it was quieter. They continued to run until they were out in the open, far away from the town and castle. They came to a farmhouse belonging to a Wallachian family. Imre knocked on the door.

A man answered and let them in. He was one of the volunteers who had fought in Belgrade, and he recognised Imre.

"I need to buy your horses," the latter said, putting a gold coin in the man's hand.

"Why?"

"The castle has been attacked. I must save the lord's daughter. Please keep calm and help us. If the soldiers come here looking for us, tell them you haven't seen us. You need not fear anything. They're after us, not you."

"I only have two horses."

"It'll do, *barátom*. Thank you."

The man led them to the stable and gave the animals to them

and the gold coin back to Imre. "I won't take money. Lord Szilágyi has looked after us and protected us. This is a way to repay his family."

"God bless you. I'll return the horses to you as soon as I can."

Imre rode one of the animals with the two children clinging to him, Margitka in the front and Endre behind him. Erzsi and Dragoslava mounted the other. They were not sure where to go, so they just followed the road that led southwest.

They had left Sándor's estate a long way behind as dawn was breaking. They stopped in a small town. Imre took them to the local inn, where they had a chance to rest and stay hidden for the remainder of the day until they decided what to do.

"What happened in the castle?" Erzsi asked him as soon as the others went to sleep. They had been running all night, and he had refused to say anything in front of the children.

"The army came to arrest Sándor on the king's orders. I don't know why. He asked me to take all of you and some important papers from the castle and leave. When I went to the miners' village, two men who had come from the town said that the king's soldiers were attacked by the garrison, and that fights broke out inside the castle."

"Good Lord!"

"I don't think the garrison attacked. Sándor commanded them not to. Something else must have happened."

"And what about him?"

"I don't know," Imre said hesitantly, "but I fear he's been arrested."

Erzsi put her hand over her mouth. She looked at Margitka, who was sleeping peacefully. "What am I going to tell this child when she wakes up and asks for her daddy?"

"I don't know, Erzsi. I'm heartbroken that I wasn't there to help him. And that I left my men and ran instead."

"He asked you to save his daughter. You did what you had to do."

Imre nodded, but sadness contorted his face. "We must decide where we are going to go soon. It won't be long before they come looking for us."

Erzsi lay on the bed beside Margitka. She loved the child as much as she had loved her mother, and now she was afraid of what the future might bring. This unexpected twist of fate had ripped the little girl away from a loving home and turned her into a refugee.

Erzsi was woken up by someone's touch on her shoulder. "What?" she said, but Imre's hand covered her mouth.

"Soldiers," he whispered. He signalled to the women to help him turn one of the beds sideways. Erzsi, Dragoslava and the children hid behind it while Imre stood by the door with his dagger drawn.

Erzsi's heart thumped. Their ordeal was far from over. What else was going to befall them? She held Margitka tight in her arms. The little girl let out a small whine. "Shh, *édesem*. Bad people are coming. Be quiet, or they'll hurt us."

Footsteps approached, and then the door burst open. Imre

locked his arm around the soldier's neck, holding the dagger against his throat. "Drop your sword, and don't make a sound!"

The man obeyed. Imre pressed his fist against the base of the soldier's throat, making him lose consciousness. He pulled him towards the middle of the room and then took his weapons. "Draga," he called his wife. "Remove his boots and socks and throw them into the fire. Give me the shoelaces first." He used these to tie the man's hands behind his back.

"Someone's coming!" Erzsi warned him.

He jumped up and rushed to the door. A second soldier had already entered the room. Imre sprang on him, pushing him against the wall. He pounded at his face. The man fainted. Blood ran from his nose and mouth.

They tied him too and burned his shoes and socks. Even if the soldiers came round and freed themselves, it would be extremely difficult to give chase in bare feet.

The innkeeper appeared in the doorway. "What the devil?"

"Stay out of this!" Imre warned him. He handed him three silver coins. "We'll leave soon."

The man nodded and withdrew.

"Please, husband, let's go!" Dragoslava begged.

"In a moment. I need to know about my friend's fate first. You can gather your things and prepare in the meantime."

Imre slapped the first soldier a few times and shook him by the shoulders. The man opened his eyes and called for help. "Shut your mouth, or you'll die!" Imre held the dagger against his throat. "What happened in Szentimre?"

"Give yourself up, Gerendi. Your lord is dead."

Erzsi felt like all the air had left her lungs. She held on to Margitka tight.

Imre did not look in a better condition either. At length, he gathered himself and shouted, "Who killed him?"

"I don't know. But he was a traitor. He deserved it. And you are a criminal too because you have abducted his daughter. Her relatives want her back."

"Not in a thousand years!" Imre growled. He punched the man in the face so hard that he left him unconscious once again.

He rose, shaking with rage and unable to utter a word. He staggered about with his hand on his forehead.

"God rest my lord's soul," Erzsi whispered and crossed herself. Letting go of the little girl, she slumped on the bed.

"Where is my daddy?" Margitka snivelled.

Dragoslava and Endre hugged her and stroked her hair and face, trying to calm her down.

"Will your parents give us shelter?" Imre asked his wife.

"I'll beg them. I have husband and child now. I hope they help."

"We must go." Imre's voice quavered. "The most important thing is to keep this little one safe... Come." He turned his gaze upwards and whispered, "One day, you'll be avenged, *kedves barátom*. God's wrath will fall upon those who deserve it."

***

Dragoslava put on the blindfold and gingerly moved about with outstretched arms. Margitka and Endre teased her with their laughter and shrieks. The little boy tugged at his mother's skirt. The woman bent forward, trying to catch him, but he escaped her. "Fooled you, mama!"

Margitka covered her mouth with her hand and giggled.

Dragoslava took off the blindfold. "There are you are, little elves!" Endre gripped Margitka's hand. They ran towards the end of the garden. The woman caught up with them, and they all embraced and jumped up and down.

Sitting on the porch steps and watching the joyous scene, Erzsi wiped a tear from the corner of her eye. She wrapped her cloak tight around her. Winter was on the way.

Imre came out of the house and sat beside her. "My father-in-law's old workshop is ready. It's now a proper home for you and little Margit. A warm and safe home."

She put her hand on his arm. "How can I thank you, Imre? You're a good man and a loyal friend. You saved this child's life. God only knows what her aunt and cousin would have done to her if she had stayed in Szentimre. Or if those soldiers at the inn had taken her from us... But you've put yourself in danger. There's probably a price on your head now."

"Don't fret. We're a long way from Transylvania. I'm sure it'll all be forgotten soon, and we'll get on with our lives here in Belgrade."

She turned her gaze back to the children. They were now playing with a puppy. They had no care in the world. "Her happiness makes me glad and sad at the same time. I fear that she'll forget. She's stopped asking for her father."

Imre smiled. "Let her be, dear Erzsi. She's only a child – a tiny ray of hope that has come out of those dark and sinister moments. Let her be happy and free of care for now. You needn't fret. Her parents still live in her. You and I must make sure she remembers that when the time comes."

Margitka ran towards them, screaming and holding something in her hands. "Erzsi! Uncle Imre! He's dead!"

She was out of breath, with despair all over her face. Endre and Dragoslava followed her.

"The poor birdie fell out of the sky," the boy explained. "Father, can you do something?"

Margitka handed the little creature to Imre.

"I'll try to revive him," he said. He rubbed the bird's chest with his fingers for a few moments and then shook his head. "I'm sorry. Your little friend's gone."

"No, no." The girl's eyes filled with tears.

Imre stroked her hair. "There's nothing I can do, dear. He's gone to Heaven. He'll be happy there. The angels will look after him."

Sucking her lower lip, Margitka brushed her tears away. She took the bird in her hands and rubbed his chest earnestly. Her eyes were fixed on the creature with resolve beyond her years.

"Wake up, birdie," she whispered. "Wake up. Fly to my daddy." She rubbed and rubbed and rubbed...

The bird twitched and faintly moved his wings.

Erzsi crossed herself. "A miracle! The child is blessed!"

Margitka smiled, raised her hands and opened them.The others watched with mouths agape as the bird flapped his wings more and more vigorously until he raised himself in the air and soared into the sky.

THE END

The Szilágyi of Szentimre (fictional) coat of arms.

Illustration by Sigrid Whelan. A variation on the 15th century Szilágyi of Horogszeg family crest, adapted to suit the origins of this novel's fictional family. The sun and crescent moon added to this coat of arms are the symbols of the Székely people.

ACKNOWLEDGEMENTS AND THANKS

I would like to thank the following people who helped me on my writing journey:

My brother, George Vavoulidis, for being the first person to read the first draft of my novel.

Emily McGregor-Allan, Sherry Vernick Ostroff, James Conroyd Martin, Adela Shockome, Lisa Caywood for providing feedback on the opening chapters.

My beta readers for their valuable comments and advice: Maria Avramidou, Yvonne Albericci, Elysée Yhuel, Richard Bradburn, Sigrid Whelan, Luke Captain, Jane Rogers, Kathryn Helstrom, Kerry Brunson, Gábor Szántai and Mark Andrew.

Richard Bradburn of www.editorial.ie for the developmental edit and the first round of editing.

Kathryn Helstrom for the second round of editing.

Sigrid Whelan for the illustration of my protagonist's family coat of arms.

Paddy Shaw for the illustration and border patterns on the cover.

Dee Marley of the White Rabbit Arts, the exclusive graphic design company at The Historical Fiction Company, for designing the front and back cover, and the book formatting.

AUTHOR NOTES

The main characters in this story are fictional, but the historical, political, social and cultural background is real. Historical events – such as battles – have been slightly altered to allow the participation of these fictional characters in them.

The dialogues and speeches of real historical figures and their interactions with the fictional characters are the product of my imagination. However, they are based on research of primary and secondary sources, and as such, they are not impossible or out of character.

Some liberties were taken with the timeline of the events in order to fit the story. For example, I have not been able to establish if János Hunyadi was in his residence when Sándor and Margit visited him in winter 1440. Recent scholarship has suggested that Mihály Szilágyi was probably too young to command the left wing of the crusader army in Varna - this was more likely led by a different commander named Mihály in the sources. However, since he is a recurring character in the story, I have placed him there instead of introducing a new character just for this one battle. Finally, Mihály Szilágyi's attack on Beszterce has been brought forward by a few months.

In the Appendices, I have listed a selected bibliography of the primary and secondary sources that I used in my research.

HISTORICAL BACKGROUND

This story was inspired by the border lords of the fifteenth-century Kingdom of Hungary. Although mercenaries had always been employed in Hungary, the men of middle and lower nobility, serving powerful overlords like Hunyadi, were the backbone of the feudal armies of the period. Very few of them made it into the chronicles and history books. Their lives must have been hard: a constant struggle to run their own estates and protect them from the relentless Ottoman raiding as well as from attacks by other local lords while also leaving home for long periods to campaign with the king and his barons.

The main character, his estate and immediate family are fictional. Yet, Sándor embodies all those heroic and battle-hardened figures of the Borderland, who defended the kingdom for centuries. While Hungarian noblemen only had an obligation to take up arms within the borders of the kingdom, the frontier lords were forced by the nature of their location to be constantly at war.

Coming from a modest background – and possibly of Wallachian origin – János Hunyadi rose to power very quickly, thanks to his military successes against the Ottomans. He is considered a hero not only in Hungary, but also in many countries of the Balkans. In addition, Hunyadi was probably one of the first army commanders in Hungary to use mercenaries on a larger scale. His son, King Mátyás, set up a proper standing army of mercenaries, which was retrospectively called "The Black Army".

Much larger in size than the modern-day country, fifteenth-century Hungary extended from Southern Poland to Belgrade and from Croatia to Central Romania. By the middle of the century, neighbouring countries – which served as 'buffer zones' between the expanding Ottoman Empire and the Kingdom of Hungary – had become 'vassals' of the Sultan, and the two countries ended up sharing a border. During that period, the previous raiding and plundering expeditions of the Ottomans developed into larger-scale invasions of Hungarian territory. The southern frontier (Croatia, Slavonia, Southern Transylvania and the parts of Serbia that were still under Hungarian control) was frequently attacked and its defences tested to their limits.

Transylvania in the 15th century

Fifteenth-century Transylvania was a multi-ethnic province of the Kingdom of Hungary, which comprised Hungarians, Wallachians, Saxons, Székelys, Slavs and other ethnic groups, and was ruled by the Voivode (military governor), who was one of the most powerful barons of the kingdom. After an unsuccessful peasant rebellion in 1437 against increased taxation and the monetary policy of the government, the three 'privileged' classes of Transylvania signed an agreement to support each other against any future resistance. Called the 'three nations' of the province, they were the following:

1.   The Saxons were people from various German territories who migrated to Southern Transylvania from the 12th century

onwards, originally as border guards. Later on, more immigrants arrived, who held a variety of occupations, such as mining experts, merchants and craftsmen. Their population expanded quickly, and their areas became known as the Siebenbürgen, ('Seven Fortresses' – which also became the German name for Transylvania in general). This name possibly derived from the fact that there were seven major German towns in Transylvania.

2.   The Székely people (pronounced Seh-ke-y) are a Hungarian-speaking ethnic group, living mainly in the 'Székely Lands' of Eastern Transylvania. They served as border guards and soldiers in the medieval Kingdom of Hungary, and their main occupation was agriculture and animal husbandry. They lived in communities of various sizes, where the land was held and cultivated in common. Although they were not nobility, they were exempt from taxes in return for military service. Theories about their origin vary from the ones claiming they are descendants of Attila's Huns to those (more likely ones) stating they are early Hungarians who settled in the Carpathian Basin before the 'Conquest', i.e., the arrival of the Magyars in the Carpathian basin at the end of the 9th century AD.

3.   Any remaining lands of Transylvania which were not the property of the king belonged to the nobility, who were predominantly of Hungarian (Magyar) origin. In addition, a number of Wallachian (Romanian), Moldavian and Southern Slavic families who had become 'magyarised' and Catholic, were granted lands by the king for their military service and joined the ranks of the nobility.

APPENDICES

1. Glossary of Terms

Akinji (Turk. akıncı): irregular light horseman of the Ottoman army. Akinjis mostly came from Anatolia and operated as raiders on the frontiers of the Ottoman empire and as skirmish units during battles. Their main weapons were bows and arrows, but they also used spears, swords and battle axes

Anatolia (Turk. Anadolu): the provinces of the Ottoman Empire situated on the Asian continent

Azap (Turk. azap): irregular foot soldier serving in the peasant militia of the Ottoman army. The Azaps were volunteers and came mostly from Anatolia. Their main weapons were polearms, maces, bows, sabres and crossbows

Banderium (plural: banderia – from Latin): a military unit in medieval Hungary, consisting of noblemen, knights and mercenaries, who fought under the banner of the king or of a particular high-ranking noble or prelate

Despot: the ruler of the Serbian Despotate, a medieval Serbian state which emerged during the first half of the 15th century, as a successor of the collapsed Serbian Empire

Erdély (Hung. pronounced er-dee): the Hungarian name of Transylvania

Janissaries (Turk. yeniçeri): the elite infantry of the Ottoman army. Mostly made up of boys from the conquered lands, who were enslaved and converted to Islam, the Janissaries underwent strict training and became the first modern professional standing army in Europe

Rumelia (Turk. Rūm-ėli): the provinces of the Ottoman Empire situated on the European continent

Sipahi (Turk. sipâhi): professional cavalryman of the Ottoman army. Although Sipahis were considered heavy cavalry and similar in rank to the European knights, they wore lighter armour. The Rumelian Sipahis were usually equipped with round shields, swords, javelins, maces and axes. The Anatolian Sipahis carried the same weapons except they used bows instead of javelins or lances

Voivode (Hung. vajda): military governor. The Voivode of Transylvania was the fourth most powerful man in the medieval Kingdom of Hungary

2. English translation of the Hungarian names in the story (approximate pronunciation in brackets)

In the novel, I have used the "western" order of names for the convenience of English-speaking readers. In Hungarian, the order is the reverse: the family name precedes the first name.

First Names
Sándor (Shan-dor, *s* like sh and á like in *father*) = Alexander
Margit (Mawr-git, *a* like in *call*, *g* like in *get*) = Margaret

Miklós (Mik-lowsh, *ó* is a long *o* similar to *ow* in *low*) = Nicholas

István (Isht-van) = Stephen

Imre (Im-re, *i* like in *sit* and *e* like in *get*) = possibly the Hungarian equivalent of the German name Emmerich / sometimes translated as Henry in English

Erzsi (Er-zhi, *zs* like the *s* in *leisure*) = Lizzie - full name Erzsébet (Er-zheh-bet) = Elizabeth

Márton (Mar-ton) = Martin

Endre (End-re) = Andrew

János (Ya -nosh) = John – and also Jankó (Yan-kow) = Johnny

László (Las-low, *sz* like the *s* in *sit*) = Ladislaus

Lajos (Law-yosh, *j* like the *y* in *yet*) = Louis

Mihály (Mi-ha-y, *ly* pronounced in the same way as the *j* in the middle of the word, but like *y* as in *hey* when it is at the end of the word) = Michael

Mátyás (Ma-tyash, *ty* like in *courtyard*) = Matthias

Tamás (Taw-mash) = Thomas

Pál (Pahl) = Paul

Péter (Peh-ter) = Peter

Kálmán (Kal-man) = Coloman

Balázs (Baw-lazh) = Blasius, Blaise

Family Names (main characters)

Szilágyi (Si-la-dyi, *gy* like the *dy* in *woodyard*)

Bátori (Ba-to-ri)

Gerendi (Ge-ren-di)

Hunyadi (Hoo-nya-di, *ny* like in *lanyard*)

Place names

Fictional:
Sasfészek (Shawsh-feh-sek) = Eyrie
Szentimre (Sent-im-re) = Saint Imre

Real:
Hunyadvár (Hoo-nyad-var), a town in Transylvania –
modern-day Hunedoara in Romania

Segesvár (She-gesh-var), a town in Transylvania – modern-
day Sighişoara in Romania

Szeben (Se-ben), a town in Transylvania – modern-day Sibiu
in Romania

Gyulafehérvár (Dyoo-la-fe-hehr-var) = White Castle of
Gyula, the capital of medieval Transylvania – modern-day Alba
Iulia in Romania

Temesvár (Te-mesh-var), a town in Temes County – modern-
day Timişoara in Romania

Beszterce (Best-ertse), a town in Transylvania – modern-day
Bistriţa in Romania

Ialomiţa (Ya-lo-mitsa), a river in Romania

Nándorfehérvár (Nan-dor-fe-hehr-var), the Hungarian
name of Belgrade, capital of Serbia

3. Selected Bibliography

Primary sources:

Aeneas Silvius Piccolomini's Europe c.1400-1458, trans. R. Brown (Washington, 2013)

Antonio Bonfini: A Magyar Történelem Tizedei (Rerum Hungaricarum Decades), Hungarian trans. P. Kulcsár (Budapest, 1995) – online version: https://www.tankonyvtar.hu/hu/tartalom/tkt/magyar-tortenelem/adatok.html

https://hungaricana.hu/en/ - Hungaricana: Hungarian Cultural Heritage Portal – Hungarian National Archives Database

János Thuróczy: Chronicle of the Hungarians, trans. F. Mantello (Bloomington, 1991)

The Annals of Jan Długosz: A History of Eastern Europe from AD965 to AD 1480, trans. and abridged M. Michael (Chichester, 1997)

The Laws of Hungary, Series I, Vol.2: The Laws of the Medieval Kingdom of Hungary 1301-1457, trans. and ed. J.M. Bak, P. Engel and J.R. Sweeney (Budapest, 1992)

Secondary works:

Bak, J. M., 'Hungary: Crown and Estates' in C. Allmand (ed),

The New Cambridge Medieval History, Vol. 7 (Cambridge, 1998), pp. 707-726

Bánlaky, J., *A Magyar Nemzet Hadtörténelme (The Military History of the Hungarian Nation)* (Budapest, 1928) – online version: edited by Arcanum Adatbázis Kft. (2001) - http://mek.oszk.hu/09400/09477/html/index.html

Engel, P., *The Realm of St Stephen: A History of Medieval Hungary 895-1526* (London & New York, 2001)

Erdélyi, L., *A Magyar Lovagkor (The Hungarian Age of Chivalry)* (Gödöllő, 2013)

Fraknói, V., *Szilágyi Mihály, Mátyás Király Nagybátyja (Mihály Szilágyi, The Uncle of King Mátyás)*, (Budapest, 1913)

Fügedi, E., *The Elefánthy: The Hungarian Nobleman and his Kindred* (Budapest, 1998)

Held, J., *Hunyadi: Legend and Reality* (New York, 1985)

Imber, C., *The Crusade of Varna, 1443-45 (Crusade Texts in Translation)* (Aldershot, 2006)

Laszlofszky, J., Nagy B., Szabó P., Vadas A. (eds.) *The Economy of Medieval Hungary* (Leiden & Boston, 2018)

Rady, M., *Nobility, Land and Service in Medieval Hungary*

(Hampshire and New York, 2000)

Pálosfalvi, T., *From Nicopolis to Mohács: A History of Ottoman-Hungarian Warfare, 1389–1526* (Leiden, 2018)

www.hungarianottomanwars.com : online blog by Szántai Gábor

HISTORIUM PRESS
www.historiumpress.com

CPSIA information can be obtained
at www.ICGtesting.com
Printed in the USA
LVHW022024060222
710389LV00019B/3082